Praise for

KATE RHODES

'Clever, atmospheric and compelling, it's
another masterclass in plotting'
WOMAN'S WEEKLY

'Rhodes is a published poet and every one of her sentences sings'
FINANCIAL TIMES

'A vividly realised protagonist whose complex and
harrowing history rivals the central crime storyline'
SOPHIE HANNAH

'An absolute master of pace, plotting and character'
ELLY GRIFFITHS

'Kate Rhodes has cleverly blended a tense plot with a
vivid sense of the raw, beautiful landscape of the Scilly
Isles, and every character is a colourful creation'
RACHEL ABBOTT

'Kate Rhodes directs her cast of suspects with consummate
skill, keeping us guessing right to the heartbreaking end'
LOUISE CANDLISH

'Expertly weaves a sense of place and character
into a tense and intriguing story'
METRO

'Rhodes does a superb job of balancing a portrayal
of a tiny community oppressed by secrets with
an uplifting evocation of setting'
SUNDAY EXPRESS

'One of the most absorbing books I've read
in a long time – perfectly thrilling'
MEL SHERRATT

'Fast paced and harrowing, this gripping novel
will leave you guessing until the end'
BELLA

KATE RHODES

DEVIL'S TABLE

**SIMON &
SCHUSTER**

London · New York · Sydney · Toronto · New Delhi

First published in Great Britain by Simon & Schuster UK Ltd, 2021

Copyright © Kate Rhodes, 2021

The right of Kate Rhodes to be identified as author of
this work has been asserted in accordance with the
Copyright, Designs and Patents Act, 1988.

1 3 5 7 9 10 8 6 4 2

Simon & Schuster UK Ltd
1st Floor
222 Gray's Inn Road
London WC1X 8HB

Simon & Schuster Australia, Sydney
Simon & Schuster India, New Delhi

www.simonandschuster.co.uk
www.simonandschuster.com.au
www.simonandschuster.co.in

A CIP catalogue record for this book
is available from the British Library

Hardback ISBN: 978-1-4711-8991-3
Trade Paperback ISBN: 978-1-4711-8992-0
Ebook ISBN: 978-1-4711-8993-7
Audio ISBN: 978-1-4711-8995-1

Typeset in Sabon by M Rules
Printed and bound by CPI Group (UK) Ltd, Croydon, CR0 4YY

For Amanda Grunfeld,
a wise and brilliant friend

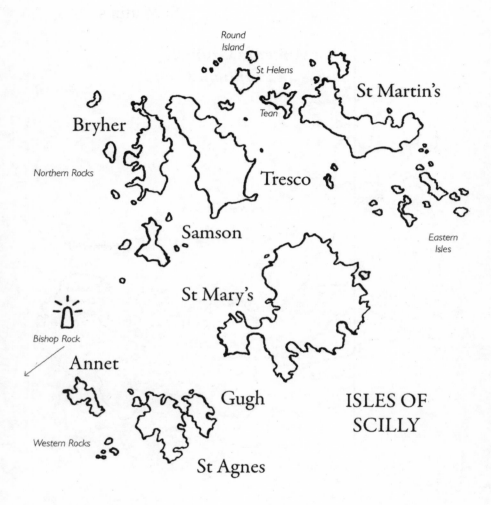

Round
Island

St Helens

St Martin's

Bryher

Tean

Northern Rocks

Tresco

Samson

Eastern
Isles

St Mary's

Bishop Rock

Annet

Gugh

ISLES OF
SCILLY

Western Rocks

St Agnes

St Martin's

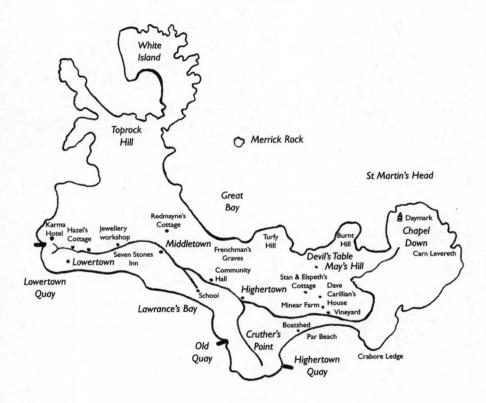

White
Island

Toprock
Hill

Merrick Rock

St Martin's Head

Great
Bay

Redmayne's
Cottage

Karma
Hotel

Hazel's
Cottage

Jewellery
workshop

Middletown

Turfy
Hill

Burnt
Hill

Daymark

Chapel
Down

Carn Levereth

Seven Stones
Inn

Frenchman's
Graves

Devil's Table

May's Hill

Lowertown

Community
Hall

Stan & Elspeth's
Cottage

Dave
Carillian's
House

Lowertown
Quay

School

Highertown

Minear Farm

Vineyard

Lawrance's Bay

Boatshed

Cruther's
Point

Par Beach

Old
Quay

Highertown
Quay

Crabore Ledge

PART 1

'No one heals himself by wounding another.'

St Ambrose

Sunday 18 December

The twins wait until the house falls silent. Outside their bedroom window the storm is gathering force; whirls of sea mist race past as the darkness thickens.

'Come on,' Jade whispers. 'The note says to be there by midnight.'

Ethan wants to refuse. Neither of them know who left the message, and their father's punishments will be harsh if he catches them, but his sister is already grabbing her red gloves and scarf. When Jade opens the window then drops onto the flat roof below, Ethan follows, even though he'd rather stay warm and safe. His body jolts as he lands on his heels, the cold air against his face telling him there's no going back.

The boy's anxiety soon turns to excitement. Mist blinds him as he chases ahead, but nothing can slow him down – he learned to walk on this path, each bump and tree root imprinted on his memory. The twins pause beside a field of narcissi. The flowers' odour is heady tonight, a mixture of jasmine and ripe oranges, thousands of blooms yielding their sweetness to the dark. St Martin's is bathed in moonlight that turns the flower fields silver, until a new wave of fog rushes inland, masking the horizon.

'Race you to the beach,' Jade yells.

'Stay on the path. Dad'll know we spoiled the flowers!'

'Who cares? Come on, hurry up.'

Jade copes better with their father's punishments, even though they both fear him. Ethan watches her trample through knee-high blooms, with broken petals sticking to her jeans. The boy glimpses her crimson scarf just once before she vanishes into the fog. Instinct tells him to follow, because he was born second, destined to play catch-up forever. Jade has always been the leader, and his voice, on days when he can't speak.

Ethan is halfway across the field when Jade screams, then all he can hear is the wind racing through hedgerows. There's no reply when he calls her name. His sister loves spooking him, but Ethan is already afraid. Ghosts dance before his eyes, the dark playing tricks on him.

'Where are you?' he shouts. 'Stop messing around.'

A hand touches Ethan's shoulder, the grip suddenly so harsh that each finger leaves a bruise. Someone kicks the backs of his knees, sending him sprawling. It can't be Jade: his sister isn't that strong. Ethan yells for help, but his attacker pushes him to the ground, tainting the air with booze and cigarettes. Jade screams again, telling him to run, but her voice sounds far away. Ethan can't see past the wall of fog that's hiding the stars. When he tries to shout for help, his voice has stopped working again. Just for a second his attacker's face comes into focus. It's familiar, yet his mind can't accept the truth. He fights hard to get free, but the arm around his waist is too powerful to escape. It's only when he bites his attacker's hand that its grip finally weakens.

The boy seizes his chance of freedom. He sprints home, tripping over the rutted ground. He tries to shout Jade's name again, but no sound emerges. All he can do is pray she's found a safe place to hide. His eyes are wide with panic when he clambers back up the drainpipe. Ethan gazes down from the window, searching for his twin, but fog has blindfolded the house again, hiding the fields from view.

1

Sunday 18 December

My grandfather valued beauty over safety. He could have built his home anywhere in Scilly, but he chose Hell Bay on Bryher's western coast, at the mercy of every Atlantic squall. My girlfriend, Nina, seems oblivious to tonight's storm, calmly writing Christmas cards at my kitchen table, even though it's almost midnight. She's decorated the house with fairy lights and tinsel, plus a large tree in the living room, making the place look more festive than it ever did during my childhood. The view outside is much less appealing. Rain is pouring down the window and breakers are hammering the shore fifty metres away. My dog, Shadow, gambols at my feet, begging for a final walk.

'No chance, mate. It's pissing down out there.'

'Don't be mean, Ben,' Nina says. 'Let him have a run.'

When I open the front door the wind rocks me back on my feet, but Shadow is overjoyed. He streaks outside

7

at top speed like he's seeking the eye of the storm, leaving me shaking my head. Four months ago he was so badly injured, it took two operations to stem the internal bleeding, followed by weeks of pain as his wounds healed, yet he never came close to giving up. The vet said that wolfdogs are a tough breed, and he must be right. The only difference in Shadow's behaviour since his near-death experience is his tendency to stay close to my side, apart from occasional forays across the island. I can see him chasing the tideline, tail wagging, while he looks for something foul to drag home.

'He's better, but still not a hundred per cent.'

'PTSD,' Nina replies. 'Give him time to recover.'

'Do dogs get depressed, like humans?'

'They have emotions, that's for sure. Shadow lets you know when he's pissed off, doesn't he?' A gust of wind rushes inside, blowing her envelopes from the table. 'Shut the door, for goodness sake.'

I can tell she's only pretending to be angry. She moved to Scilly in August, and it's taken me months to second-guess her moods. Her shield of mystery is so impenetrable I'd need an X-ray machine to discover what else lies beneath. Nina's serenity is rarely disturbed, but I know she's still affected by her husband's death nearly three years ago. She spends every weekend with me yet values her independence too highly to compromise. I asked her to live with me weeks ago, and I'm still waiting for an answer. Tomorrow she will return to St Martin's, a twenty-minute boat ride away, where she's house-sitting for a local couple who are spending the winter abroad. The arrangement suits her perfectly. She can study for her counselling diploma, do gardening duties, and keep me at arm's length.

Nina is stacking her cards in an orderly pile, giving me time to study her again. I can't explain why she's stuck in my head like a tune I can't stop humming. She never bothers with her appearance, apart from running a comb through her chocolate-brown hair, which hangs to her shoulders in a neat line. She's dressed in old Levi's and a white T-shirt, the olive skin she inherited from her Italian mother a shade darker than mine.

'Don't stare, Ben. It's distracting me.'

'Why are you writing cards now? They'll never get there in time.'

'It's the thought that counts. You should send some.'

'Christmas is a marketing conspiracy. When's the last time anyone gave you something you actually need?'

'That's such a narrow, blokeish thing to say.' Nina rolls her eyes. 'Stop bugging me and play the piano instead.'

'Is my conversation that bad?'

'I'd prefer some music to end the day.'

I haul myself upright with a show of reluctance. Nina handles her violin like it's an extension of her body, while I make constant mistakes on the piano my dad inherited from the island's pub. I taught myself to play by ear out of boredom as a kid, copying songs from the radio, because my parents refused to buy a TV. I can still pick out tunes, but conjuring one from memory is harder. I play the first notes of 'Someone to Watch over Me' in the wrong tempo, then muscle memory kicks in and life gets easier. Before long I'm following the storm's music instead, echoing the wind's high notes, and the waves' slow heartbeat.

When I finally stop, Nina is curled up on the settee, smiling. 'Not bad, for a man who never practises.'

'They offered me lessons at school, but rugby got in the way.'

'You're a natural then.'

'Why are you flattering me?' I say, closing the lid of the piano. 'Do you need a lift to St Martin's tomorrow? I'm off duty, so I can take you there.'

She shakes her head. 'Ray's cooking me breakfast, then we're going in his speedboat.'

'The old boy's sweet on you. Don't break his heart, will you?'

My uncle Ray is a hard man to impress; a lifelong bachelor, who returned to Bryher after years at sea, to build boats. He's famous for enjoying his own company, yet Nina can spend hours pottering around his boatyard, without being asked to leave.

'Are you jealous, Benesek Kitto?' She only uses my full name to mock.

'Not at all, I've got one hell of a weight advantage if he wants to fight it out.'

Nina stands up abruptly. 'Stop boasting and come to bed.'

10

'Is that your best line in seduction?'

'Take it or leave it, my friend.'

'Maybe I should play the piano more often.'

I don't put up a fight when she leads me to the bedroom. The sex between us is less frantic these days, but I still want her badly enough to grit my teeth while she peels off her clothes. My hefty, carthorse build embarrassed me as a kid, but the way she looks at me removes self-doubt. She takes her time undoing my shirt, stripping away layers of fabric, until nothing separates us, except the overhead light that exposes every detail. I love watching her move, and the emotions flowing across her face. It takes effort to hold my shattered senses together, but when I see her finally let go, it's worth the wait.

Her eyes are still cloudy when we collapse onto the pillows, her amber gaze softer than before. 'That's clinched it,' she murmurs.

'About what?'

'I choose you, not Ray.'

'Thank God.'

'But I wish you'd say how you feel now and then.'

'I just showed you, didn't I?'

'It was lovely, but its words that hold a relationship together.'

'I can't force it.' Voicing my emotions isn't easy, and working undercover taught me to hide my feelings. It's a habit I've found hard to shake off.

She touches my face. 'Just remember I'll listen, whenever you're ready.'

I stand up to turn off the light, her eyes closing when I slip back under the covers. Nina's hunger for sleep still amazes me; she can remain unconscious for twelve hours straight without moving a muscle. She shifts towards me, mumbling something under her breath.

'Changes are coming, Ben. You have to be ready.'

'How do you mean?'

I wait for a reply, but hear only her slow breathing, and the gale rattling roof tiles overhead. Her oval face is as calm as a statue in the moonlight filtering through the curtains. I'm still digesting her words when Shadow scratches at the front door, the sound reminding me of the squealing car brakes that often woke me in London. I moved back to the house where I was born two years ago, but still remember the city's hectic pace. My dog's fur is soaked when I get him inside, so I rub him dry with an old towel, then he lies at my feet, warming himself by the fire's embers. When I look around, Nina's belongings are scattered across my living room. A copy of *Persuasion* lies on the coffee table, her rucksack by the door, and the violin her husband gave her just before he died is propped against the wall. She's even begun leaving clothes in my wardrobe, which must signal progress. When I finally get to meet her parents I'll know she means business.

Shadow doesn't complain about being left alone when I return to bed, content to stay warm by the hearth. My girlfriend's warning is already half-forgotten; my life has already changed beyond recognition. I was alone for five years, apart from a few meaningless flings, but now Nina's here, and I'm not prepared to let her go. When I peer out of the window for a final time the storm is worsening – fog presses against the glass, trying to find its way inside.

2

Monday 19 December

My phone rings before I'm fully awake. Emergency calls come through to me when the police station's closed, and I recognise the woman's voice. Gemma Minear is phoning from St Martin's; the line is patchy at best, her speech broken by a hiss of static. She informs me that her eleven-year-old daughter Jade is missing before the connection fails. When I call her back it crosses my mind to advise her not to worry: kids love solitary adventures, and the island is just two miles long, but the fear in her voice forces me to act.

'Stay there, Gemma. I'm on my way.'

I hiss out a few curses before hanging up; my day off has just been cancelled. It's 6.30 a.m. and Nina is still fast asleep. It's pitch dark when I peer out through the curtains, but at least the gale has blown over. The sea looks unnaturally calm, with a pall of mist covering the ocean, the islands of Gweal and Illiswilgig bathed in moonlight.

14

I take a shower and bolt down some toast before scribbling a note for Nina, explaining what's happened. Shadow leaps outside the moment I open the door, desperate for another hit of freedom. I felt the same when I worked undercover in the Murder Squad, hemmed in by skyscrapers, stress, and polluted air. I'd prefer more time in bed, but mornings like this remind me why I came home to Bryher. I've got the island all to myself, the sea murmuring its greeting, as low waves drag shingle further inland. Hell Bay Hotel is the only building in sight, with a single light shining from the bar, a ten-minute walk along the shore. My closest friend Zoe grew up there, and she's back from her new life as a music teacher in India for a pre-Christmas visit. I haven't seen her yet, but there should be time to drop by this afternoon, provided Jade Minear gets home soon.

My house looks shabby when I glance back from the path. My mother kept the one-storey building spotless while Dad worked at sea, but now it's crying out for attention. The moonlight exposes broken tiles on the roof, and window frames desperate for a coat of paint. Nina was right about things needing to change, starting with basic maintenance, but the DIY must wait. My boss would be outraged to hear that one of Scilly's richest families has been kept waiting.

Shadow bounds ahead when I walk east towards Church Quay. My short journey takes me over Shipman Head Down, my torch beam exposing land covered in heather and bracken, with no sign of the wild garlic,

15

poppies, and vetch that bloom there in high summer. I walk through the minute village, which qualifies as a town on Bryher, but the place is hibernating. The closed sign outside the Vine Café will stay there until April, when the season's first day-trippers arrive.

My uncle Ray is already up when I reach his boat-yard at 7 a.m. He's wearing paint-stained overalls, inspecting a brand-new dinghy that needs to be sanded smooth before its first coat of resin. The man is almost as tall as me, his steel-grey hair cropped short. He's in his sixties, with a hard-boned face and rangy build. When he turns to face me, there's more anger in his eyes than I've seen in years, his voice a gruff baritone.

'Why build a boat, if you're going to neglect it?' he asks.

'Sorry, Ray, I should have called you.'

'Last night's storm almost smashed her apart.'

'I meant to put her on the trailer.'

'You said that last time. I had to winch her up the slipway, in the pissing rain.'

'I'll give you some labour as payback.' I can see his bad mood fading, even though he shakes his head in mock-despair.

'How about finishing off this dinghy for me now? Or have you got better plans?'

'I'm needed in St Martin's. A kid's run off without telling anyone.'

'Who's that?'

'Jade Minear.'

He shakes his head. 'Scott won't be happy; he expects obedience from all his kids.'

'I'd better get moving then.'

'Take care in this fog.' My uncle's sea-blue eyes fix on me again. 'It's not done with us yet. We're stuck in a weather cycle; it'll keep coming back.'

I'm in no position to argue. Ray understands the ocean's moods better than anyone, after years in the merchant navy. He leads me further inside the boat-yard, where my bowrider lies on a trailer. I built the twenty-foot motorboat from cedar and spruce last spring, under Ray's guidance. I let my uncle choose its name as payback for his help; he christened it Morvoren, which suits the territory. It's Cornish for mermaid, and the islands have plenty of folk tales about mythical singers, tempting sailors to their deaths. My boat has a more practical purpose. It's essential to my job as Deputy Commander of the Island Police. I rely on it to deliver me to the station on St Mary's, espe-cially in winter, when the inter-island ferries are less frequent. I feel bad about failing to protect my sole form of transport, but time with Nina wipes everything else from my mind.

It's the wrong time to ask my uncle for a favour, but he's my best option. 'Can you keep Shadow for a while, Ray?'

'He may not want my company.'

'Hang on to his lead good and tight when I cast off.'

The dog is whining already, sensing abandonment. I

start the engine then sail into the mist, with Shadow's howls of protest echoing across the sound. I'd prefer to take him with me, but I can't visit one of the most powerful families in Scilly with a badly behaved wolf-dog in tow.

The temperature drops when my boat leaves shore, with the forelight on full power, cutting a swathe through the dark. Sea mist hangs over Tresco's western coast: the island's hills are blurred, the pale sand of Appletree Bay barely visible. I keep my distance when the Chinks loom in front of me, piercing the water's black surface like broken teeth, waiting to shred the hull of any vessel that strays too close. It's a reminder that this stretch of water is thick with shipwrecks, from four-hundred-year-old frigates to modern yachts blown off course. Once I reach Tresco's southern tip I can breathe easily again, steering into Crow Sound, then heading east for St Martin's. The horizon is turning pink, and the only noise comes from the grind of my boat's engine, the sea as calm as a basin of mercury. When the mist billows past, its breath leaves droplets of brine on my skin.

I'm chilled to the bone by the time St Martin's rises from the fog. It has the same dark history as Scilly's other four inhabited islands. Centuries ago the islanders were prepared to kill to evade the customs men. St Martin's 140 inhabitants have grown more law-abiding since the days of smuggling, and the mild climate works in their favour. Dozens of people make a living from working on the Minears' flower farm all year round, shipping daffodils, pinks, and agapanthus to the mainland in winter. The rest rely on tourism. St Martin's boasts the high-end Karma Hotel, an art gallery, a bakery, and several flourishing cafés, but almost everything shuts in winter. Plenty of locals work on trawlers or oil rigs during the coldest months, if they can't find work as seasonal flower pickers. A third of the population leave for the mainland every November, only returning when the holiday season restarts.

St Martin's jagged profile fills the horizon as I reach Highertown, bathed in pure morning light. The island offers two contrasting faces to the world; its curved axis is split by a ridge of high ground that runs from Top Rock in the west, all the way to Chapel Down. I let my engine idle as I approach the island's sheltered southern side. St Martin's has some of the most beautiful bays in Scilly: my brother Ian and I often played on Par Beach as kids, burying each other in white sand, or picking cockles by Crabore Ledge. The tide is high when I moor on the quay, but when the water recedes you can still make out the foundations of a Neolithic village.

My clothes are wet with spray, making me shiver as I hurry inland at 8 a.m., passing a well-kept cricket green with a pavilion the community built themselves. The island's vineyard lies to my left as I walk uphill to the village, its dormant grapevines waiting for spring sunlight to revive them. I scan the landscape for the missing girl, but she's probably run home already, hungry for breakfast. My curiosity rises when I see the sign for Minear Farm. I used to work there during school Christmas holidays, alongside my brother. Scott and Gemma Minear run the island's biggest enterprise, with a controlling stake in many of St Martin's businesses. Their farm looks prosperous when I open the gate — the fields are thick with yellow narcissi, their lemony scent filling my airways. The flowers will soon be harvested, then flown to the mainland as gifts for Christmas and New Year. The Minears' farmhouse is the biggest on St Martin's, grey and imposing, built from local granite with a slate roof, the front door glossy with scarlet paint.

Gemma is waiting for me in her porch, drawing on a cigarette like it's her sole source of oxygen. I don't know the family well but rumour has it that she and Scott are millionaires. Her clothes don't reveal any sign of wealth; a grey tracksuit clings to her thin frame, dyed black hair pulled into a ponytail, as she grinds out her fag with the heel of her trainer. Gemma is a decade older than me, around forty-five, with delicate features. She used to be one of the island's beauties, but it looks as though years of worry have left her cheeks hollow, and her skin a shade too pale. Her voice crackles with anxiety when she greets me.

'Thanks for coming over, Ben. I'm getting worried, it's not like Jade to run away.'

'Let's warm up inside. You can give me the details.'

The hallway is less pristine than the farmhouse's exterior, and there's very little Christmas cheer. I can't see much sign that the family are looking forward to the holiday season, just Wellington boots heaped by the door, three badly framed seascapes on the walls, and quarry tiles worn thin by generations of footsteps. Gemma rushes down the corridor like she's training for a sprint race. The first thing I see in her kitchen is a family photo that must be several years old. All four Minear kids sit with their parents in a photographer's studio. The teenage boy and girl look uncomfortable, but the twins are beaming. The pair of them are around six years old, and so similar it's uncanny, with dimpled cheeks and blond hair combed flat, their hands folded neatly in their laps.

Gemma remains silent as she pours coffee into mugs, keeping her back turned. I'd like to know why she's so upset, when her daughter is probably just enjoying herself. I used to love solo adventures, and my parents never worried about it, on an island with no record of crime. When Gemma sits down opposite me, it looks like she's been on edge for months, her shoulders hunched tight around her ears. Family tension could be to blame, not her child going AWOL.

'Jade's a strong character, more like a teenager than an eleven-year-old,' she says. 'But she's never done this before.'

'Do you know what time she left?'

'The storm woke me around three a.m. I looked

in the twins' room then and her bed was empty.' She swallows a gulp of coffee. 'I checked her clothes just now. She must be wearing her red bomber jacket, with matching hat and scarf.'

'Sounds like red's her favourite colour.'

'It's all she'll wear at the moment. Jade likes to be noticed, unlike her brother.'

'Does she have a phone?'

She shakes her head. 'Everyone here's agreed not to let our kids have them before they start secondary school.'

'Good plan. Have you called your parents yet?'

Gemma looks embarrassed. 'I'm not in Mum's good books right now. We haven't spoken for a while, but she'd call me if Jade turned up at the crack of dawn.'

'Where else could she be?'

'The twins love visiting Will and Maria Austell. They've been renting the farm manager's cottage since Will started working for us. He's a friend of yours, isn't he?'

'We were close at school, but I haven't seen him in years.' Gemma still looks so anxious, I'd like to know what other factors are adding to her distress, but I need to focus on bringing the girl home. 'Text your parents if that's easier than phoning. She'll be there, most likely, or at a mate's house.'

She shakes her head, frowning. 'Jade wouldn't visit anyone in the middle of the night.'

'What's Ethan saying?'

'Nothing, as usual – his sister helps him to speak. That's why I want her home soon. He was awake when I checked on him, but he couldn't answer. Ethan's struggled to talk for years, and he's not keen on writing either; he does his schoolwork, but I can't get him to write down what he's thinking. I'd hate him to lose the confidence he's gained this year.'

'She's bound to turn up, safe and sound. Maybe Ethan's staying quiet to keep her out of trouble.'

I'm still reassuring Gemma when Scott Minear barges into the room. Ten years ago the farmer looked like a Hollywood star, with a chiselled jaw and high cheekbones. Minear still carries himself like the island's unanointed king, despite being several stone overweight, with brown hair in a razor cut, his skin reddened by working outdoors. He's been St Martin's mayor for years, facing down rivals for the position. Some believe he's a force for good, while others say he's a control freak, but everyone knows he doesn't suffer fools. Rumour has it that he runs his empire by harsh rules. When I worked for him two decades ago he would always fire the slowest pickers, sparing no mercy for anyone who needed the income to support their families.

'Welcome to the madhouse, Inspector,' he says, grinning like he's told a first-class joke. 'My wife's wasting your time, Jade's always playing tricks on us.'

'Better safe than sorry,' I reply.

'The girl's a real drama queen. I don't mind that,

to be honest. At least she's strong-willed, but she's picked the busiest time of year to wind us up.' Minear parks himself on a chair, so close our knees are almost touching.

'Why do you think she's run off, Scott?'

'She's got my warped sense of humour; it'll be some kind of prank.'

'There's been no trouble at home?'

'None whatsoever.'

Gemma leans forward, her expression anxious. 'Tell Ben about the window, Scott.'

'That was nothing.' Minear looks scornful. 'Some tosser lobbed a stone through our living room window last week. It scared the living daylights out of Gemma, and it cost me a bloody fortune to replace. A few folk here envy our success, but it could have been a kid on a dare. That's why it didn't bother me.'

'When did it happen?'

'Last Wednesday, about six in the morning. I looked outside, but they'd scarpered,' he says. 'It was a bloody great lump of rock, with "Devil's Table" scrawled on it, with a marker pen.'

'That's a strange message.' The Devil's Table is an ancient rock formation shaped like an altar on Chapel Down, five minutes north of the farm.

'Christ knows what it means. I took a walk up there, but it looks the same as ever. If I find the culprit I'll return the favour.'

'Let us sort it, Scott. Did you keep the stone?'

'I threw it back on the beach, where it belongs. You'll never find out who chucked it. Who's going to own up, in a place this small?' He lounges back in his chair, amusement on his face. 'I hear you've got a new girlfriend – a classy brunette, by all accounts. Why's a city woman like her staying at the Redmaynes' place?'

'She's house-sitting while they're in Spain.'

'Nice work if you can get it.' The farmer's dark eyes glitter like chips of wet slate. 'Psychologist, isn't she?'

'Nina's training to be a counsellor.'

'I'd pay her good money to fix Gemma's nerves.' Minear's statement is delivered with a laugh, but his wife flinches. 'She's always fretting about stuff she can't fix.'

'Doesn't everyone?' I reply.

'You'd need a grenade to disturb my sleep, and Jade's bound to walk through that door any minute.' Minear rises to his feet again, but I can tell he's rattled. 'Stay for the harvest, if you like. The wages are better since last time you picked for us. We still lay on cider and a decent lunch.'

'Thanks, but I'll head back to Bryher, once Jade's found.'

'She'll show up, sooner or later.'

'There has to be a reason, Scott. She's never done this before.' Gemma's voice is low and placatory.

Minear stares at his wife. 'The little bugger was horsing around in the top field last night – dozens of plants were flattened, and I know why. Those twins

25

are spoiled rotten. They spend hours playing bloody computer games; I was in the fields every spare minute at their age, or I got a clip round the ear.'

'Life's improved since then, thank God,' she mutters.

Scott swings round to face me. 'Let me know if you need help,' he says, nodding at the fields outside. 'A hundred crates want filling today, or our supplier in London will drop his prices. When are you coming outside, Gemma?'

'Not till Jade's home. Luke's helping you, and the pickers will be here soon.'

He scowls at her. 'Where's my harvest knife?'

'Probably where you left it, in the cutting house, with all the rest.'

Scott Minear marches away without saying goodbye. I feel sure he's concerned about his daughter, but too macho to admit it. When I look outside he's talking to his oldest son, Luke, but the discussion appears one-sided. The young man is keeping his chin up, while his dad bawls in his face. Luke absorbs his father's tirade with a fixed expression. I've seen him playing football for the local team – he's St Martin's best striker at just eighteen – but there's no sign of his athletic prowess today. Gemma's eyes are glossy when I study her again.

'Is Luke okay? He looks tired.'

'Harvest time's gruelling for all of us.' Her gaze lingers on the view from the window. 'Luke was here with me and Scott when that stone came through our window. It's unsettled him too.'

'Where do you think Jade's gone, Gemma?'

'God knows, I'm just scared something bad's happened.'

'Like what?'

'You should speak to Dave Carillian. The twins were playing near his house yesterday afternoon. They're fascinated by him for some reason, but he gives me the creeps . . .' Her words fade into silence. 'The bloke was watching them from his front window, until I called them away.'

'Do you know him?'

'No one does. The bloke's lived here three years without mixing with anyone. Why would a man lock himself away like that?'

'None of the islanders are on the Sex Offenders' Register, if that's your point. Local police are kept informed if they enter the neighbourhood.'

'That's good to know, but he's a still a weirdo. I keep telling the twins to steer clear. I hope to God he's not laid a finger on Jade.'

'I think that's unlikely, but I'll visit all your neighbours, if Jade isn't home soon.'

Gemma's words echo the standpoint of a minority of islanders. Most people in Scilly accept newcomers gladly, but the rest remain suspicious. Incomers have to adapt fast, by volunteering at local events and keeping an open door. Loners always stand out in a tiny community.

'I'll drop by the cottage first. It's time I said hello

to Will and his wife. Contact the rest of your family, please, and ring me if Jade shows up.' I stand up to put on my coat. 'It's cold out there, maybe she doesn't fancy joining the harvest. She could be hiding in a mate's loft.'

'Let's hope so.'

The stress on Gemma's face shows no sign of lifting when I take my leave.

3

Ethan is still in bed, keeping his eyes closed. He hardly slept last night, and now he's afraid to face his family. Words clogged in his throat when his mother asked about Jade; he wants to explain what happened, but his voice has failed him again. Guilt presses on the centre of his chest like a lead weight. Why didn't he make Jade ignore the note, inviting them down to the quay at midnight? She tucked it in her pocket before they set off, so he can't even show it to his mum. Anyone on the island could have sent it, then waited in the field to catch them. Pictures float through his mind like last night's fog. Even with eyes screwed shut he can see the excitement on Jade's face, then shadows dancing in the mist. His heart beats too fast when he remembers the stranger's hand gripping his shoulder. He tries to recall his attacker's face, but it hovers, just out of reach.

When the boy forces himself out of bed, his hopes rise suddenly. It looks like his sister has returned, but it's just his own image glimpsed in the mirror. A child with a slight build and sandy hair stares back at him. The reflection could almost be Jade, yet there are subtle differences. He's never witnessed that much fear in his sister's eyes.

Ethan takes his piccolo from the shelf and plays a few notes, the sound light and soothing. He walks over to the window, standing in a shaft of winter light that carries no warmth at all. When he shuts his eyes and concentrates, his sister's heartbeat still drums beside his own, a little weaker than before. He can hear the murmur of her breathing when they're apart, her thoughts echoing inside his skull, but now there's only silence.

The fog has lifted when he stares down from the window. Pickers are already at work in the nearest field, their movements quick and precise as they harvest flowers into sheaves, tying bunches of fifty with brown twine. Ethan knows he should run down to help, but it feels like his feet are stuck to the floor. He can only remain by the window, scanning the horizon, like a soldier on guard.

4

The old farm manager's cottage lies beside the Minears' top field, set back from the lane. It's showing its age, like my place; the lead flashing round the chimney is falling apart, the roofline sagging. Two mountain bikes by the porch are the only hint that the place is newly occupied. When I glance through the front window into the kitchen, a man in his thirties is kissing a dark-haired woman with so much enthusiasm, they're oblivious to the outside world. I give them a moment to enjoy themselves before lifting the door knocker.

When Will Austell finally appears, I barely recognise him. He comes from a family of easy-going hippies, but no one would guess it now. His nose piercing has gone, and the blond dreadlocks that fell past his shoulders have been replaced by a neat haircut, but his body language is the same. His movements are still fluid and graceful as a dancer's when he reaches out to hug me.

'Jesus, Ben, it's great to see you. Were you always that tall?'

'Six foot four, last time I checked.'

'You're built like a bloody giant.' He steps back to welcome me inside. 'Come and meet Maria, I've been meaning to bring her over to Bryher.'

The woman standing in the couple's rented kitchen has a face that's memorable, rather than beautiful. Her bone structure is delicate, with wide-set eyes and lips that dominate her face. Maria's features only make sense when she steps towards me with her hand outstretched, the warmth in her smile making it hard to look away.

'You must have magical powers,' I say. 'How did you persuade this rebel to get married?'

'It wasn't easy. Luckily I'm a patient woman.'

'He was a restless soul, back in the day.'

'Lots of girlfriends, you mean? Tell me his secrets, please.'

'That could take hours.'

Maria's soft Spanish accent adds to her charm. She tells me that Will is so glad to be home, he goes for walks late at night just to smell the air and reconnect with the landscape. I glance around their kitchen while we talk. Will's guitar is propped against the wall, and their pinboard is covered with photos that prove how far they've travelled, with selfies taken on Caribbean beaches and in a dozen exotic cities.

'I just need to check if either of you have seen Jade Minear last night, or this morning?'

Will looks puzzled. 'The twins came by early

evening, to check out our new bikes. They love any-thing mechanical.'

'That was about six,' says Maria. 'We were making dinner.'

'Not since then?'

'We've been busy, mate,' Will replies. 'We only just got out of bed.'

When his wife blushes, his laughter carries me back two decades. Will was a tearaway back then, living in a caravan on St Martin's, playing in a band, and dating the prettiest girls. I remember him dancing beside the bonfires we lit each summer, head back, lost in the rhythm. He seemed like a free spirit, dreaming of adventures, until his family left suddenly and we lost touch.

'Did you make it to art school in the end?' I ask.

'No such luck. Reality caught up with me – the army was my only option.'

'Are you kidding? I can't imagine you in a uniform.'

'It never felt right,' he says, quietly. 'I thought you'd be an English teacher by now. Your head was always stuck in some big American novel.'

'My shelves are still full of them. What made you come back to Scilly?'

'Maria was nursing in a field hospital when we got together. I told her about the islands and she wanted to see why I love it here.'

'I start a temporary job at St Mary's hospital in the New Year,' his wife adds, placing her arm round her husband's waist. 'Will's doing building work for the Minears. We'll give the lifestyle a try for a year, to see if it suits us. But you wanted to know about Jade, didn't you?'

'She's run off somewhere. If you see her, can you ring me, please?'

'That kid seems fearless to me, I bet she's fine.' Will accepts my card, glancing at the words. 'You can't be the Deputy Commander of the Island Police. You were a gangly teenager when I left, too tongue-tied to ask girls out.'

'Things have improved on that score, thank God.'

'Bring your other half round for a drink soon, or meet us at the pub,' Will says, following me down the hall. 'Call us, won't you, if we can help look for Jade?'

'I will, and let's have a drink soon. Nina will enjoy meeting your wife.'

'Everyone does. I must have done something good in a former life.'

Will Austell squeezes my shoulder, but doesn't linger. He races back to the kitchen to find Maria. My old friend's happiness is obvious, but the visit has brought little fresh information about Jade Minear's disappearance, except that she and Ethan called by early yesterday evening.

My next visit is to a property that lies a few hundred metres north of Minear Farm. Dave Carillian is one of the few permanent residents on St Martin's that I don't know by sight. I've met the majority of Scilly's two thousand inhabitants since joining the island force, but never had reason to visit his property. His ugly chalet-style house lies halfway up May's Hill; it looks like a bungalow, with the first floor nailed on as an after-thought, the roof covered in mismatched tiles. I peer through the picture window into Carillian's lounge while I wait in his porch. It's painted magnolia, with few distinguishing features, except the swirling pattern on his brown carpet. There's no TV, only shelves loaded with books, and an old-fashioned radio.

The man who appears in the doorway seems shocked by my arrival, peering out through a six-inch gap. Carillian comes from a generation of men that still wear a shirt and tie seven days a week. His cardigan looks like it was hand-knitted decades ago, corduroy trousers several inches too short. He's in his sixties with a thickset build, almost completely bald, apart from a few tufts of grey hair scattered across his scalp. I get the sense that he'd rather send me away than allow a stranger over his threshold.

'Can we talk please, Mr Carillian? I'm DI Kitto, from the island police.'

'Come inside, if you're coming. The heat's rushing out the door.' The man's voice is a low Cornish growl when he finally allows me over his threshold.

His kitchen looks like a seventies time warp. There's a Formica table with a single wooden chair, an old-fashioned fridge droning in the corner, the doors on his units hanging at odd angles. His only Christmas decoration is an artificial tree in the corner that must get dragged out every year, shedding more plastic needles each time, until most of the branches are bare. Carillian has arranged his home to deter visitors, forcing me to remain standing, and I can tell he takes cleanliness seriously. The air reeks of bleach, as if the lino and work surfaces have been scoured recently, which makes me uneasy. The temperature in his home feels icy, or it could just be the impact of his stare. His small eyes are so focused on me, it feels like I've been placed under a microscope.

'Your home's in good order, Mr Carillian. It's far neater than mine.'

'Tidiness brings peace of mind, doesn't it?'

'I've never managed to find out.'

His smile is fraying at the edges. 'Are you here for a reason, Inspector?'

'I'm looking for Jade Minear. Have you seen her recently, please?'

'Is she one of the twins from the farm?'

'Their mother saw them playing by your house yesterday afternoon.'

'I spotted them, but took no notice. I didn't see them again until last night.' He remains motionless, arms hanging at his sides.

'Was she with her brother?'

'The pair of them were running across the field when I closed my bedroom curtains.'

'What time was that?'

'About eleven thirty, I always go up then.'

'Can you remember which way they were going?'

'Towards Highertown Quay, I think. One of them was dressed in red, I saw the gloves and scarf, but the fog soon hid them again.' He peers at me more closely. 'It didn't seem like anything to worry about. Those two are always off gallivanting.'

'How do you know?'

The old man's gaze slips from mine. 'I often catch sight of people on the lane.'

'Even at night?'

'Only if I happen to look, but I know how kids behave. I went on midnight adventures myself as a boy.'

'You may have been the last person to see Jade, before her mother realised she was missing at three a.m.'

'It was purely by chance.'

'Do the Minear twins ever call on you?'

'Why would they?'

'To be neighbourly, perhaps? Their mother says they often play on the lane outside.'

'I wouldn't open my door if they knocked.' His voice becomes strident. 'My mother humoured the neighbours all her life, much good it did her. Their real opinion only came out at her funeral. Do you know how many people attended?'

'I can't guess.'

'Five, including me. The rest never even sent apologies.' A look of rage appears on the man's face, then vanishes again.

'I'm sorry to hear that. Did you have a job on the mainland?'

'How else would I survive?' Carillian appears irritated by the simple question. 'I was an architectural draftsman in Truro, until computers made me redundant. That's when I moved back to Mousehole, to care for my mother, ten years ago.'

'It can't have been easy giving up your home.'

'My past has nothing to do with what's happened, Inspector. That girl's situation isn't my problem.' The man's bad mood sharpens his tone of voice.

'She may have been hurt, so it's everyone's problem, until she's found. If you do see Jade, can you call me please?'

Carillian mutters a few angry words under his breath, his manner getting odder by the minute. When I pass him my card, he shunts his glasses further up the bridge of his nose before examining it. 'Benesek is an unusual name. Do you know its origin?'

'Only that it's Cornish.'

'It's derived from the Latin word *benedictus*, meaning "blessed by God". Your parents must have welcomed your arrival.' His statement wrongfoots me, but I manage a smile.

'They were hoping for a girl, but settled for me. Thanks for your time, Mr Carillian.'

The man's cryptic speech and touchy manner could explain why the islanders avoid him. Some would say he fits the stereotype for a child molester: isolated, watchful, with limited social skills. But there are plenty of oddballs in Scilly, and his standoffishness could stem from shyness. People often drift to the margins if they can't fit in, believing that life will be easier in a small community, at the edge of the world. They don't realise how much resilience you need to survive the long winters. I've got no reason to believe that Carillian has hurt either of the Minear twins, despite their mother's suspicions, but his awkward manner and obsessive cleanliness stick in my mind.

It's 9 a.m. when the conversation ends. My boss will be rearranging ornaments on his desk at the station on St Mary's, a half-hour boat ride away. I know from experience that DCI Madron likes to hear about threats before they materialise, but his tendency to panic forces me to handle every conversation with care. My senior officer goes into meltdown at the smallest hint of being overlooked. He listens in silence when I ring him to share the news that Jade Minear is missing, then draws a sharp breath.

'Don't offend her father. I know how hot-headed you are, Kitto.'

'No one's ever complained about my conduct, sir.'

'It's only a matter of time. Did you hear me? Scott Minear could make our lives a misery.'

'In what way?'

'He uses his role as mayor to undermine council decisions. Minear supports local causes like the primary

39

school, but he loves upsetting the applecart, just for the hell of it.' The DCI sighs loudly. 'I'll send Eddie over now. Talk to the islanders, and find out what's happened.'

'I'm doing that already; the last sighting of the twins seems to have been around eleven thirty last night. They were spotted together.'

'That's a start, I suppose. Don't waste time, Kitto. Bring that girl home today.'

My boss rings off without making a single helpful suggestion, leaving me to walk back to Minear Farm alone. A shape appears in an upstairs window when I approach the building. A fair-haired child is staring out at the fields; he's holding a small flute in one hand, the other pressed against the glass like he's trying to claw his way out.

5

Ethan knows the policeman's name. The other kids talked about Inspector Kitto for days after he visited school, with his grey dog that looks like a wolf. The policeman reminds him of a black-haired giant, but his arrival raises the boy's spirits. Maybe the police can find Jade today, and bring her home safe.

Ethan lifts his piccolo to play a few scales, the sound quick and effortless, making him wish that words came as easily as musical notes. He's still holding the instrument when footsteps pound across the landing. His father storms into the room, eyes blazing, just like when he fights with his mum. Ethan's dad has only shaken his fists at him until now, but his mother gets worse treatment. It feels like a matter of time until it's his turn. The boy can feel anger flowing from him in waves.

'Put that bloody whistle down and do some work for once.'

The boy stands still, hoping to be left in peace, but his dad stoops down until their faces are almost touching.

'You and Jade trampled on the flowers last night, didn't

41

you? I had to give her a slap yesterday, for talking back. Is that why she's sulking?'

Ethan thinks of a reply, but nothing leaves his mouth except a hiss of air.

'Pretending to be dumb again, you little fool?'

His father grips his arm then shakes him, as if the words stuck in his throat could be dislodged, but it has no effect. It feels like his mouth is packed with sand.

'What's wrong with you, boy? Fetch Jade home, before your mum loses it. I want you both in the field today.'

Ethan grabs his clothes fast, to avoid the back of his father's hand, but his thoughts spin like a broken compass. He's still shaking when his father leaves the room. Once he's alone again Ethan retrieves his piccolo, then slumps back onto his bed, cradling it against his chest.

6

Pickers are arriving when I return to Minear Farm, the group in high spirits. The peak harvest season begins in November, but the farm always needs extra help over the Christmas holiday. It's a family event for most of the island population once the kids break up from school. Dozens of people will spend the next week gathering the Christmas harvest, dressed in ancient jeans, walking boots, and waterproofs. A buzz of laughter rises from the crowd; if any of them have heard that a child is missing, no one seems alarmed. I'd like to interview Ethan immediately, to find out what he saw, but Gemma's description of his speech problems makes me cautious. I don't want to make matters worse, so I'll leave it for another hour. There's every chance the girl will run home soon without putting a sensitive kid through the wringer.

The first face I recognise belongs to Hazel Teague. She's one of a handful of community nurses who travel between the islands, treating medical complaints, from bunions to heart disease. She's a single mum in her mid-thirties, with a waterfall of chestnut hair flowing past her shoulders, her gestures animated as she chats to a friend. Hazel has brought both her teenage kids along: Ivan is tall with a strong build, his rock-star haircut obscuring his eyes. He did a week's work experience with me last summer, after his GCSEs. The lad struck me as mature for his age, prepared to try any task, and today he's observing his mum's flamboyance with a look of amusement. I felt the same at his age. My mother was always first to get drunk and dance at parties, until my father died, and her joie de vivre withered overnight. Hazel helped to nurse her when she became housebound with MS, so I'll always be grateful. Her younger child is watching the pickers arrive; Polly Teague is around thirteen, standing close to her brother like she's taking shelter. When I raise my hand to wave, Hazel beckons me over.

'Are you picking today, Ben? Be warned, you'll ache like hell tomorrow. Ivan and me are in the cutting shed this year, but it's Polly's first time in the fields, isn't it, love?'

The girl's cheeks flush with embarrassment. 'Stop going on about it, Mum. I'll be fine on my own.'

'You'll enjoy it,' I tell her. 'I bet you pick more than everyone.'

Polly gives a shy smile, but doesn't reply.

'How's it going, Ivan?' I ask. 'Still thinking of a police career?'

'It's my first choice, but my teachers want me to do an economics degree.'

'Stockbrokers get better wages, that's for sure. But could you handle being stuck behind a desk?'

He shoots me a mischievous grin. 'I'd hate every minute.'

'Me too. I'll write you a good reference, if you decide to join us.'

The lad mutters a quick thank you before disappearing into the crowd with his sister tagging along, in search of younger company.

'They grow up so bloody quick,' Hazel sighs. 'Ivan's got another year of sixth form, but he spends every waking moment with his girlfriend or messing about in the shed. Sneaking a cigarette, most likely. I've caught him smoking more than once. Polly's already stealing my make-up.'

'Things move fast these days. Does your daughter know the Minear twins?'

'Ethan and Jade are a few years younger, but they hang out sometimes.' Hazel falls into step beside me as the crowd forms a queue, collecting baskets and knives from the cutting shed. 'I used to think all that stuff about twins was rubbish, but those two are joined at the hip. They do everything together.'

'Jade left home around eleven thirty last night. No one's seen her since, from the sounds of it.'

'Is that why you're here?' Her keen gaze scans my face. 'The last time I saw her was when they stopped by last week, after school. The twins played on the Xbox with Polly for a while.'

'Apparently she's never run off like this before.'

'Have you tried her gran?'

'No luck there – Gemma's texted me to say no.'

'Ethan depends on Jade to communicate. Do you need help looking for her?' The concern on Hazel's face has grown during our conversation.

'Can you ask the other pickers if they've seen her this morning? Give me a ring if there's news.'

'Of course I will.'

The nurse is as good as her word, quizzing another woman about Jade straight away. I walk towards the barn before anyone else can catch my eye. I don't want to spread panic, but the rocky landscape is full of hazards; the girl could have fallen somewhere in the fog. I'll have to scour the island if she's not back soon, in case she's lying somewhere unconscious.

There's an old sign above the barn door, with the words 'Cutting Shed' chiselled into the wood. The building has served the same purpose for over a hundred years. The harvest is brought here, so the flowers can be packed, then loaded onto a delivery boat and flown to the mainland from St Mary's. I notice a change in atmosphere inside the barn. Scott Minear's oldest son is working alone. Luke is stacking plywood boxes on one of the tables, then lining them with cellophane and tissue paper. He reminds me of his father during his heyday, except for his slimmer build and a midnight-blue tattoo on his hand. The teenager has the same chiselled features as Scott, sandy hair spilling over his collar, but his temperament seems calmer. Luke is working at a rapid pace. He's so focused, my arrival goes unnoticed until I call his name. The boy appears startled, like he's just surfaced from an intense dream.

'Can we have a chat, Luke? It won't take long.'

He carries on lining the boxes. 'Do you mind if I keep going? Once the pickers start, there's no let up all day.'

'Go ahead, I know how busy it gets. I worked here every Christmas years ago, but I wasn't great. The experienced ones picked twice as much.'

Luke shrugs. 'Every little helps. We're growing different varieties now: Soleil d'Or, Paper White, and Grand Monarch. They give more blooms than the old types.' His hands fly as he completes his work.

'Can you think where Jade might be hiding?'

'Mum said she's run off somewhere.' His gaze finally lifts to meet mine. 'She seemed happy enough last night, I can't think where she'd go.'

'Not even a theory?'

'She's got no reason to run away.' The boy's tone lacks conviction.

'If there's been a row at home, I need to know. Your dad said Jade can be headstrong.'

'That's rich, coming from him. They clash because they're so alike, but she's still his favourite.'

'How about you? Do you get on okay with the twins?'

'Of course, but me and Amy are so much older,

we're more like extra parents.' Luke hesitates before continuing. 'Gran should know about Jade. The twins go up there most days. Mum doesn't like it, but she can't stop them.'

'Why does that upset your mum?'

He shifts on his feet. 'It's more about Dad than anything; they've never seen eye to eye. I try to keep out of it.'

'Thanks for the info. I'll call by for a chat with your grandparents later. Is there anywhere special the twins like to play?'

'Up by the daymark, flying their kites.'

'I'll take a look there later. Isn't Amy helping you today?'

'She lives at the vineyard now, so we hardly see her.' Luke's already working again, cutting more cellophane. 'It took her weeks to plan her escape.'

I want to ask what he means, but Gemma acknowledged there's conflict in the family too. It's possible that Jade has run away to escape the tense atmosphere. I'd like to know why Amy Minear has flown the nest much earlier than most of the island's young, but my presence is slowing Luke down. He's so focused on his task, his movements are robotic. When I glance back from the doorway he's still working at a relentless pace. Luke's hands are a blur of speed, never settling on anything for long.

7

Eddie Nickell is waiting for me outside, his choirboy face alight with anticipation. My deputy achieved the rank of sergeant about eighteen months ago and still loves wearing his uniform, even though his high-vis jacket swamps his thin frame, blond curls spilling from under his cap. We've grown close since I joined the island force, despite the decade between us, and his insistence on calling me 'sir' while we're at work. He's breathless with excitement when he greets me.

'The DCI sent me, boss. He said it was urgent, but didn't give details.'

'We need to find Jade Minear. It sounds like the twins ran across the fields about eleven thirty p.m., but only Ethan came back.'

He listens to my plan to interview every member of the Minear family, then extend our search to their close contacts. I was hoping to avoid quizzing Ethan about his late-night excursion with Jade, but the need to find her is getting more urgent. There's a good chance the boy knows exactly why his sister didn't come home.

We find Gemma in the farmhouse kitchen, loading sandwiches onto trays for the pickers' lunch. A fresh wave of anxiety crosses her face when I ask about Ethan. She explains that he's refusing to come downstairs, and hasn't said a word all morning. Gemma still looks reluctant when I tell her we need to conduct an interview. She seems afraid of upsetting him further, but the kid's our only clear source of information, and he might talk more easily to someone outside the family if there's tension at home.

Gemma only agrees after some gentle persuasion. The twins' bedroom door creaks loudly when she pushes it open, making me wonder how they left the farmhouse without being heard. It's obvious they enjoy beachcombing, their shelves heavy with driftwood, weathered glass, and oyster shells. The room even smells of the ocean, the air sharp with brine and seaweed. Two narrow beds lie separated by a metre-wide gap. The boy is curled against the headboard, with his face pressed against his knees, his small flute clutched in his hand. Gemma steps forward to speak to him first.

'Ben and Eddie want to ask you a few questions, sweetheart.'

She pats his shoulder, but he shrinks from her touch, keeping his face averted.

'You're not in trouble, Ethan,' I say, quietly. 'Did you

and Jade go down to look at the sea last night? I don't blame you. We had some tall breakers on Bryher, too.'

The kid's body language relaxes by a fraction, but shyness or misery is making him close down. After five minutes I stop throwing out questions. The direct approach isn't working; he's in such delicate shape, three adults invading his space must be terrifying. I can see the twins' escape route last night when I look out of the window. They could easily have jumped onto the flat roof below, then shinned down the drainpipe. Gemma waits until we're back on the landing before speaking again.

'Ethan hates being without Jade. That's why the twins share a room, even though we've got loads of space.' She presses her fingers to her lips, her skin paler than before. 'He's only spoken to Jade since he turned six. Ethan can say a few sentences without her help now; I don't want him set back.'

'Hazel Teague might be able to bring him out.'

Gemma's face brightens. 'That could work, the twins have known her forever. I'll ask her to come up.'

She scurries back downstairs, leaving me and Eddie alone. My deputy's habitual smile is missing, and I can guess why. No one likes seeing a kid slipping beyond reach, and he's been the world's most committed dad since his daughter was born. When I look at him again, his gaze is solemn.

'Do you know much about Scott Minear, boss?'

'He's rich, with plenty of business interests.'

'That's not the half of it.' Eddie's speech drops to a stage whisper. 'Gemma and him are the biggest land-owners on St Martin's; the power's gone to his head. He throws his weight around if anyone challenges him. Even his twin keeps out of his way.'

'I didn't know Jason and Scott were twins.' I've seen Scott's brother unloading his fishing boat in Hugh Town harbour on St Mary's, or drinking at the Atlantic by himself, keeping a low profile.

'Hard to believe, isn't it? They're chalk and cheese,' Eddie replies. 'Rumour has it Scott's a ladies' man too. There's a woman he visits on the mainland.'

I have no time to reply, because footsteps are coming up the stairs. Gemma Minear and Hazel Teague are around the same age, but Gemma looks far older, her face marked by cares. I can tell she trusts her friend deeply when she allows us both to speak to Ethan, with me staying in the background, to avoid overloading him. Hazel gives me an encouraging smile. She must have faced worse crises in her nursing career than a young boy unwilling to speak.

'Gentle encouragement should do the trick, but let's not push too hard while he's vulnerable,' she whispers.

I sit down in the corner, while she perches on the boy's bed, addressing him in a soft voice. Hazel chats about Polly working in the fields today, like she's talk-ing to a friend, informing him that everyone's keeping busy, with ten crates already filled. I notice her edging closer to Ethan, then laying her hand on his back. It seems odd that the kid accepts her comfort, after reject-ing his mother's.

'It's all right, love,' she murmurs, her tone low and soothing. 'No one's mad at you. We're just wondering if you saw where Jade went last night. You don't have to talk until you're ready. Okay?'

Ethan Minear doesn't reply, but a new sound fills the room, making me certain he witnessed something bad happening to his sister. He's begun to cry, with his head on the nurse's shoulder. The noise cuts straight through me. It's a dry, wrenching sound, like fabric being torn apart.

8

Memories flood Ethan's mind like the incoming tide. Jade has always been the brave one, dragging him along on her adventures. She climbed the tallest tree on the island when they were seven years old, while he waited below, terrified she'd fall. Jade can swim faster too, her arms scything through the water, laughing when she wins every race. Ethan prefers to answer the teacher's questions in his head, while his sister calls them out loud. The only time he feels confident at school is in music lessons, one to one with his teacher. His best days are spent playing his piccolo while Jade sings, or together on the beach. Sometimes they only find tangled fishing twine, plastic bottles, and discarded flip-flops. But on a good day they bring home dried-out starfish, and weathered glass that shines like diamonds. His earliest memory is building sandcastles with Jade, their thoughts united, with no need to speak. His sister is separate from him yet still connected, their hearts beating in time.

Ethan can feel the nurse's hand on his back, her touch soothing, but his fear has grown. He understands what danger smells like since last night: booze and cigarettes, a sour whiff of sweat catching the back of his throat. He tries to recall the attacker's face again, but his memory's stopped working. Frustration makes tears course down his cheeks, forming wet circles on his jeans. If he could picture that face again, he could bring Jade home. All he wants to do is sleep until she returns, but monsters appear whenever he shuts his eyes.

9

Ethan Minear looks too small and fragile for an eleven-year-old. The sight of him crying stays with me as we return downstairs, where Hazel reassures Gemma about his state of mind. The child's muteness may have returned due to stress. I feel sure the kid witnessed something that's left him terrified; Jade may have had an accident, or been attacked in front of his eyes. If someone can make him speak, he could lead us straight to her, but we risk leaving him even more traumatised. Gemma barely responds to the nurse's advice to let him rest. Her hands are clutched so tightly in front of her chest, I can see her nails whitening.

'We'll carry on looking for Jade,' I tell her. 'Kids go missing for days sometimes, then come home safe.'

Gemma's smile has worn thin. When she walks past I catch a whiff of cigarette smoke and vodka; it's only mid-morning but she's already had her first drink. I can't tell if it's a one-off, giving her Dutch courage to cope with this crisis, or part of a habit. We leave her carting cans of cider and lemonade outside with Hazel's assistance, the pickers' lunch placed on trestle tables in the farmyard. You could hear a pin drop inside the Minears' property, but it's business as usual in the cutting shed. Luke is showing a dozen temporary staff how to wrap the flowers, then pack them inside gift boxes, before sealing each one. People chat as they work, their voices cheerful, like nothing could disturb their peace.

Scott Minear is in the nearest field, knee-deep in the yellow and white narcissi that cover his land. The man is bent double, cutting blooms without damaging the plants, so they can flower again. He rarely looks up, his jaw clenched with concentration. Minear could afford to appoint a farm manager, but seems to enjoy the hard labour. I had no idea that he's seen as a womaniser, but it makes sense for a man with restless energy, oblivious to public opinion. He probably sees himself as a loveable rogue, while his family fear his temper.

We're halfway up May's Hill to visit Jade's grandparents before Eddie speaks his mind. 'The lad's suffering, isn't he?'

'His mum's not in a great way either. She had booze for breakfast; I could smell it on her breath.'

'Me too. She seems worried sick about Jade. What do you think's happened?'

'Let's see the rest of her family before we form an opinion. There's no proof she's been attacked. She could have fallen somewhere on her midnight adventure, or gone into the sea.'

'It's a shame to upset her gran. Elspeth's had a rubbish year.'

'Do you know the Hicks well?'

'Her and Stan were like extra grandparents when Dad worked on their farm. Those two have supported a lot of youngsters over the years.'

'How do you mean?'

'It's easy to go off the rails here, isn't it? Old people end up in care homes on the mainland, so youngsters don't always have their grandparents around. Elspeth keeps an open door and she's a good listener. Kids often turn to her in a crisis.'

Eddie increases his pace to match mine, clearly eager to make progress. We've got little concrete evidence about Jade Minear's absence, apart from her brother's panic. It's possible that the twins argued and she's found somewhere to hide until the dust settles, yet there's a nagging feeling in my gut. Instinct tells me she'd have run home by now unless she's been hurt. Dave Carillian is standing by his window as we pass his property on our way to visit Gemma Minear's parents. The old man doesn't bother to raise his hand in greeting, and his appearance is unsettling; his skin's so pale, he looks like an apparition.

Stan and Elspeth Hicks's home lies a hundred metres further up the lane. Their detached Victorian house stands on top of May's Hill with one of the best views in Scilly. I can see Chapel Down rolling east from their gate, covered in dark green heather, and a swirl of seabirds hovering above White Island.

Elspeth Hicks appears in her doorway wearing a look of curiosity. I don't know her well on a personal level, but she's a respected member of the community, and a lifelong sea swimmer like me. She competed in the islands' swimathon last summer, winning a medal in the seniors' class. Elspeth's a tall, no-nonsense woman of around sixty-five, with grey hair cropped short. My gaze catches on the gold crucifix around her neck, then her thick sweater and black trousers, no doubt chosen for practicality, rather than style.

'Come in and warm up, both of you,' she says, her face brightening. 'It's lovely to have visitors.'

'Thanks, Elspeth. Has Gemma contacted you today?'

'I got a cryptic text about Jade, that's all.'

She leads us through to the kitchen, which is far more welcoming than her daughter's home. One wall is covered in cards and tinsel, the windows decorated with sprigs of holly. She smiles again when my gaze lands on an advent calendar, which features a herd of cartoon reindeer.

'The twins chose that, and they decorated the place too,' she says, studying each of us in turn. 'What's all this about?'

'We think Jade went out late last night with Ethan. She's not come home.'

She studies me more closely. 'Maybe they fell out. The smallest argument feels like a tragedy at that age, doesn't it?'

'Has Jade run away before?' Eddie asks.

59

'Not to my knowledge. Those two are happy, so long as they're together. Jade'll be fine, I'm sure, she's got good common sense.'

'Has she seemed upset by anything?'

'She can be a handful sometimes, but she never gives us any trouble,' Elspeth says. 'The twins come here if things are difficult at home. Stan's been confused since his stroke, but he still loves seeing our grandkids. The four of them visit us all the time.'

'Gemma mentioned that you and her aren't talking right now.'

Elspeth's face saddens. 'That's her choice, not mine. I told her a few home truths, but it's Jade that matters now, isn't it?'

'You can't think of any reason why she's hiding?'

'The farmhouse isn't a calm environment. That's what we give them here, whenever they need it.'

'Ethan plays the flute, doesn't he?'

'It's a piccolo. They're half the size of an adult flute.' The woman seems to relax for the first time. 'I recorded the twins playing last week. Would you like to hear?'

Elspeth presses a button on her phone before I can answer. A girl's piping voice is delivering one of Scilly's old folk songs, a piccolo in the background carrying the same slow melody, echoing the islands' tides.

'That's a beautiful sound.'

Her face glows with pride. 'Jade can carry a tune, but Ethan's got real talent. Suzie Felyer's been coaching him after school.'

'Do you know what triggered Ethan's speech problems, Elspeth?'

'Scott can be a hard taskmaster. It affects the whole family; Gemma's depression doesn't help either. I begged her to have counselling, but she took it as an insult.'

I get the sense that Elspeth won't be drawn any further on the state of her daughter's marriage, despite tension between them, but her concern is obvious. She only speaks again as we walk back down the hallway.

'Would you mind saying hello to Stan before you leave? He loves seeing visitors. It would make his day.'

Elspeth opens the door to her front room before I can reply. I haven't seen Stan Hicks since his illness began six months ago, so his appearance takes me by surprise. He used to be a fit-looking man, always working in his garden, with a jovial manner. He's retained his powerful build, but he's slumped on the sofa, his mouth hanging open like he's permanently surprised. The old man can only respond to our greetings with a moan. Eddie does his best to maintain a conversation; it's lucky my deputy has excellent social skills. I stay in the background while he talks. The room has been customised since Stan's illness; there's a hospital bed in the corner, and a plastic box on the table, full of different types of medication. The man's stroke appears to have robbed him of everything except his TV, his wife's devotion, and the ocean view outside his window.

Eddie is still delivering a monologue about the

islands' lifeboat rescuing a stranded trawler from the Northern Rocks in last night's storm. Stan's expression quickens, but the puzzlement on his face shows that he's fighting a losing battle to understand each sentence. The old man's condition reminds me of his grandson's muteness, both trapped behind an invisible wall.

My respect for Elspeth increases when we say good-bye. The woman's been caring for her husband with no sign of strain, despite his sudden decline.

'You'll have made his day. Stan's physical strength's come back, but everything else is a struggle. I can tell he loves having young people around. It makes him feel connected to the outside world.' Her smile reappears as she opens the front door. 'I'll let you know when Jade arrives. The twins always run here, if there's trouble.'

The wind is picking up as we leave the cottage, explaining why the twins come up here to fly their kites. I scan the open land, looking for any sign of Jade Minear. My eyes fix on the daymark: its conical shape is unmissable against the dark green of Chapel Down. The structure is eleven metres high, built three centuries ago to warn passing mariners not to stray too close, in the days before lighthouses. Its vivid red-and-white horizontal stripes are visible from miles away.

When I look out to sea it's a reminder that St Martin's has no protection from the elements. The nearest land mass lies thousands of miles across the Atlantic, and the weather is constantly changing. Mist is rising from the sea again, obscuring the jagged rocks below the cliff face. The Minear twins may have strayed too far for comfort last night. If Jade fell into the sea, the breakers would have dragged her under before her brother had time to blink.

10

A surprise is waiting for us at the bottom of May's Hill. I recognise Shadow's loud bark before he emerges from the mist; my dog chases towards me, tongue lolling, with his lead trailing the ground. The creature makes a desperate attempt to lick my face, before subjecting Eddie to the same treatment. Nina and Ray must have brought him over this morning, his sense of smell so acute he could track me across miles of open country. I'd have preferred to keep him safe at home, but he seems thrilled to join the search. He looks up expectantly when I call Jason Minear on St Mary's. I want to speak to every member of the family today, but the twins' uncle isn't answering.

'Where are we going next, boss?' Eddie asks.

'Let's see Amy Minear.'

'Michelle knows her,' he says. 'I think she's been having a rough time with her dad.'

'It sounds like she's not alone.'

Scott Minear's immediate family may find him hard

to tolerate, but Shadow is oblivious to any concerns. He's trotting a few paces ahead, sniffing the air, like he's relishing the scent of flowers.

The island's divided personality shows as we pass Little Arthur's Farm, heading for Par Beach. Its northern side consists of rocky terrain and beaches that receive the full force of the Atlantic; the soil is too thin for cultivation, rising to the peaks of Chapel Down and Turfy Hill. The southern side has a softer personality, sheltered by the high ground that forms the island's backbone. St Martin's three settlements and the Seven Stones pub all lie to the south, hemmed in by acres of the Minears' farmland.

There's no sign of Amy when we reach the vineyard. The grapevines look so like charred bones protruding from the ground, it's hard to believe their gnarled forms will ever bear fruit. The girl could be helping her family bring in the flower harvest, when there's nothing urgent to do at the vineyard, yet she's chosen to keep her distance. I hear singing as we approach the nearest barn. Amy's belting out an old Lady Gaga song, her voice loud and tuneful, proving that another member of the Minear clan is musical. She stands with her back to us, removing empty bottles from cardboard boxes. This is where wine is laid down for the season, the air spiced with musk, and the acidic tang of alcohol. A row of wooden casks line the opposite wall, purpled with stains from last year's vintage.

When Amy finally notices us she's still grasping an

empty bottle, embarrassed to be caught singing. The seventeen-year-old still looks like a sixth former, desperate to seem original, her style a cross between punk and Pre-Raphaelite. The girl's hair is dyed traffic-light red, falling in long curls, her green eyes heavily made up. She's dressed entirely in black, with rows of silver earrings glittering in the overhead light.

'That sounded great,' Eddie says. 'You should be on *The Voice*.'

'I'll stick to karaoke, thanks. How's Lottie doing? I've been meaning to come and see her for weeks.'

'She's a chatterbox these days,' Eddie replies. 'Michelle's working at the nursery again, but she'd love to see you. Come over, any weekend.'

'I will.' The girl's expression has grown serious, as if she's just twigged that the arrival of two police officers might mean bad news.

'We're looking for Jade,' I say. 'Has she been here lately?'

Amy's eyes widen. 'No one told me she's missing. Is Ethan okay?'

'He's shaken,' I reply. 'It looks like the twins ran towards the quay last night, but Jade hasn't come home.'

'I haven't seen the twins all week. Mum should have texted me.' Panic echoes in her tone of voice.

'Don't you ever visit Ethan and Jade?' I ask.

'I'd love to, but Dad ran me off the farm back in October,' the girl says, biting her lip. 'He thinks Neil's too old for me, which is bollocks. Luke gets my share of the flak since I left, the poor sod. Dad's even turned Mum against me. We live half a mile apart, but you'd think I'd emigrated.' Amy takes a step closer. 'When did Jade leave home exactly?'

'About eleven thirty we think. She was seen crossing the flower fields.'

Amy's shoulders twitch suddenly, the wine bottle she's holding slipping from her grasp. It shatters on the flagstones, the sudden noise sending Shadow running for cover. Amy Minear's body language is still jittery when she goes to fetch a broom. Once she's swept up the fragments I ask her to sit with us, on some upturned wine barrels in a corner of the barn.

'Something's upset you, Amy. What is it?'

Her eyes blink shut. 'It reminded me of when I tried leaving home in Luke's old Wayfarer dinghy.'

'I remember seeing you both fishing in it, years ago.'

'Luke still keeps it in the boatshed, but it doesn't get much use now.' She looks down at her hands. 'I almost drowned in it the summer I turned thirteen.'

'Where did you go?'

'Halfway to Tresco, before the riptide dragged me into the shipping lane.'

'That sounds dangerous.'

You'd have to be miserable at home to take such a risk. Stricken lobster boats have been cut in half by freighters that never spotted them in the dark.

'A passing yacht found me, thank God.' Amy's gaze darts to the window, like her sister might be drifting on the open sea. 'Jade never leaves Ethan by himself. We ought to look for her straight away.' The girl stares first at me, then Eddie. 'Do you want me to organise a search party?'

'We'll do it, don't worry.'

'Now, please, before the fog gets worse.'

Amy's manner has changed suddenly, her father's determination to win every argument showing in the set of her jaw, but we've reached the same conclusion. I've seen every member of the Minear family, apart from Jason, who was probably on St Mary's last night, and no one can explain Jade's disappearance. The visits have only revealed that the Minear family's three generations are divided by conflict.

'We've still got a few hours of daylight,' I say. 'We'll get the pickers to stop work, then assemble everyone at Highertown Quay by three p.m.'

Amy looks calmer now there's a definite plan. She seems to share my view that Jade's absence is serious, despite our lack of evidence. Eddie and I leave her making phone calls to recruit islanders to the search, before we head back outside.

Shadow gives me a warning bark when we leave the vineyard, but it's too late. DCI Madron is already marching up the lane. He often makes surprise visits to check up on me, bringing our newest recruit with him, PC Isla Tremayne. I can feel his disapproval from a hundred metres. I wish he was more like my old boss in London, a seasoned DCI who always took responsibility for her mistakes. Madron sees himself as the islands' sole guardian, convinced that his team lacks commitment. It's lucky that Isla has a calm disposition; he will have criticised every turn of the rudder while she steered the police launch through the fog. The constable's short black hair has been ruffled by the breeze. She's dressed in a police-issue waterproof, black trousers, and heavy-duty walking boots.

The DCI's sharp voice cuts through the air. 'Tie that bloody animal to a tree, Kitto. I've warned you before about bringing him on police business.'

'He made the journey independently, sir.'

'I'm in no mood for jokes.' DCI Madron stands in front of me, chest puffed out like a sergeant major, his pepper and salt hair pasted to his scalp with Brylcreem. 'Give me a progress report.'

The DCI's grey eyes are the same colour as the mist rolling inland. The tension only lifts from his voice when he hears that the protocol for missing juveniles has been followed correctly. It's standard practice to interview family members first, then extend the search to the wider community. There are less than a dozen cars, motorbikes, and buggies using the narrow lanes that connect St Martin's three hamlets. Our best option is to enlist volunteers to sweep the whole territory on foot.

'Let's get to work,' Madron snaps. 'We haven't got all day.'

I count to ten to avoid telling him that he's the one

slowing us down. The DCI's arrival has put us all on edge, instead of helping to find the missing child. Madron believes his first responsibility is to criticise. A dull silence settles over the four of us as we make our way uphill, with the bare branches of elm trees forming a steeple over our heads.

It's a relief to reach the outskirts of Minear Farm, where pickers are back at work after their lunch break. Polly Teague is the smallest figure in the field, but she's dropping flowers into her basket at impressive speed. Scott Minear is working in the next furrow; he's cleared a wide swathe through the flowers, as if he'd prefer to reap the entire harvest alone. The DCI marches into the field without any warning. I'm amazed that he's prepared to spoil his Oxford brogues to join the farmer.

Eddie's phone rings as the two men square up to each other. I'm too far away to hear their conversation, but their movements speak volumes. The farmer is intruding on the DCI's space, jabbing his finger at his chest, while my boss stands his ground. Minear appears so obsessed by his harvest, nothing else matters, including searching for Jade. His head is buried so deep in the sand, he seems unmoved by his favourite daughter's absence. The two men are still jockeying for power when Eddie taps me on the shoulder.

'Gemma just called from the farmhouse, boss. The line broke up, but it was something about Ethan being in trouble.'

'I'll go now. See you up there.'

The fields pass in a yellow blur as I run uphill. The front door is unlocked and I can hear Gemma calling her son's name from an upstairs room when I enter. She's on the top landing, her face frozen with anxiety.

'Hurry, Ben, please. He won't listen to me.'

I climb the rickety ladder to the loft, where dust catches the back of my throat. I can't see the boy anywhere. The space is crammed with rolls of old carpet, picture frames, and cardboard boxes, with dust motes hanging in the air. I only catch sight of Ethan when the soles of his feet cross the skylight's glass opening, making my heart rate double. The kid has climbed onto the roof and shut the window behind him. There's no safety barrier to prevent him from tumbling onto the concrete eighty feet below.

11

Ethan feels better in the fresh air, with his piccolo tucked inside his jumper. He can breathe easily for the first time since running home last night, and his thoughts are calmer with no one to bother him. The boy leans against the chimney stack, legs straddling the ridge, his trainers balanced on the slate tiles. He can see the whole island, from end to end. It's the best place to look for his sister. A gull coasts past, screeching at him like he's trespassing. Ethan's hands rest lightly on the concrete ridge, but he's not afraid; in the distance he can see the dark shapes of Nornour and English Island, rising from the mist.

He shuts his eyes to concentrate on Jade. All he can hear is the breeze gathering strength and the tide's soft whisper. But his peace of mind fades when his mother appears in the yard below, her voice a thin scream, begging him to come down. His father is a distant figure in the top field, striding towards the farmhouse.

Jade brought him up here weeks ago, while the rest of the family watched TV downstairs. She said it was the best place to see the moon. They sat together, watching the sky blacken, and a million stars blinking in the dark. It was the silence Ethan loved best. The quiet stretched to infinity, apart from the hum of their breathing. But there are no stars today, only fog and confusion. The second heartbeat in his chest is weaker than before, and all he wants is to be left in peace to look for Jade. When the skylight window opens, panic surges in his chest, making him stumble to his feet.

12

'It's okay, Ethan, stay right there.'

The boy is teetering on the ridge like a tightrope walker. The only thing keeping him alive is his sense of balance. I could haul myself closer, but some of the tiles have worked loose, and the ridge pole might not support my weight. When I tell the boy to lower himself back down he sways to one side, and my heart's in my mouth until he rights himself again. The commotion below isn't helping. Pickers have rushed out of the cutting shed to see why Gemma is screaming, her shrill voice setting my teeth on edge. I grab my phone to call Eddie, telling him to get everyone back into the barn immediately, and keep them quiet.

Ethan's face is unnaturally pale, his thin frame swaying in the breeze, making me afraid he could pass out from fear. It's lucky I don't suffer from vertigo, but the drop is still daunting. Neither of us would survive a tumble to the paving below. I murmur a few words of encouragement when he returns to a sitting position, his legs straddling the ridge. The kid is facing in my direction, but he's too lost in his own world to respond. I understand for the first time how deeply the twins' lives are connected. If Jade doesn't come home, Ethan may choose not to survive. I ask him to drag himself closer, but the kid stays put, and I'm running out of options.

'I heard a recording of you playing your piccolo just now. It sounded amazing. Have you got it with you?'

The lad hesitates before revealing the thin silver instrument, tucked inside his hoodie.

'I know how you feel, Ethan. I'm close to my brother, like you and Jade,' I tell him. 'Ian's only a year older than me.'

The boy angles himself towards me at last, his gaze skimming my face.

'We did everything together at your age. Swimming, rugby, sharing the same friends. I followed him to London when I left school. He's a doctor in a flash hospital in America now. He's a lot smarter than me.'

The boy edges a foot nearer. I don't know what else to say, so I stick to the truth.

'I was upset when he left, but we're still close. Jade's going to be fine. I'll bring her home, I promise. You have to trust me on that, okay?'

The kid's only four or five metres away, but still out of reach.

'You're doing great, all you have to do is move this way. Then we can go inside together. There's no rush, just take your time.'

Suddenly a man is yelling in the yard below. Scott Minear is bawling at his son to come down, his face dark with rage. The boy makes a sudden movement, his foot dislodging a rooftile. We both see it skitter past the guttering, then smash on the stone floor below. Now there's abject panic on the kid's face. If he follows the same route, his body will be shattered in seconds.

'Focus on me, Ethan, nothing else. I won't let you fall.'

The boy rises to his feet suddenly, like a gymnast on a beam. He's so unsteady, it takes all my self-control not to yell at him to sit back down. When his foot slips, time clicks into slow motion while I watch the kid clawing at thin air, desperate for something solid. Instinct makes me lurch forward. I manage to knock him sideways, so he lands on his chest, his legs kicking out. He's clutching the ridgepole with his fingertips, and I don't have long. I'll have to risk my whole weight on the roof's fragile structure to stop him falling. The wood groans as I edge forward, more tiles smashing into the guttering.

'Hang on tight for me. Don't let go.'

The kid's grip is weakening. He's starting to slide when I grab his wrist, then haul him into my lap. His weight makes me overbalance, my gaze skimming the concrete below while I struggle to right myself. We'll both fall if I slip up now.

'You're safe,' I mutter. 'Good lad. Now, keep still, okay?'

The kid's body is limp in my arms. He's too weak

with shock to cling to me, so I keep a tight grip on him as I lever myself backwards. It seems to take forever to lift him over my shoulder then climb down through the skylight, where Gemma is waiting. She still looks terrified, but it's the boy that concerns me. His brown eyes are jacked wide open, pupils dilated, staring at something only he can see. The kid's right hand is clenched around his piccolo like it's his only shield.

When I lay him down on his bed, he doesn't move a muscle, even though I repeat my promise to find Jade. He doesn't seem to register his mother stroking his face either, but she's soon calm enough to remember my existence. Gemma launches herself in my direction, wrapping her arms round me in an unexpected embrace. I can smell the booze on her breath again when she finally speaks.

'You saved my boy,' she whispers. 'I can never repay you.'

'Ethan can't be left alone for a minute, until Jade's found. If you and Scott need help, I'll start a rota.'

Her hands are still gripping my sleeve. 'I'll stay with him, I promise.'

'Be careful, please. Don't have another drink today.'

Her cheeks flush with embarrassment or outrage. 'I don't need lectures from you, or anyone.'

'Your son's welfare matters more than your pride, Gemma.'

I didn't mean to confront her so directly, but part of me is still on the roof, fighting to grab Ethan's hand.

She turns away immediately, returning to her son, but someone else got there first. Shadow has slipped through the door, his muzzle resting on the kid's shoulder. I can't tell whether Ethan welcomes his version of canine comfort, but it looks like he's got no choice. When I call Shadow away, he gives a soft whine, refusing to leave the child's side.

Shock catches up with me when I go back downstairs, my legs turning to jelly. I could easily have fallen from that rooftop, with the kid in my arms. Eddie is struggling to control the crowd out in the yard when I glance through the window, but I'm not ready to face them yet. I lean against the kitchen counter, steadying myself with a few deep breaths. Ethan's vulnerability proves that his fate is linked to his sister's in ways I don't understand. I cast my gaze around the kitchen, desperate for a hit of glucose. I cram a biscuit into my mouth from a plate on the table, then swallow a leftover sandwich from the picker's lunch in two bites, and pocket more for later.

I'm still dazed when I walk outside. Scott Minear's field workers have downed tools, the packers still clutching scissors and lengths of ribbon. The farmer is standing at the back of the crowd, his expression furious. DCI Madron is at his side, clearly trying to keep him calm. People call out my name and applaud the rescue, making me uncomfortable, but I know why they're excited. We've all experienced that primal impulse that turns drivers into rubberneckers, keen to witness the carnage of a traffic accident. Ethan Minear's antics have provided enough drama to fuel the island's gossip mill for weeks. People are still congratulating me on saving the kid's life, but they'd be less impressed if they could tell I'm still shaky with adrenaline. I was no braver than the boy, terrified of having his death on my conscience.

When I raise my hand to call for silence, the crowd soon falls quiet. I learned years ago that being built like a rugby full back has one major advantage. People expect you to take charge, simply because you're the biggest guy in the room, even if you're least qualified. I reassure them that Ethan Minear is safe, but his twin has been missing since late last night. No one looks surprised by the news. Hazel Teague has told people about the missing girl, as I requested, the information spreading like wildfire. When I ask who can join the island-wide search for Jade, they all raise their hands, which relieves some of my stress. St Martin's population has a reputation for teamwork, banding together to build their community hall and cricket pavilion. Everyone understands the need for safety in numbers in a place where the sea is your closest neighbour.

'Meet us at Highertown Quay at three p.m. please. Wear thick coats and walking boots, and bring torches. It'll take us a few hours.'

The pickers hurry away to collect their gear, ready for the search in half an hour's time. That's when

Scott Minear strides up to me, leaving Madron in the background. He looks outraged that his workforce is deserting him. My boss makes a calming motion with his hands, like I should pour oil on troubled water, but a truce is out of the question. Minear's face is crimson, an ugly knot of veins throbbing in his neck. He's muttering expletives, too angry to make sense.

'You can forget your flowers for today,' I inform him. 'Searching for Jade takes priority.'

'That's my decision, not yours. What the fuck were you doing just now, on my roof?'

'Rescuing your son.'

'Who let him up there in the first place?'

'I'm not a childminder, Scott. We've been hunting for Jade all morning.'

The man's stare intensifies. 'I saw you outside Dave Carillian's house earlier. Has he touched her?'

'It was just a routine conversation. Why not let me do my job, Mr Minear?'

'That bloke's a freak. You think he's hurt her, don't you?'

'We've got no proof your daughter's been harmed.'

The man is so close, I can see the dark stubble on his jaw when he yells at me again. 'If he's laid a finger on Jade, I'll beat the living shit out of him.'

'Ethan almost died just now. It's him and Gemma that need your attention.'

'Are you telling me how to run my family?' The man's fists are balling at his sides.

'Just stating the obvious. Jade's still missing, remember? There's no time to waste.'

'You smug bastard.'

I see his fist flying just in time, dodging the blow before it lands. I catch hold of his arms and band them at his sides, aware that the DCI is watching, like a referee, about to blow his whistle.

'Behave,' I hiss. 'Go and support your wife, before she takes another drink.'

Scott Minear's face is still flushed with anger, and I suspect it's been years since anyone faced him down. He holds my gaze for a long interval after I let him go, then struts indoors, muttering curses. The DCI is still observing me with eyebrows raised. I don't know whether his expression signals anger or approval, but right now I don't care.

Eddie is holding an animated conversation with Luke Minear, whose reactions seem the opposite of his father's. He looks relieved the search is happening. The teenager nods in agreement while Eddie explains that we'll spread out across the terrain, making sure every field, beach, and back garden is checked. Luke is already dressed for the outing, bundled up in scarves and waterproofs, a torch sticking out of his pocket.

I'm about to head for the quay when I remember something Minear said earlier. He claimed that the twins had crossed his top field, trampling plants on their way, but when I peer over the hedgerow, the damage is hidden. Pickers have churned deep furrows between each line of flowers. It's only when I look closer that a seam of broken plants is visible, running diagonally across the field. I pick my way along the fault line, between narcissi plants already budding with fresh blooms.

Jade and Ethan seem to have followed each other so closely, they've left a single trail. There are no properties in sight, except Dave Carillian's halfway up May's Hill, and the Hicks' place right at the top. When I look down again, there's a two-metre-wide circle where plants have been flattened. There's no point in looking for an attacker's footprints; the pickers have erased them by labouring up and down the furrows all morning. It looks like the twins chased each other to the middle of the field, then ran back the same way. Ethan may be my only chance of finding out exactly what happened to Jade last night, but our drama on the roof might have silenced him for good. My chances of getting him to talk seem slimmer than ever.

I crouch among the ruined plants, where petals lie scattered, but nothing catches my interest until something glitters between broken leaves. There's a glass bottle lying in the mud. The miniature boat trapped inside is a traditional clinker vessel with an open hold, like the luggers used for two centuries by local lobstermen and crab-catchers. I've helped Ray build several and even the smallest details are correct, including the seamed lapping, bait baskets, and raised prow. Constructing it must have been a labour of love for someone, and it was built to last. The model has survived its fall intact. I feel sure it was made years ago; the paint on the boat's prow has faded with age, the cork stopper crumbling, with red sealing wax holding it in place.

I pull an evidence bag from my pocket to collect it, the boat resting easily in the palm of my hand. There's no evidence that it belonged to the missing girl, or to someone that pursed her and Ethan across the field, yet instinct tells me it's connected. When I look up at Dave Carillian's house I expect to see the man's pale face at the window, but the glass only contains a reflection of the clouds overhead.

13

The bottle is still in my pocket, wrapped in its evidence bag, when Eddie and I reach Highertown Quay. DCI Madron has sailed back to St Mary's alone, leaving Isla Tremayne marshalling the islanders into teams. Our new constable may only be twenty-two, but she has a natural authority, the crowd quick to follow her instructions. The young woman heads in my direction; her short black hair is tucked under her cap, freckles littered across her cheeks, her keen gaze assessing me.

'I've split them into three groups, boss. Word got round pretty quick about the missing girl; some of the off-islanders have sailed over to help.'

I can think of few situations bad enough to bring so many islanders together in bad weather, apart from a missing child. Members of almost every family have arrived, even though Scott Minear has squeezed their businesses for years. Around sixty people stand in huddles on the beach, their faces pinched with cold. The crowd's high spirits before the flower harvest this morning have faded. Some of them are marching on the spot, trying to keep warm or dispel tension. We're all keen to find Jade Minear before the tide comes in, and the fog returns. I catch sight of Nina standing with Ray on the far side of the circle when I get up to speak.

'Thanks for coming, everyone, especially if you've travelled over from Tresco or Bryher. It'll make our work much easier. We've divided the island into three sections: Eddie Nickell will lead his team from here to Chapel Down, my group will search from Par Beach to Knacky Boy Carn, and Isla Tremayne's group will cover Middletown to Top Rock Hill. Remember that Jade's been missing since before dawn. She'll be exhausted, and she could be lying hurt on one of the beaches. Walk fast, please, but stay focused. Check every cave, outhouse, and barn.'

I watch the crowd disperse, with Isla shepherding them. My own team contains a mix of young and old; they all appear focused on the task as we head for Cruther's Point. Mist is rolling over the island in waves, blurring the coastline, but the boulders that lie in jagged formations along the shore are still visible, like giant building blocks. It strikes me again that Jade Minear could have drowned, if she fell last night while watching the storm's brutal energy.

I'm still scanning the headland when I catch sight of Amy Minear, hand in hand with Neil Kershaw, the vineyard owner. I can see why her parents worry about their relationship. She's wearing an electric-blue leather coat, but he's dressed in dark waterproofs, his cap pulled low, like he's trying to disappear. Tongues have been wagging about the twenty-year age gap between them since the couple's romance began, which is the disadvantage of living in a tiny community. There's no privacy, especially in winter, when there's plenty of late-night gossip in the island's only pub. Amy doesn't acknowledge her father's presence. Scott has joined the search alone, leaving Gemma caring for Ethan. No one would guess that the pair are related. The farmer is ignoring his oldest daughter, keeping his back turned, as Amy joins my group. It interests me that plenty of islanders seem to be avoiding him, despite turning out to find the missing child.

Someone taps my shoulder before I can take another step. When I swing round the woman standing there is unmistakeable, despite her six month absence. Zoe Morrow was my closest childhood friend. Our relationship even managed to survive the fierce crush I had on her in my teens. She's dressed in a yellow oilskin, six feet tall in her wellingtons, hair dyed Marilyn-Monroe blonde, still gorgeous enough to stop traffic. My stress levels plummet when she flings her arms around me. Whatever happens next, at least one member of my team is a hundred per cent behind me.

'I sneaked into your group,' she whispers. 'Don't tell Isla I swapped places with Hazel Teague.'

'I was going to call by this afternoon . . .'

'. . . But you're busy, big man, and you've been having fun. I saw Nina just now; it sounds like things are good on the romance front.' Her cat-like eyes glitter with interest.

'How come Dev stayed in Mumbai?'

'He's setting up a new street school for the foundation. It's brilliant, but he's exhausted.'

'It's great to have you back, even for a few days.'

'I needed to see you, and all of this, before visiting my folks on the mainland.' She gestures towards the rocky coastline. 'I think about the islands when it's too hot to sleep, and traffic's roaring in my ears.'

'I thought you loved Mumbai.'

'I do, but this will always be home.'

We walk on together in silence, and I know what she means. Ten years of city living made me long for Scilly's clean air, big skies, and pure white beaches.

'I'll buy you a drink, after we find Jade Minear.'

'Why would a young girl leave home in the middle of the night?' she asks.

'She was with her brother. Maybe they were meeting someone.'

'Or just fooling around. We tore round Bryher on our bikes, or drank cider on the beach till dawn, didn't we?'

'Not in midwinter, at that age.'

'It sounds like you're still living dangerously. I heard about your escapade on the farmhouse roof.' Zoe falls into step as the path takes us round to Old Quay, where the island's historic jetty is crumbling onto the beach. 'People say you rescued Ethan from certain death.'

'He got up there alone, so he'd probably have saved himself. Look, Zoe, I should check everyone's okay. Can we talk later?'

'Give me an update on Nina first.'

I carry on scanning the shoreline. 'What do you want to know?'

'Details, stupid.' She gives me a light punch on the arm.

'She's stalling on me. I asked her to move in weeks ago, but she won't give me an answer.'

'Raise your game, sweetheart.' Zoe's smile widens to a grin. 'Treat her like a princess, then slide a big glittery diamond onto her finger. You'll have to cover the floor in rose petals and go down on one knee to clinch the deal.'

'She'd laugh at me.'

'You're wrong about that, any girl would love it. You're punching above your weight, my friend. Wake up and smell the coffee.'

Zoe is laughing as she lopes away to speak to Amy Minear. My head is too busy thinking about the missing girl to spare much time on her advice, even though it echoes Nina's prediction that changes lie ahead. I've never considered a big wedding with all the bells and whistles, but I may have to adjust my position.

The light's fading when my group walks along Old Quay Beach. The tide is still out, leaving slabs of granite exposed, my boots slipping on wet seaweed, but so far there's no evidence of the girl's presence. The search party is strung out across the beach, torch beams trained on the ground, looking for anything that could belong to Jade Minear. A shout goes up just as we head back inland and I catch sight of Neil Kershaw jogging across the sand. When the man comes to a halt beside me it looks like he's paid a high price for his relationship, his eyes circled by shadows. There's tension in his body language too, shoulders down like he's expecting an ambush.

'I just checked the boatshed,' he says. 'One of the gigs is missing.'

Kershaw's statement pricks my interest. It's odd timing for one of the island's racing boats to vanish, on the same night a young girl goes missing.

'Can you show me please, Neil?'

The low-roofed hangar smells of seaweed and bitumen, an abandoned pot of varnish lying by the door. There's no electric light, so I shine my torch around the interior, where a dozen canoes lie on metal stacks. Everything looks normal until I see an empty cradle beside three of the island's racing gigs. The huge rowing boats are based on a Viking design. Two hundred years ago men raced boats like these out to frigates in need of pilots, to guide them through outcrops that make local waters a deathtrap for unwary mariners. These days the gigs are used for recreation only. The islands' teams compete in regular competitions, using titles handed down generations ago. The boats' names are painted in ornate lettering on their prows. I can see *Dauntless*, *Iron Maid* and *Dolphin*, but the *Galatea* is missing.

'The doors were open, that's why I checked,' Kershaw says. 'I left them shut yesterday around six p.m. when I heard a storm was forecast.'

The vineyard owner makes an unlikely captain of the

racing team, too mild-mannered for a natural leader, but I can see why he'd check the gigs were secure. The boathouse doors were left open two years ago, and one got damaged by a freak high tide. Nature isn't to blame this time. A row of dinghies lie in an orderly row, with Luke Minear's old Wayfarer closest to me, in need of an overhaul.

I spot another glass bottle where the missing gig lay, and crouch down for a closer look. It contains a perfect replica of the *Galatea*, complete with minute oars, as fine as toothpicks. This model looks brand new, unlike the one I found earlier. The paintwork is so fresh it could have been completed yesterday. The sight of it makes something shift in my chest. If the girl's been abducted, the culprit may have stood exactly where I am now, leaving the ship in a bottle for me to find, like the one in Minear's field, at the spot where she was taken. Whoever took the gig may have been watching the twins for months, planning their attack.

I run my torch beam over the other three racing boats. They look well-maintained and I know their exact specification, from helping Ray build one years ago. Each gig is made of elm wood, thirty-two feet long and five feet wide, so durable that each vessel can last a hundred years. They're ideal for racing, with thin prows that cut through rough waters. But why would Jade's attacker drag a heavy boat down to the shore, just as a storm took hold?

14

It's dark when something startles Ethan awake, a shaft of moonlight streaming through the window. The bedroom appears empty, but when he sits up the policeman's dog is still at his side. The creature gives a soft moan before licking his hand. The boy strokes his spine, reassured by his presence. Shadow whines again, but falls silent when Ethan makes a hushing sound. He closes his eyes to concentrate on Jade. He's certain that his sister's still alive, but further away now, drifting out of reach.

When Ethan rises to his feet, the dog stays close. The boy circulates the room, touching the items he loves most, starting with his piccolo, the smooth metal settling his nerves. He picks a starfish from the shelf, its dried surface as rough as sandpaper, before touching a nugget of amber. It warms quickly in his hand, as if the tiny creatures trapped in its resin might come back to life. Ethan dips his hand inside a shoebox full of tin soldiers, until his fingers meet polished glass. His ship in a bottle is one of his favourite possessions. He holds it up to his eye, inspecting it in the cold moonlight. The tiny captain stands on deck, with hands braced on the wheel, certain of his destination. Ethan wants to crawl inside the galleon and join his voyage, but can only hide the bottle in his pyjama pocket, to keep it safe.

Ethan comes to a standstill, checking for noises before he lifts the rug that lies between the two beds, with the dog sniffing at the exposed wood. The boy uses his fingertips to prise up a loose floorboard. He's performed the action so often, there's no need to turn on the lights. He slips his hand through the gap and pulls out a mobile phone. The screen lights up, but there are no messages, filling him with disappointment. He's about to attempt a call when he hears someone marching along the hallway.

The boy drops the rug back into place as footsteps batter upstairs. He hides the bottle under his pillow just before his mother enters. Shadow has settled on his bed again. He rises onto his paws when she comes closer, giving a low growl, with teeth bared. His mum puts out her hand to calm him, but Ethan can see anger in her eyes.

'You need to sleep now, and Shadow should be outside,' his mother says. 'Something's upset him, hasn't it?'

He strokes the creature's fur, trying to calm him down. The boy can smell something unpleasant on his mother's breath. It's the same odour he picked up when Jade was taken, strong and cloying.

'Give me the dog, Ethan.'

He grips Shadow's collar tighter, until the dog relaxes enough to let her come closer.

'I'll let him stay for one night, but at least try to eat

something. You've had nothing all day. I've brought you sand-wiches.' His mother fusses over him again, smoothing his hair back from his forehead. 'Did you see what happened to Jade, is that why you're upset?'

He screws his eyes shut, and the face he saw in the field almost comes into focus, before slipping out of reach. When his eyes open again his mother looks angrier than before. She scares him almost as much as his dad, because her mood is always changing. There's little warmth in her gaze tonight.

'The police will question you again. Try and answer them, Ethan, but tell me first, okay? If you remember anything at all, I want to know. Promise not to let me down.'

Ethan is too afraid to risk annoying her again. He nods obediently, then takes a sandwich from the plate. The boy swallows a mouthful, but the bread is as dry as sawdust.

15

We spend the next two hours searching from Old Quay Beach to Turfy Hill. I ask my group about the missing gig as we walk, but no one can explain. It would take an individual a combination of muscle and ingenuity to drag it down the slipway, unless a vehicle was used to haul it to the sea. Dave Carillian is the only islander to raise my suspicions so far, but with no hard evidence, he can't be named as a person of interest, and I doubt he could have completed the task alone.

I try to focus my thoughts on Jade Minear. The longer we take to find her, the more likely she's in danger. Dusk has already turned the sky pewter grey, making our search more challenging. My team is walking at a slow pace, heads down as they fan out across the beach, giving me a moment to check for information about ships in bottles on my phone. Wikipedia informs me that the tradition of placing highly prized items in bottles began in monasteries, when monks recreated scenes from the Bible on a minute scale. Sailors and fishermen took up the craft in the 1700s, to fill the long winter months, and it has a strong tradition in Cornwall. The museum in Penlee owns a collection of ships in bottles that goes back centuries. None of the information explains why someone would leave them on the ground, after abducting a child, like clues in a treasure hunt.

I'm scouring the path with my torch beam when Will Austell falls into step, leaving his wife chatting to Zoe.

'Jade's probably hiding somewhere, isn't she? It's the kind of stunt we pulled as kids,' he says.

'She may be sulking in someone's barn.'

'This place is too peaceful for anything bad to happen.'

'I'm afraid accidents and crimes happen everywhere.'

He releases a quiet laugh. 'You sound like a real cop. It's one hell of a change from the old days.'

'No one ever told me why you left here so fast.'

'Sorry I didn't say a proper goodbye, it wasn't my choice.' The sadness in his voice resonates. 'I loved my time on the islands, even though my parents struggled. They thought renting a caravan and growing their own veg would be paradise, but it didn't work out.'

'The three of you seemed happy from the outside.'

'Things soured months before we left. My parents split up when their self-sufficiency dream failed. Dad lost contact once we moved back to the mainland, and mum lives in a council flat now.'

'But you've turned it round. You did well, finding Maria.'

'She's my silver lining. Let's hope I don't screw it up,

like everything else. I was hoping for tranquillity here, not a hunt for a missing child. I walk to Porth Seal most nights, to soak up the peace and quiet.'

'It's one of my favourite spots. Where did you go with the army?'

'Two tours in Afghanistan. It was a lot worse than you see on the news.' His voice flattens. 'I joined Voluntary Services Overseas after that. They sent me to Yemen, to teach kids carpentry and building skills, which felt better than destroying enemy targets.'

'That sounds satisfying.'

'It helped me recover, and I can't regret anything with Maria around,' he says, quietly. 'Let's hope Jade turns up before it gets any colder.'

Will slips back to his wife's side, leaving me struck by his honesty, which has remained the same since we were young. He seemed indomitable back then, the kind of lad that shifts easily into manhood, never fazed by obstacles. There's something reassuring about his story. It proves that a life can fall apart, then heal over, with little permanent damage.

I lead the team through Highertown, checking every shed and garden, as well as peering inside the island's fire station. It's just a glorified shed that accommodates a tractor and a water tank. We pause outside the few houses where lights are still glowing to ask for sightings of the missing girl, but the islanders who are too frail or old to join the search have no fresh information. We've traced St Martin's perimeters, its fields sheltered by tamarisk hedges and hawthorn bushes, with no sign of Jade Minear.

The group slows down as we reach Great Bay, where a new band of fog hangs on the horizon, waiting to smother the island again. We're crossing a section of the downs that's called Frenchman's Graves. The spot always scared me as a kid; my brother claimed that the bodies of forty French sailors were buried on the beach, after a shipwreck on Merrick Rock. The bay looks empty tonight, apart from breakers pounding the shore, and a row of ancient cairns. I shine my torch inside an entry grave, but find only dried leaves and seagulls' skeletons. The team revives when I call time on our search, but my own spirits are on the floor. I'd like to keep going, even though there's little point, now the light's gone.

We head to the Seven Stones Inn, in Lowertown. The island's only pub has a reputation for its warm welcome. The old building looks too small to accommodate such a large crowd, with Eddie and Isla's teams already packing the place. My group has to squeeze through the doors, into a room that resembles Santa's Grotto. Bunting hangs from the ceiling, alongside streamers announcing Yuletide cheer and a massive tree covered in artificial snow, but the atmosphere is less celebratory. There's a buzz of subdued chatter, with everyone's attention still on the search.

Scott Minear is standing with his elbow propped on the bar, holding court. The farmer gives me a hard stare before downing the last of his beer, suggesting that he holds me responsible for Jade's fate, but that's the least of my worries. The islanders are all swapping theories about the missing child, ignoring the elephant in the room. People have disappeared from the islands before. Five years ago a young girl on St Mary's was swept away by a freak wave; she drowned long before the lifeboat found her body. Then a pregnant woman got caught out by the tides on Tresco two years later, dying in a sea cave called Piper's Hole. The Atlantic is the islands' worst threat. It stole my father's life during a fishing trip, but it will kill anyone who fails to take care. The resignation I see on the old-timers' faces proves that some are already blaming nature, not humanity, for the girl's absence. It's the wrong time to share my growing belief that Jade's been abducted.

The crowd falls silent when I hold up my hand to catch their attention.

'Thanks for your help, everyone. We've done a thorough search, but there's a chance we missed something, with the weather against us. My team will look for Jade again in the morning when the fog clears. I need you all to stay vigilant. It's possible she doesn't want to be found. Jade knows the island well enough to keep one step ahead, but she's been outside almost twenty-four hours. Does anyone have questions?'

A male voice calls out from the back of the crowd. 'When can we get back to the harvest?'

'Tomorrow morning, but ring us if you see Jade, or anything unusual, please. No one can leave St Martin's without my permission until she's found.'

It crosses my mind to mention the ships in bottles, but I don't want to distract anyone from our primary goal, to bring Jade home safe. 'One more thing, before you go. The *Galatea*'s missing from the boatshed. Does anyone know where it's gone?'

Scott Minear steps forward, his frown deepening. 'I sponsor that gig. Why wasn't I told?'

'We only just found out.'

The rest of the crowd gaze back at me blank-faced, while Minear grumbles curses. I need to understand the link between the missing boat and Jade's disappearance, but it won't happen tonight. News that the *Galatea* is missing has lowered the islanders' spirits even further. The gigs have been part of our heritage for centuries, and the races are popular fixtures in everyone's diaries. No one can answer my question, but the crowd lingers, and the landlord must be overjoyed. More than half have stayed behind, keeping warm by the log fire in the inglenook, knocking back beer.

When I scan the room again, there are dozens of familiar faces. Zoe is chatting with old friends, easily the tallest woman in the room, lighting the place up with her hundred-megawatt smile. Felicity and Rob Paige, the owners of St Martin's jewellery workshop, are sitting in the corner. Felicity is around forty, pretty, with a cloud of ash-blonde ringlets. Her husband Rob makes an odd contrast: he's wearing a black eyepatch, hunkered in his seat like a bad-tempered pirate. I noticed earlier that he and his wife went out of their way to avoid Scott Minear on the search. They're still keeping their distance now, but Rob glances at him occasionally, monitoring his behaviour. Suzie Felyer is sitting with the Paiges. She's run the island's primary school with complete dedication for years. I'd like to ask her about Jade's recent behaviour, but Eddie and Isla are heading in my direction. My deputy's enthusiasm shows in the width of his smile, but the younger officer is a born observer, always taking stock before revealing her opinion. My mother would have described Isla as an old soul, wise beyond her years, while Eddie races through every duty like a medal's waiting for him at the finishing line.

'We haven't found anything yet, boss,' he says. 'Isla and me have collected the names of everyone on the island last night.'

I run my eyes over the list and the number seventy-nine scribbled at the bottom. If anyone harmed Jade Minear deliberately, her attacker must be somewhere on the list.

'There's a new dimension,' I say. 'Jade's disappearance and the missing gig must be linked, because someone's leaving us calling cards.'

When I produce the two ships in bottles from my coat pocket, the young officers take time to absorb the information. Eddie's excitement shines even brighter, but Isla's face is solemn.

'We can talk about details tomorrow,' I tell them. 'Don't try sailing home in this weather.'

'We've taken rooms here, boss,' Isla says. 'Saul gave us our pick.'

'Good work, now talk to as many people as you can. We need information to work on tomorrow. I'm going back to Dave Carillian's to ask a few more questions.'

Neither of my team members reply. We all know that Carillian matches the stereotype for a child abductor, but I'm withholding judgement – being an oddball doesn't make him a criminal. My team members attack their task by different means. Eddie heads for the nearest table wearing his habitual smile, while Isla clutches her notebook like a shield, but I don't care how they work, so long as they get results.

There's no time to speak to Nina or Ray before I slip outside the pub. The beauty of life in Scilly is that neighbours can be visited in the blink of an eye. My only obstruction is the fog that's thickening again, just as Ray predicted. I stick to the island's only tarmacked road, which links its three small communities. Middletown looks deserted, a few granite cottages hiding behind drystone walls with upstairs windows lit, as the owners prepare for bed. There's nothing unusual to report in Highertown either. Polreath's tea room is closed for the season, and a sign in the post office window announces that water is in short supply. It's a reminder that nothing can be taken for granted in Scilly; basic utilities are hard to access, with natural resources stretched to the limit.

I come to a halt by the turning for Minear Farm. The north wind is rising, and gulls are shrieking overhead, but now there are footsteps too. When I turn round a wall of fog blocks my view. My follower has chosen a good night for a chase, the thick air muffling every noise. The sound stops when I continue up May's Hill. It could have been one of the islanders making their way home from the pub, my senses heightened by a day of tension.

Lights are on in Dave Carillian's house; he should still be awake because it's only 10.30 pm, an hour before his normal bedtime. The old man takes a long time to appear, and his movements are sluggish when he greets me, as if he's been napping by the fire. I can only see him in silhouette at first, but closer inspection reveals that his appearance has been transformed since this morning. One of his eyes is puffed shut, with ugly swelling distorting his cheek.

'Who did that to your face, Mr Carillian?'

His hand flies up to conceal the damage. 'I tripped going upstairs an hour ago.'

'You should press charges with those injuries.'

'No one else was involved, I simply lost my balance. Why have you come back, Inspector?'

'I need more information.'

I can hear a radio playing through the open door of his kitchen, the smell of paint drifting down the corridor. He stands in his drab hallway with arms folded. The wounds on his face look worse under the overhead light, and I find myself disliking Scott Minear more than ever. There's no proof that he beat the old man up because of his suspicions, but who else would target him?

'Let's talk in your kitchen, please. It must be warmer in there.'

The old man mutters a protest when I brush past. The room still smells of bleach, the floor and surfaces gleaming, but it's become a workshop since this morning. Radio Three is blaring out classical music, and a spotlight shines down on his table, which is crowded with pots of paint and pieces of balsa wood. I come to a standstill when I see that he's constructing a tiny boat, just like my own bowrider, based on a photograph. The speedboat is two inches long, its deck shiny with varnish.

'I didn't know you made ships in bottles, Mr Carillian.'

'You never asked.'

'That boat's just like mine.'

'I spotted one in St Mary's harbour. I enjoy building exact replicas.' He watches me intently through his thick spectacles when I produce the glass bottle I found in the field, still wrapped in an evidence bag.

'This was found near where Jade Minear disappeared. Is it one of yours?'

'The craft's a Cornish tradition. Other people must make them too.'

'Look at it closely, please.'

He inspects the bottle again, taking a long time to reply. 'It's not mine. I'd say it was made decades ago, when people used wax instead of glue to seal the bottles. The colours need retouching. Someone's kept it on a windowsill, in direct sunlight. They should have taken more care.'

I produce the other model from my pocket. 'How about this? It's a real beauty. It could almost be the *Galatea*.'

'That's definitely mine, I've copied all the racing gigs. Fine old-fashioned vessels, aren't they?'

'Did you give it to Jade?'

'I've never spoken to those twins. I told you that already.' His trembling hands give him away.

'She may have dropped it last night, running across the field, opposite your house.'

'Anyone could, my models are easy to find.'

'How do you mean?'

'Children's vision is better than adults; they don't need a magnifying glass to appreciate the fine details. It's a shame to hoard them here when kids could be enjoying them ...' Carillian's voice slows, like he's run out of steam. 'Those twins are curious by nature. They came to my kitchen window, to watch me work, but I never let them inside. I saw them flying kites by the daymark the next day, so I left two of my models there. A gift, you might say, with no strings attached. The next day, when I went back, they'd gone.'

'What made you give them presents?'

'I had few toys as a child, but my father taught me how to put ships in bottles. It's a patient task, using needles, pins, and twine. I leave them scattered around the island, whenever there's a surplus.' He picks up the miniature bowrider and holds it on the palm of his hand like a peace offering. 'I know how much pleasure they bring. I sell them through gift shops on the mainland, but keep a few dozen to give away each summer.'

'When did you start leaving them outside?'

'Three years ago, soon after I arrived.' I've got no proof he's lying, and something in the man's eyes almost convinces me it's true.

'We may need to speak again, Mr Carillian. Call me if you decide to press charges against Scott Minear. A nurse should look at that black eye.'

The old man flinches at the sound of Minear's name. 'I'm perfectly capable of looking after myself.' He pauses by his front door, his tone softening. 'Is the boy safe and well? He must be missing his twin.'

'Ethan just wants her home. Stay indoors tonight, please. Don't go anywhere.'

Carillian's bleak expression remains fixed in my mind. The starkness of his house is striking, and its unnatural cleanliness. If he's harmed Jade Minear, he's had the entire day to scour away evidence, so there's little point in searching until I can get a warrant, or forensic help arrives. I'm probably the only person he's spoken to in months, and his concern for Ethan Minear looked genuine. I find it hard to imagine him overpowering the girl; he's frail, and she's quick on her feet. Carillian's so isolated. Who would help him drag the *Galatea* down to the sea? When I glance over my shoulder the old man is still framed inside his doorway, and the fog has returned, a fresh wave of it hiding him from view.

16

The atmosphere has relaxed when I return to the pub, the punters' tension dissolved by good beer, the fire's heat, and Wham's 'Last Christmas' drifting from speakers above the bar. It's 11 p.m. and the place is emptying. I'm relieved that Scott Minear has gone home; he may enjoy public spats, but I need to remain professional. It's a pity the farmer is so aggressive – I'd like his opinion on why the gig he sponsors went missing the same night his daughter disappeared, but he's only happy when he's in control. I doubt he'd spare me the benefit of his opinion. I can't help wondering if Jade has been taken to punish him. It's becoming clear that the man is either feared or disliked by many on the island, including his own family. You'd need a twisted mind to hurt a young girl in order to attack her father, but anything's possible. It nags at me that I've been searching for Jade all day, yet we've uncovered no hard evidence.

My gaze catches on a large ship in a bottle, displayed

on a shelf above the bar, and it strikes me that the objects are commonplace. I played with one as a child, and many houses on St Martin's probably have one on their mantelpiece. If they're linked to Jade's disappearance, it may not be easy to find the culprit.

Eddie and Isla are still talking to the island's diehards, who are nursing their last drinks of the evening. I can tell from their body language that my two officers have found no new leads; Eddie's taut shoulders signal frustration, while Isla's head is bowed, her eyes scouring her notebook for clues. We have a quick debrief about Carillian's hobby of making ships in bottles, but none of us are convinced that he could drag a heavy boat down to the shore without assistance. My junior officers are starting to flag, so I send them up to their rooms. I'll need them fresh tomorrow morning, when our hunt for Jade Minear will start again.

Nina has texted me, inviting me to the cottage she's house-sitting, but the landlord, Saul Heligan, beckons me to the bar. He's a friend of my godmother Maggie, who runs the Rock pub on Bryher. Most of the landlords and hoteliers in Scilly get on well, because they're not in competition. There's a high demand for rooms all over Scilly during the summer season. European visitors flood here to birdwatch or visit the Abbey Gardens on Tresco, so no one runs short of business. Saul is famous for his bonhomie, and his love of dressing up, serving drinks in a tuxedo on Valentine's Night. He was born on the islands but trained as an actor, only returning to St Martin's when work dried up. I can tell he's been enjoying his own hospitality a little too much; he can't be much over forty, but his face is ruddy from good living. Heligan's clothes look theatrical when he steps out from behind the bar. Greying hair flows down to his shoulders, and his scarlet waistcoat announces his big personality long before his booming voice echoes in my ears.

'Have one for the road, Ben. Don't make me drink alone.'

'Whisky would be great, thanks.'

The landlord pours us both large measures of single malt. I normally avoid spirits, but too many unanswered questions gives me an excuse. He watches with eyebrows raised while I sip my drink.

'I could have forecast this,' he says. 'Money doesn't fix human woes, does it? That family's loaded, but they're at each other's throats. We call them the warring Minears on St Martin's.'

'How do you mean?'

'It's like *EastEnders*. Scott treats Gemma like dirt, and hates his twin brother. That man's got a finger in every pie, so no one dares to criticise. Their kids get a hard time too, except Jade, who's a strong character by all accounts. It's Gemma I worry about. Do you remember her, back in the day?'

'Not well, I'm afraid.'

'She was beautiful and bright too. We were together for a while, many moons ago. She studied languages at university, but never got a chance to travel. Scott dazzled her into marrying him straight after she graduated, so I missed my chance. She tried to escape with her two kids when they were babies, but he lured her back. The poor girl's been paying for it ever since.'

'That must have been a long time ago.'

'Fifteen years at least. But why did she marry him in the first place? Women fall for the bloke, hook, line and sinker. He's had half a dozen flings over the years, the lucky sod.'

'You must get opportunities, Saul.'

'Not in living memory. If you find any rich, good-looking widows on the island, give them my number.' Heligan's laugh is grating, his voice raw with booze and cigarettes. 'Rumour has it Scott's been chasing two women at the same time.'

'Is that right?' It crosses my mind that such behaviour would have repercussions in such a small community, where extramarital affairs are difficult to hide. It's possible that a wronged husband could be seeking revenge against Minear by abducting his favourite child.

'He visits Suzie Felyer's house at night, bold as brass,' Heligan says. 'The man spent a fortune replacing the school roof last year, and he never hands out money from the kindness of his heart.'

'You think Scott and Suzie are having an affair?'

'He prefers Felicity Paige now, by all accounts. That's a mistake, if you ask me. Scott had a punch up with Rob outside here last weekend. If I hadn't intervened things would have got nasty.'

'What was it about?'

'Jealousy, I suppose; the green-eyed devil affects us all. Rob wouldn't take kindly to being a cuckold.'

'How well do you know Gemma Minear now, Saul?'

'It's such ancient history, I barely recognise her. She looks so fragile. If anything happens to Jade, she'll fall apart.'

'The island's only two miles long. We'll find her, soon enough.'

Heligan shakes his head. 'I don't blame Jade for running away, like her sister. There are good reasons why people fear Scott's temper.'

'I'm just focused on finding Jade. Thanks for the drink, but Nina's expecting me.'

'You did well there, my son. She's gorgeous, with a real air of mystery.' The landlord emerges from the bar again. 'It may not be relevant, but Scott's brother was on the island last night; his fishing boat was heading for the harbour when I took a stroll after closing time. Jason hardly ever comes over from St Mary's, but he must have found a place to stay till conditions improved. He'd have been mad to attempt the trip back last night; his boat's too old to weather a hard storm.'

'Thanks, Saul. You're a good man to know.'

Heligan's wide smile reveals unnaturally white teeth. 'People always tell me their darkest secrets. You know where I am, if you need information.'

When he opens the door, the fog is so thick I can only see a few metres ahead.

'This bloody nislow won't shift,' Saul mutters.

'That's Cornish, isn't it?'

'Nislow's the kind of fog that keeps coming back. Get yourself home, Ben, before it settles in your bones.'

I turn on my torch, but the beam blinds me with swirling white air. Shadow must still be with Ethan Minear. He normally appears whenever I've made a long visit, but his loyalties have changed. I shove the torch back into my pocket, hoping that instinct will guide me to Nina's cottage.

17

Ethan and Jade are together in his nightmare, fighting the same demons, but he wakes alone, panting for breath. The dog is curled at the foot of his bed, but he's too wired to go back to sleep. He's used to his sister's breathing, and the rustle of sheets when she turns over. Silence presses down on him now, the panic in his chest tightening.

A sudden noise breaks the quiet. Someone cries out, the sound so thin and pitiful it makes Ethan clamber out of bed. The dog wakes up and tries to follow, but the boy leaves him shut inside. He tiptoes across the landing, then downstairs, hoping Jade has returned.

Sounds are coming from the kitchen, so he edges down the hallway. When Ethan peers through the crack in the door, his parents are facing each other, and there's no sign of Jade. His mother's eye make-up has trailed down her cheeks like raindrops on a dirty windowpane. There's a metre of space between his mum and dad, but the air is humming, and Ethan wants to call out a warning. Something, or someone, is about to get broken.

'My parents were right about you.' His mother spits out the words. 'This is your fault, not mine.'

'Look at yourself before you cast blame.'

'Why should I? You never do.'

'There's nothing to see. Your looks went years ago.' Ethan's dad gives a mocking laugh. 'You're so full of booze, you don't give a shit about Jade.'

'I love the twins more than anyone, you bastard. I'll take them with me when I leave.'

'If you try that again, they're staying with me.'

'Get outside and look for her now, if you love her so much.'

'She's hiding from your black moods, Gemma.'

'You made me like this, no one else.'

'That's bollocks and you know it. See a shrink and sort yourself out.'

'I'll get custody when the courts hear about you.'

'Shut up, you silly bitch.'

Ethan witnesses the moment when the fight starts. His mother loses control first; she flies at his dad, hands clawing at his face. Her fierce cry makes Ethan press back against the wall, hoping to disappear. When he looks through the door again, his father has caught her by the shoulders. His mother looks like a rag doll, apart from the tears rolling down her cheeks. The boy is too afraid to move when his dad lands a blow on her stomach, until he sees Luke at the top of the stairs, beckoning him up to the landing.

Luke crouches down until their faces are level, an odd excitement burning in his eyes. 'Ignore them, mate. It's their mess, not ours, and it won't last forever. If he touches either of us again I'll knock him senseless.'

Ethan is too tense to listen properly. Luke helps him back into bed, but his heart is beating too fast for sleep to arrive.

18

I take a wrong turn and stumble a few times, but music guides me to Nina's door. It's after midnight when the high call of her violin leads me through the muffled air. The Redmaynes' cottage is one of the oldest in Scilly: the property has stood at the edge of Middletown for three centuries, built from local stone and slate, with shuttered windows to protect it from the Atlantic's worst gales.

Nina has left the front door unlocked, warm air hitting me as I walk inside. She's made herself at home during her month of house-sitting, her books stacked on the table beside a vase of narcissi. My girlfriend is swaying in time with the slow melody she's playing, and it dawns on me that Zoe was right. She's beautiful, smart, and out of reach. She only notices my arrival when the tune ends, smiling at me before putting the violin back in its case. I normally enjoy the way she only speaks when necessary, instead of filling every gap, but tonight we're out of step. I'm buzzing with adrenaline while she seems totally relaxed.

I watch her languid movements as she makes herbal tea in the kitchen. I hate the stuff, but she insists it will do me good. Nina looks more comfortable in this sleek, well-designed kitchen than she does in mine, settling in the chair opposite, with an expectant look on her face. She was in Eddie's search party and returned to the cottage after one drink at the pub, so she's heard nothing since. There's disappointment on her face when I explain that we're no closer to finding the missing girl, and my frustration increases. I push my mug of tea away and walk over to the window.

'Jade must be out there somewhere. No one's left the island.'

Nina peers at me from her chair by the range. 'You won't find her in this fog, and you can't work without sleep.'

'It feels wrong to stop looking, that's all.'

'Something's got to you, hasn't it?'

'I promised Ethan to bring his sister home. Those twins are inseparable, and his family's a mess. What'll happen to him if Jade's not found?'

Her face grows solemn. 'All kids react differently, but I've read an impact study about twins that lose their siblings as juveniles. Kids don't always understand the boundaries between themselves and their twin, unless they get counselling. The ones left behind often feel like a part of themselves has died. It can raise the risk of teenage self-harm, and adult depressive illnesses later in life.'

I think about Ethan Minear teetering on the roof beam. 'I'll have to bring her back safe then, won't I?'

'Your whole team's responsible, Ben, not just you.' She studies me again, her amber stare impossible to avoid.

'I'm almost certain Ethan saw someone attack Jade last night. Can you try getting him to talk? The kid's musical, so you've got that in common, and you're training to be a counsellor.'

'I think his mutism's come back for a reason; maybe he's afraid to remember.' She turns in my direction. 'How old were you when your brother left the islands?'

'Sixteen. Why?'

'Does this remind you of him leaving you behind?'

'Ian didn't die and he's not my twin. He went to medical school; our whole family was proud of him. I'm not a case study for your dissertation, remember?'

'It can't have been easy, after being so close. You didn't see him for a long time, did you?'

'He was studying hard. Ian likes to be top of the class.'

'It almost sounds like another bereavement. How did you react?'

'I went into my shell for a bit, that's all.' I sit down again and take a sip of her tea, its sourness catching the back of my tongue.

'If we stay together, we have to be able to discuss the past.' Nina's hand skims my wrist. 'Why do you hate admitting you've been hurt?'

The question pulls me up short. My father died at sea, then my brother ran off to the city, leaving our mother drowning in grief. Somewhere in my mid-teens my feelings switched off. I worked in Ray's boatyard in my spare time, because he never asked questions. I could learn carpentry skills, work up a sweat, and watch raw timber become a thing of beauty. The rugby field helped too. There was something cathartic about the crowd's cheers and the brutal tackles. I thought scoring tries would make a man out of me, but now I'm less certain. Every one of my girlfriends has complained about me being too remote, until I lose interest and walk away. This time it's different; I'm not prepared to let her go.

'Aren't you even going to mention the risk you took, to save Ethan's life on that roof today?' Nina asks.

'What would be the point?'

'To release some stress, and let me comfort you.'

'I did my job. It's what I'm trained to do.'

'You're not a robot, Ben. It's natural to feel shaken by something that huge, and to enjoy being seen as a hero. Did it even occur to you that I might be scared?'

'That's why I kept quiet.'

'It was all round St Martin's in five minutes. I wish you'd told me first. I've already lost one partner, remember?' Her voice is cracking, making me reach for her hand.

'Nothing happened, I'm safe and sound.'

'But still a closed book.' A brittle smile appears

on Nina's face. 'What have you done with Shadow? I thought he was with you.'

'He stayed with Ethan Minear.'

She settles on my lap, wrapping her arms around my neck. 'That dog's got more emotional intelligence than his master.'

'Is that right?'

'Therapists sometimes use dogs with traumatised kids. It might have helped you, after losing your dad. Animals give unconditional love without taking anything in return.'

'You think Shadow's volunteered himself as a therapy dog?'

'I wouldn't be surprised, he's pretty smart.'

I pull her closer, until we're eye to eye. 'Help the boy talk, Nina, please. He could lead us to his sister.'

'You never give up, do you? No one should force him, if he's not ready, and I won't even be qualified till Easter.'

'You're the only one here with counselling experience. I know he'd trust you.'

'We can't risk his mental health. It's not a game, Ben.'

'I know, and he's the one that's suffering most.'

'Let me think about it.'

She drops her head onto my shoulder, ending the exchange. When I check the clock, it's 1 a.m., and tiredness nags at me. This time when we go to bed, the touch between us is about comfort, not sex, with Nina curled against my chest. She falls asleep in moments, while I gaze at the ceiling. My brain is thick with ideas about the missing girl. The wind has stopped blowing and the only sounds I can hear are the foghorns of passing frigates, crossing the Atlantic. Their calls are so deep and melancholy it reminds me of whales singing for company through miles of empty ocean.

19

Tuesday 20 December

Something wakes me an hour before dawn. The noise is loud and ugly, like a pickaxe smashing a windscreen. It takes me a moment to remember that I'm in the Redmaynes' cottage, not at home on Bryher. The carpet is littered with fragments of glass. Nina's awake too, rubbing sleep from her eyes.

'What the hell was that?' she asks.

'The window's broken.'

My first thought is to blame the storm, a sudden gust of wind breaking the sash, but wild nature had nothing to do with it. Shards of glass cling to the frame like broken teeth, and a chunk of rock is lying beside the bed. The words 'DEVIL'S TABLE' have been scrawled on its surface. It looks like a child's writing, with mismatched capital letters, making a knot form in my gut. It matches Scott Minear's description of the one they received, days before Jade vanished. Someone on the island has used brute force to send me to Chapel Down when they could have knocked on the door. I grab my shirt before running outside, but all I can see is darkness and the sea mist that never goes away. I can't chase through the village searching for the culprit in my boxer shorts, so I go back inside, but the cold has left me wide awake. Eddie's voice sounds groggy when I call him at quarter past seven, telling him and Isla to meet me by the Devil's Table.

Nina is reluctant to stay indoors, but I insist she keeps the place locked while I find out what's happened. She's already half dressed, but the stone might lead to a booby-trap and I can't put her in danger. Last night's fog has thinned to a watery mist when I set off at a jog, with my torch beam catching on white spirals that linger on the air. I follow the island's main road west, the tension in my stomach hardening as I run. Someone could be playing a joke, but that's not likely while an eleven-year-old girl is missing, unless they've got a sick sense of humour. I'm breathing hard as I pass Minear Farm. The place looks oddly peaceful when I pause to scan the fields. The farm is still surrounded by narcissi, nodding their heads in the breeze as the sky lightens from black to grey. There's no one in sight as I pass the vineyard either, the whole island asleep, apart from whoever shattered my dreams with a lump of granite.

The mist thickens again as I run up May's Hill, then over grassland; covered in bracken and faded heather, the ground soft underfoot. I stop to catch my breath as the incline steepens. Scilly's peaks were mountaintops and the islands were attached to the mainland, in the days before sea levels rose. They're still strewn with ancient burial sites. I almost trip over the opening to an entry grave that's big enough to crawl inside, suddenly aware that I'm on sacred ground.

I come to a halt near the Devil's Table. I don't know how it got its name, but it looks like a huge sacrificial altar, and something is lying on the basalt slab. The platform is mounded with hundreds of yellow flowers. When I push them aside, I see denim fabric splashed with dark red stains, and my head swims for a moment. It looks like the missing girl's body has been placed under a floral shroud after last night's search ended. I scan the surrounding area, aware that the killer may be hiding in the dark, revelling in the drama. Ethan Minear's face flashes into my mind, but I try not to focus on his vulnerability. The child is so close to the edge, he might never recover from such a terrible loss.

At times like this it's better to follow protocol than let emotions dominate, my thoughts steadying as I use my phone to take pictures for the coroner. There's still no sign of Eddie and Isla when I pull a set of plastic gloves from my pocket. My first responsibility is to check whether the child is still clinging to life, even though there's no sign of movement. I clear away more flowers, but the sight that greets me is a shock. The victim isn't the missing girl after all.

A fully grown man gazes up at me through the sea of narcissi, dark eyes stretched so wide open it takes me a moment to recognise Scott Minear. A line of blood is trailing from the corner of his eye. My head spins as I take in details, forcing me to look away until the nausea clears. I want to shove the blossoms covering his body to the ground, so I can find out why he died, but that would break every crime-scene protocol. The table may hold vital forensic clues, even though expert help may be out of reach for days.

Eddie is calling my name, and the mist is lifting again. I can see past the Devil's Table to the Atlantic, where slate-grey waves are retreating from the island fast, like they're trying to avoid contamination.

PART 2

20

The three of us huddle beside the Devil's Table, looking down at Scott Minear as the sky brightens. I'm still keen to find the cause of death, but can't risk disturbing the scene again before the pathologist arrives. It's a struggle to believe that the most powerful man on St Martin's has been killed, but he was feared by many. I'm almost certain he left those ugly bruises on Dave Carillian's face, and then there was his fight with Rob Paige. How many more families had he alienated? Scott's killer may have chosen the Devil's Table to suggest that he was an evil influence. The farmer was too macho to admit that Jade's disappearance hurt him, but now his whole family appears to be under attack, and the responsibility for finding his killer rests with my team alone.

Ferries don't sail from the mainland in winter, because of rough seas, and the helicopter and Skybus can't risk flying in poor weather. No extra officers or forensics experts can travel here until conditions improve, and judging by the wisps of fog dancing over Minear's body like poltergeists, there's more on its way.

I ask Eddie to inform DCI Madron of the death, but my biggest concern is that an early morning jogger or dogwalker could stumble across the murder site before it's secured. Sergeant Lawrie Deane will bring the crime scene kit when he ferries the pathologist over from St Mary's to confirm cause of death. It's still only 8.30 a.m., the sun just risen, but I need to tell Gemma Minear the news, before anyone hears.

'Isla, I want you to act as family liaison. You understand the role, don't you?'

'Of course, boss, and Gemma knows me pretty well. I worked on the farm for a whole season before I left for uni.'

'You'll need to take care of the family until we get an outcome, but you'll be observing them too. There's been a lot of conflict in that house, especially between Luke and his dad, so the investigation starts there. In murders like this, a family member's often involved.'

'I'll keep a close watch, sir.'

'Let me know if you see or hear anything suspicious.'

The young constable looks apprehensive. 'There's something you should know before we tell Gemma, boss. I saw Scott last night from my bedroom window at the pub. I sat there for a while, after I went up. Fog was coming over in waves, but I'm certain it was him. He left the Paige's house by the back door.'

'What time was that?'

'Around midnight.'

'Saul Heligan says Rob Paige had a fight with Scott recently – the rumour is Minear had his wandering eye on Felicity. I'll follow that up after we've seen Gemma.'

Eddie will have to guard the body alone until backup arrives. He may have disliked the victim, but he's always quick to empathise. My deputy listens to my instructions with distress on his face, then positions himself by the huge stone table, straight-backed, like a sentinel.

Isla doesn't speak as we walk downhill to Minear Farm. Silence has been her default position since she joined the island force six months ago, keen to absorb every detail, but she's already proved her worth. Her serious manner makes people trust her instantly. I'm glad of the peace and quiet today, giving me time to prepare myself. Every cop has their least favourite duty, and this is mine. I don't enjoy sharing information that will mark someone forever, but there's no avoiding it today. It doesn't help that Isla is watching me as we cross the farmyard, like she's expecting me to showcase the ideal method for giving bad news.

When I glance through the cutting shed doors, it looks like a parallel universe. Luke is with Ivan Teague and for once he looks relaxed. Ivan is trying to construct flower boxes as quickly as his friend, while Luke laughs at his attempts. It's ironic that the boy has found his sense of humour on the day we've discovered his father's body; I'd rather be working alongside him than tearing the whole family's world apart. I have to swallow a deep breath before approaching the farm-house door and pressing the bell.

Gemma is dressed in the same drab work clothes as yesterday. A look of hope crosses her face, then vanishes. We'd be wearing smiles if her daughter had been found. It bothers me that there's vodka on her breath again, so early in the morning. If she's finding life hard now, it's going to feel worse in five minutes' time.

'Watch you don't trip,' she says. 'The kitchen's a minefield. I'm getting the pickers' lunch ready.'

We navigate past a crate of Coke cans and baking trays loaded with pasties, ready for the oven. Gemma looks preoccupied when she invites us to make ourselves comfortable at the kitchen table.

'Scott went out early, but I can ring him, if you want.' She fumbles a cigarette from her packet, but doesn't light it. 'Is this about Jade?'

'Sit down for a minute, please, Gemma.'

Her gaze clings to mine. 'Tell me if she's hurt, please. Don't make me wait.'

'It's not about your daughter. We found Scott just now, on Chapel Down.'

'Why's he up there?'

'I'm afraid it's bad news, the worst kind possible.'

She leans forward, the cigarette crumbling in her hand. 'He's been injured?'

When Isla touches her arm there's no need to speak again. Gemma can read her husband's fate on the young constable's face.

'Where is he?' She's on her feet, grabbing her coat. 'There must be something I can do.'

I block her way to the back door. 'It's too late, Gemma. Scott was killed, I'm so sorry.'

'Was it an accident?'

'I'm afraid not, we believe he was attacked.'

She draws a long breath but her silence only lasts for thirty seconds. Gemma releases a piercing cry, like she's waited years to vent her misery. The wailing sound continues when Isla wraps an arm round her shoulders. The noise is so high and pitiful, it makes me want to back away, but there's no avoiding the truth. Scott Minear was in rude health yesterday, running the harvest like a military campaign, dealing out summary justice to anyone that crossed him. But his wife doesn't seem to care how much upset he caused, her sobbing loud enough to reach every room. She tries to regain control when I crouch beside her.

'Is there anyone I can call?'

'Ethan needs company, he can't be alone.'

'Hazel will help out and Isla's staying here too. I'll tell Luke and Amy what's happened this morning. Can you remember what time Scott went out this morning?'

'I didn't hear him leave.'

'How about Luke? Was he indoors last night?'

'Of course, my son never went anywhere.' Her blank face hides the reality that she may have drunk herself to sleep, too comatose even to notice her husband getting out of bed, but she still deserves justice.

'We'll find out who did this, Gemma, I promise.'

I'm rising to my feet when Ethan Minear appears in the doorway, dressed in a hoodie and jeans, his piccolo sticking out of his pocket. His face is flushed with shock. I know immediately that he overheard the news of his father's death. Ethan dashes through the back door at full pelt; I could give chase, but he'd only outrun me. All I can do is watch the boy sprint across his family's land, miles of yellow flowers swallowing him before I can catch my breath.

21

It's after 9.30 a.m. when Ethan huddles by the edge of a field, tears streaming down his face. He's never felt more alone. None of what he heard makes sense, his heart thumping too hard in his chest. His father is too powerful to die; no one on the island has enough strength to kill him. The boy can hear pickers calling greetings to each other from the lane, like it's a normal harvest day, but everything has changed.

Ethan feels guilty about leaving his mother, but he had to escape. He shuts his eyes and pulls his knees up to his chest, trying to block out every sound, but noises reach him anyway. First a woman's laughter, then a door slamming, and a tractor's engine revving further inland. His nerves are so frayed, he rams his fingers into his ears. Now he can only hear the hum of his own breathing, until a dog's soft bark reaches him. Shadow is bounding across the field when his eyes open. The dog must have followed him outside. Shadow curls at his side, keeping him warm.

There's no way to help his father, but Jade feels closer now; her pulse is stronger than yesterday. Ethan pulls his piccolo from his pocket and plays one of her favourite tunes, the music steadying him at last. Soon he's calm enough to follow a path down to the shore, praying not to be seen. If he can find out who hurt his father, the answer might lead him to Jade.

22

Luke Minear is in the cutting shed, scribbling numbers on packing crates at a hectic pace. Ivan Teague is further away, lining a row of boxes with tissue paper for today's harvest. It feels like a rerun of yesterday, with Luke's reluctance to quit showing in the rigid set of his shoulders. I feel almost certain that his dad's temper explains his strong work ethic.

'Come outside with me for a minute, please, Luke.'

'Can it wait? The packers will be here soon.'

'It's urgent, I'm afraid.' He drops his pen and follows me out to the yard. 'You'll have to send your workers home.'

'Why? It's our busiest time of year.' The young man stares up at me.

'There's bad news, I'm afraid. Your Mum's very upset.' I pause to let him absorb the idea. 'Your dad's been killed. I found his body on the moor an hour ago.'

Emotions flow across the lad's face, then quickly vanish. 'What happened to him?'

'The details will come out soon, so I'd better tell you now. I'm sorry, but it's very likely his death wasn't an accident. Can you tell me what happened at home, after the search for Jade?'

The boy's gaze is blurry with shock. 'Mum and Dad were talking in the kitchen after I went to bed.'

'What kind of time?'

'Around one, I think.'

'It must have been loud if you heard them upstairs.'

'Everyone knows they argue,' he replies, frowning. 'They were yelling, as usual.'

'Did you go outside at all, during the night?'

He shakes his head. 'I slept till my alarm rang at six. It seemed odd that Dad wasn't out here, I thought he was checking the fields . . .'

'Can you think of anyone who'd target him?'

He rubs his hand across his jaw. 'Dad's upset a lot of people over the years. Most of the pickers only show up because they're short of cash.'

'I need his phone, Luke.'

'I'll look in his office, but he normally keeps it on him.'

The young man's voice has fallen to a low monotone, and he doesn't react when I touch his shoulder. Eventually he goes inside, stumbling like a sleepwalker, yet something about his reaction doesn't ring true. He could have lost control, after so long as his dad's whipping boy. He's got enough wiry strength to haul Scott's body onto the Devil's Table. It's rare for a son to kill his father, but Luke's suffered for years. He could have lured Scott to Chapel Down then launched an attack. The Minears' farmhouse is a battlefield, like Saul Heligan suggested. When someone dies so violently, it's almost always the result of an intense conflict, with a killer they know intimately.

I don't have time to wait for Luke to find his father's phone. My pace is rapid as I head for Lowertown, with the fog blurring my thoughts. It takes effort to concentrate on the task in hand. I need to see the Paige family before the pathologist arrives from St Mary's, to find out why Minear paid them a visit hours before his murder. I also want to know about any conflict between Rob and Scott.

Felicity and Rob Paige live with their daughter above their jewellery workshop. It's a big whitewashed cottage, with a well-kept garden. My head is full of ugly details from the scene at the Devil's Table, but their plot looks like something from *Gardeners' World*. It's crammed with flowers, ferns, and dwarf palm trees, flourishing in Scilly's mild climate. The Paiges' front door stands ajar, like most homes in Scilly. The workshop specialises in sea-inspired jewellery, and Christmas must be a busy time for their online business.

I can smell hot solder, paint, and freshly brewed coffee when I step inside, where my eyes catch on a display case. It's full of pendants, bangles, and earrings shaped like glittering oyster shells. It crosses my mind that I could commission an engagement ring. I spot

Rob Paige hunched over his workbench, too focused on the red-hot metal he's hammering to notice my arrival.

Rob takes off his visor once he sees me, abandoning his tools. The man's appearance is striking when he rises to his feet; he's around fifty, grey hair worn in a ponytail, a leather patch covering his left eye, the scar bisecting his cheek giving him an air of danger. But his manner is too civilised for a villain, with no sign of swagger. His injury is recent, but I never heard exactly what happened. I get the sense that he'd rather no one mentioned it, but I admire how it never seems to slow him down. He still volunteers in the islands' lifeboat crew and is one of the best rowers in the gig racing team. I'd rather share the news of Scott Minear's death with all the islanders present, but the information will spread like wildfire. If I don't tell him now, Chinese whispers will arrive first, full of mistakes.

'Good to see you, Ben,' he says. 'I hate this bloody fog, don't you? Come in and have some coffee.'

The jeweller's manner is typical of the islands, where people pride themselves on hospitality. You're greeted like a long-lost relative, and never asked the reason for your visit unless you volunteer it. Rob went to art school in London, but he was drawn back to Scilly by its wide-open landscapes. The man's oil paintings adorn the walls of the studio, showing St Martin's as a ragged black line, circled by thrashing waves, under a pale winter sun. I've always preferred books to art, but one of his elegant seascapes would give my house a touch of class, if I could afford it. I accept the coffee he pours from the percolator that's bubbling in the corner with a grateful nod.

'Thanks for searching with us last night,' I say. 'I'm grateful so many people turned out in bad weather.'

'We could never stay at home with a child missing,' he replies. 'Felicity's with the pickers now. She gets cabin fever from being indoors all day, unlike me. I could sit here from dawn till dusk.'

'You've found your vocation then.' I glance down at the miniature hammer, knives, and tongs scattered across his bench. 'I've got a few questions, Rob, if that's okay. I've heard that you and Scott Minear clashed recently. Is that true?'

There's a pause before he answers. 'The bloke takes whatever he wants, without asking permission. I've never liked bullies.'

'Me neither. Why did you two fight outside the pub?'

'That wasn't my finest hour,' he says, rubbing the back of his neck. 'Scott hit a raw nerve, and I'd had a few beers.'

'What started it?'

'His tone. The guy's got no respect for anyone.'

'Did he say something about Felicity?'

'It was about our business, the usual stupid insults. He lent us a few quid and now he acts like he owns us.' The man's one-eyed stare focuses on me again. 'If he's insulted my wife, I'll wipe him all over the pavement.'

'Scott was attacked late last night, after the search.'

'That's no concern of mine.'

'His body was found by Chapel Down an hour ago. He was seen outside your house last night, after the pub closed.'

'You're saying he's dead?' His tone softens immediately. 'We weren't friends, but I never wished that on him. Was it an accident?'

'The details aren't clear yet. What was he after last night, Rob?'

A muscle ticks in his jaw when I look at him again. 'Felicity and Lauren were in bed when he turned up, after midnight, half pissed. He started throwing out accusations. Scott said I'd taken his gig, which was rubbish. I'd never harm the boats, just because we didn't get along. The bloke was paranoid.'

'You may have been the last person to see him alive. How did your conversation end?'

'I told him to leave, then threw him out.' Rob's discomfort shows in his hunched shoulders.

'I'll need to speak to your wife today. Can I see Lauren while I'm here, please? She might have information about Jade.'

The shock on Rob's face looks real when he goes to fetch his daughter, but he may just be a good actor. He's admitted to disliking the victim, and I have to put aside my admiration for the man's bravery in facing his injuries. The islands seem like the last place on earth for such a vicious murder, with kids free to play unsupervised, until someone chucks away the rule book.

We've seen several attacks in recent years, and tight communities can feel like a stranglehold when conflict erupts. It's possible that Rob's self-control was broken by Scott's goading.

Lauren Paige looks like a miniature version of her mother when she enters the room, with pale curls, a slim build, and a watchful expression. She's around sixteen, already beautiful. The girl is wearing a long dress, her feet bare, like it's the height of summer. There's no way to shield her from the truth, but I keep my statements simple. Her blue eyes turn glassy when she hears of Scott Minear's death, so I ask Rob to bring her a sugary drink to combat the shock. The girl seems unwilling to meet my eye while her dad hurries to the kitchen.

'Can you tell me about Jade? I know she's younger, but maybe she confided in you?'

'She hasn't said anything recently.'

'Has she ever seemed upset?'

'Only about Ethan sometimes.'

'How do you mean?'

'Jade worries about starting secondary school.' The girl's shy gaze fixes on my shoes. 'She's scared he'll be bullied, if she's not around.'

'She protects him, doesn't she?'

'The twins do everything together.' Lauren presses her fingers against her lips. 'Does Ethan know about his dad yet?'

'I think he may have overheard the news.'

'I can stay with him, if you want. He's known me and Ivan forever.'

'You're talking about Ivan Teague?'

She nods her head. 'He's my boyfriend. One of us could support him till Jade's found; we're both mentors at the primary school.'

'That sounds like a good thing to do.'

'I volunteered for work experience last summer, I want to be a teacher one day.' The girl's expression is so solemn it looks like her dad's injury has helped her grow up fast.

'Thanks for the offer, but the family need time alone today. I'll let you know if Ethan wants company soon. If you think of anything Jade said that stuck in your mind, please give me a ring.'

Lauren's eyes are brimming. The hot chocolate her father has placed at her side is untouched. She's able to meet my gaze now, but it's still possible she's concealing something. There's no point in pressing for information until she's ready. I give her my card, then let them both know that I'll be making a public announcement in the community hall at one o'clock. The visit has left me with too many unanswered questions. Rob steered away from the bad blood between him and Scott Minear, and I don't want to discuss the rumour about his wife's affair before talking to her. The only thing I feel certain of is his daughter's fondness for Ethan and Jade.

A call arrives from Lawrie Deane once I leave the

Paiges' home, announcing that he's nearing Highertown harbour, so I head for the quay at a rapid march. I hear the police motorboat's engine chugging before it emerges from the mist; the fibreglass motor cruiser has seen better days, with faded dayglow stripes on its sides, and a scraped prow from colliding with Hugh Town quay at high tide. Its engine rattles with age, but our annual budget won't stretch to a replacement.

Dr Gareth Keillor steps onto the quay first, his expression concerned, sparse grey hair combed across his bald patch. He's the only registered pathologist on the islands and we've worked together several times since my appointment. I know him socially, too. The man's teaching me golf, but my swing leaves much to be desired, despite plenty of lessons. Keillor looks like a retired history teacher, but he's got a keen sense of humour that rarely emerges when he's at work.

'The victim's Scott Minear, Ben. Is that right?'

'I'm afraid so.'

'A family man in the prime of his life. My day's getting worse by the minute. Our crossing wasn't great either; we almost ran aground in this fog.'

'The sea's a bloody nightmare,' Deane says, tightening the mooring rope. 'Visibility's down to five metres south of Tresco.'

Sergeant Lawrie Deane looks overjoyed to set foot on dry land. He's worked for the Isles of Scilly Police for three decades. The man struck me as a jobsworth at first, bitter from thwarted ambitions, but I was wrong.

Deane's a passionate traveller, with several European languages under his belt, teaching me to not judge a book by its cover. He grows portlier with every passing year, his red hair cropped brutally short.

I give both men details about finding Minear's body as we walk east along Par Beach, the sand wet from the high tide. It's 11 a.m. when we cross Chapel Down, with cairns rearing from the mist like startled horses. Eddie looks chilled to the bone, but he's standing guard at the exact spot where I left him several hours ago. The Devil's Table still looks like a site of ancient sacrifice, with Scott Minear's body under a mantle of yellow flowers.

Keillor circles the slab of rock before approaching the corpse, while Deane keeps his distance. I don't blame him for being squeamish. Witnessing a fatality can affect you for days, even when you're a member of the Murder Squad, but I'm obliged to stay close to the pathologist. He pulls on sterile gloves before sweeping the flowers away, scattering dozens of blossoms across the ground. There's not much point in trying to preserve the blooms to test them for the killer's DNA. The nearest forensics lab is in Penzance, but with transport closed to the mainland, the evidence would be invalid by the time it arrived.

Scott Minear's body is dressed in the work clothes he wore yesterday; jeans, and a black padded jacket. A pool of blood has collected on the rock, below his torso. Keillor's movements are gentle when he flexes the man's joints, like he's trying to avoid causing more pain. It's only now that I see the wooden handle of a knife protruding from the man's chest, the blade plunged deep. It's the type that pickers use in the fields. The initials 'S. M.' are carved into the handle, my thoughts clicking into place as the pathologist continues his work. Scott Minear has been stabbed with his own blade. I heard him asking Gemma where his knife had gone, and he's the only islander with those initials. Luke could easily have taken it from the cutting shed.

'He died between six and twelve hours ago,' Keillor says. 'It may have been from impact trauma; his skull's been shattered. Or the knife blow to his chest could have caused exsanguination. I can't tell which came first until I do a full examination.'

'What's your best guess for cause of death?'

'Unstoppable blood loss from the knife wound, but that's not certain.' Keillor turns to me again. 'The flowers are an interesting touch, aren't they? It's fitting for a man who spent his life cultivating them. My wife would know the variety, but I'm no expert.'

'I'll find out today. Is it okay to move him?'

'Let me record some details, then we'll take him back to St Mary's.'

The pathologist steps away to dictate notes into his phone. The blood that's collected under Minear's body is oxidising to a dark brown, but it's only when I step closer that something glints among the flowers. Another glass bottle has been placed near the victim's head, with a model boat trapped inside. I collect it, using an evidence bag to shield it from my prints. The colours are so bright, it could have been painted yesterday. I'm almost certain it was made by Dave Carillian.

It may have been the last object Scott Minear saw, as he lay dying. My heart rate increases when I see it's an exact replica of Minear's own speedboat, with a flower emblem on the prow. He used it to travel between the islands, its powerful engine painted a dull silver. The man's killer has taken a lot of time and trouble to reproduce every detail.

Keillor is still recording findings for his initial report, while Lawrie Deane watches the sea. Eddie has observed the whole proceedings, his ever-present smile missing for once. My hands are shaking from cold or delayed shock, and the third ship in a bottle bothers me. Dave Carillian isn't a clear suspect. It's possible that he lured Minear outside in the early hours of this morning, but his isolation continues to make me doubt his involvement. He would have needed help to lift the corpse onto the table. I place the glass vessel in my pocket, still wrapped in an evidence bag, then lean down to close Scott Minear's eyes. Witnessing the murder scene is bad enough without having to confront his furious stare.

23

Ethan feels the cold through his windcheater, the moist air damping his skin. He follows the shoreline towards Carn Levereth, with Shadow at his heels. Instinct leads him to the place where he likes to beachcomb with Jade. He needs to be calm to work out who hurt his dad. The huge rocks on the beach have been carved into sculptures by the tides. Some rise like ghosts from the seabed, while others are as sharp as needles. At least the daymark up ahead looks cheerful; its red and white stripes shine through the fog, but there's no sign of Jade. Ethan has never been apart from his twin for so long, his gnawing anxiety making it hard to concentrate.

He walks down Chapel Brow, then backtracks when muffled voices travel through the air. The boy moves closer, making a hissing sound to stop Shadow barking. Figures surround the Devil's Table, too busy to notice him crouching behind a boulder, but before he can grab the dog's collar, Shadow bounds forward to greet his master. When Ethan peers out from his hiding place Kitto rubs the dog's head then sends him away. The policeman is too busy talking to pay Shadow any more attention, so the dog returns to his side. The oldest man in the group is using complicated language. Ethan hears the words 'rigor mortis' and wonders what they mean, until he sees a dark shape lying on the slab of granite.

The boy's heart pounds as he drops behind another rock. When he peers at the Devil's Table again, the two policemen are obstructing his view, but when they finally step back, he sees his father is lying on the table surrounded by flowers, his eyes closed. His face is chalk white, lips an odd shade of blue, with blood smeared across his cheek. Ethan swallows hard to suppress his nausea. His dad is perfectly still, even though one of the men is leaning close to take photos. If his father was alive he'd shove the man away.

Ethan blunders away through the mist. The dog gives a single bark from somewhere up ahead, and he runs to catch up, tripping over a tree root in his hurry, sending him sprawling onto a bank of heather. Whoever placed his dad's body on the Devil's Table may still have Jade. The idea drags him to his feet. He runs on with the dog at his side, looking for a place to hide.

24

The palm-sized glass bottle looks like a child's toy, yet its meaning is sinister. I can't tell why the killer left an exact replica of Scott Minear's boat at the murder site, but it must be symbolic, because a trail of them is being scattered across the island. I need to understand why he left an antique model in the field where Jade was taken; the other boats have been made more recently. I can feel someone watching as I slip the evidence bag back into my pocket. The skill came to me when I worked undercover: psychologists call it hypervigilance, but it feels more like a sixth sense, offering protection in dangerous times. When I turn round no one's in sight, except my small team, preparing Minear's body for its journey to St Mary's.

I shrug the feeling off until Shadow's bark echoes through the air, high and strident, making me wish I'd paid him more attention a few minutes ago, but I couldn't allow him near the crime scene. He behaved like a normal pet during his recovery, following instructions, but now seems determined to please himself. It's a small concern compared to the island's richest family being targeted.

I can't prove that Jade Minear is still alive; she may already have met the same fate as her father, her body cast into the sea. I have to keep in mind that the abduction and the murder could have been committed by two different perpetrators. It's possible that someone has capitalised on the island's panic about Jade's absence to attack her father, but there's no evidence to support that theory. It seems more likely that one individual is targeting all the Minears, for reasons I don't yet understand. Scott's womanising may have something to do with it, or an old vendetta with someone he trampled on in the past.

The killer must be among the islanders present on St Martin's the night Jade Minear went missing, and we've already whittled our list of potential suspects down to twenty-five. Some are too old, too young, or too frail to attack a robust, fully grown man like Scott Minear. My top suspect so far is an elderly loner, with a passion for making ships in bottles, but the evidence against him is circumstantial. And surely Carillian is too smart to leave such obvious clues?

It bothers me that my team consists of just two inexperienced officers. Isla needs to stay with Gemma Minear, and keep a close eye on Luke's behaviour. I've instructed her to record the names of all visitors to the farmhouse, aware that killers sometimes ingratiate themselves with victims' families. I need to return

Ethan to his mother's care too, in case the killer is planning more attacks. I instruct Eddie and Lawrie Deane to carry the body bag containing Scott Minear's corpse down to the police launch, so the pathologist can examine it at St Mary's hospital.

I'm alone once the three men depart, leaving me to make a final assessment of the murder site. Photos of the Devil's Table often appear in guidebooks; it's one of St Martin's most distinctive landmarks, but the blood on its surface this morning makes it look chilling. The slab still bears a stain, despite our efforts to wash it away. I can't yet tell which islander is bitter enough to abduct a child and plan the brutal killing of her father. Scott Minear had enough bravado to commit such terrible acts, yet he's the victim, not the perpetrator.

A message from DCI Madron reaches my phone while I survey the scene. The man's panic resonates through his voice. He's requesting a written update, even though Minear's body has only just been found. I fire off a text, telling him he won't get his report until after the 1 p.m. briefing. I crouch down to inspect the hundreds of flowers that were strewn across the rock's surface. They're all the same variety, but different from the ones I harvested as a boy. These have six or seven flowers on every stem, white petals with a yellow corona. I collect a few blooms then drop them into an evidence bag. When I poke around in the grass there's nothing unusual, until I widen my search. An old-model iPhone is almost hidden under a clump of bracken a few metres away. Luke Minear promised to look for his dad's phone, but we may have got there first. The screen is cracked and the battery's dead, but it could still unlock the reason for Scott Minear's death, so I put it in an evidence bag.

Eddie returns while I'm still poking around in the grass. 'The fog's getting worse, boss,' he says. 'The coastguard's banned all sailing from here to the Solent apart from police and RNLI vessels. It'll take Lawrie ages to get back to St Mary's.'

'The bad weather could help us. No one can visit or leave the island.'

'Do you want me to start house to house?'

'Let's review the evidence first. This phone could be Scott's; the call log might show if someone rang him last night and lured him up here.'

My deputy gazes at me like a sixth former hoping for an A grade from his favourite teacher. His excitement grows when we discuss the murder weapon, especially the symbolism of Minear being killed by his own knife, but our only tangible clues are the ships in bottles. I want to get information from all of the islanders about the calling cards today; they might know if they belong to someone's collection. We may get fingerprints from Scott's harvesting knife too, but it could be days before items can be sent to the forensics lab. The samples may already have been in the open too long, damp air corrupting primary evidence. I wish Liz Gannick was here to assess the crime scene; the county's chief

152

forensics officer has a reputation for closing cases fast, but she can't travel from the mainland until the airport reopens.

'I want to see Suzie Felyer, before the meeting. She spends more time with the island's kids than anyone. She'll know if Jade's been upset, and there's a rumour she's had a fling with Scott Minear, too.'

I'm hoping the schoolteacher's reaction to the farmer's death will prove whether or not they had an affair. Eddie falls into step beside me, clearly relieved to be given a concrete task. My deputy never complains about doing the worst duties, but he hates inactivity.

When we walk back through Highertown, the Minears' farmhouse has its curtains drawn, signalling the family's desire for privacy. When the road forks at the edge of the village, we follow School Lane. The thoroughfare is just wide enough to accommodate the island's Jeep, which delivers goods from the harbour to every building on St Martin's during winter. The school is a small red-brick building set back from the lane, and I feel almost certain Suzie Felyer will be inside, rather than at home next door, even though it's the Christmas holidays. The outdoor noticeboard shows a picture from the nativity play at the end of term. The Minear twins are dressed in identical robes and crowns, even their smiles matching.

I catch sight of Suzie through the window. She's in the school's only classroom, sorting costumes into piles, her expression relaxed. When I rap on the glass she appears startled before raising her hand in greeting.

Suzie looks like an archetypal primary-school teacher; middle-aged with an attractive smile, her curly light-brown hair tied back with a scarf. She's wearing a pinafore dress over jeans, beckoning us closer with both hands.

'This is an honour, gentlemen. Have you come to admire the kids' dinosaur paintings?' The amusement in her voice confirms she hasn't yet heard about the murder.

'I'm after some help, Suzie. Can I ask a few questions?'

'Fire away, I'm just doing some tidying. Has Jade been found?'

'Not yet, I'm afraid.'

The teacher's smile fades when she perches on one of the miniature chairs, and Eddie follows suit, but I lower myself onto a table, hoping it will take my weight.

'How's the school year going?' I ask.

'The kids are doing well. My nine pupils are at different key stages, so SATs tests are a nightmare. But you're not here about school, are you?'

The professional pride on Suzie's face makes it harder to break bad news. Eddie watches me from the corner of his eye, as I take time choosing my words.

'Did the Minear twins seem okay at the end of term?'

'Jade's top of the class, but Ethan's made progress too. I got a speech and language therapist to help him online this term. He still hates talking to the whole group, but he's doing better one to one. His musical talent's building his confidence too; I've been giving him private lessons.'

I can tell Suzie could wax lyrical about her pupils for hours, but it's my job to spoil her day. The teacher is so shocked to hear of Scott Minear's death, her gaze slips from my face to Eddie's, checking I'm not lying. A long time passes before she speaks again.

'When the council tried to close us down, Scott was this school's biggest defender; he bought new tables and chairs for the kids, plus a dozen computers. I know he upset people, but he was generous too.'

'I have to ask an awkward question, I'm afraid. There's a rumour that you and Scott were involved.'

'Sleeping together, you mean?' she asks, her cheeks flushing with anger or embarrassment.

'Yes.'

'That's absolute rubbish. I'd never steal another woman's husband, under any circumstance.'

'I don't mean to offend you, just to find out why he died.'

'Scott wanted every child on St Martin's to have a decent education, and no one can fault that. He could be difficult, but he changed dozens of lives for the better.' The teacher's speech comes to a sudden halt, her anger finally surfacing. 'What kind of sick bastard would hurt him?'

'It must be an islander. We'll find out, don't worry.'

'And Jade's still missing?'

'She left the farmhouse before dawn yesterday,' Eddie replies. 'No one's seen her since.'

'You think she's been killed too, don't you?' Suzie's hands flutter up to her face.

'We don't have any proof that she's been hurt. Try and cast your mind back to anything different in her behaviour, please, Suzie. Details could help us understand.'

She frowns in concentration. 'Jade's just a sweet, confident girl, like I said. She's reacted well to the mentoring scheme. It's the first time my year-six kids have been mentored by teenagers like Lauren Paige and Ivan Teague. It should help their transition to Five Islands next September. She loves it when they visit.'

Every child in Scilly goes to Five Islands secondary on St Mary's, which can be a rude awakening after tiny classes on the outlying islands. I can tell we've asked enough questions for the time being; Suzie's face is drawn with shock.

'Gemma must be in bits,' she mutters. 'How can I help?'

'The family's not ready for visitors yet, but thanks for the offer.'

'I'll call at the farmhouse in a few days.'

The teacher musters a smile when we say goodbye, but her calm has vanished when I glance back through the window. Suzie's reaction to Scott Minear's death seems too extreme for the loss of a benefactor, no matter how generous. She's standing by her desk, head in hands, shoulders jerking as she sobs. The man seems to have divided opinions on the island straight down the middle. I still need to understand if he was a hero or a villain.

25

Eddie and I return to Minear Farm before going to the community hall. I want to reassure Gemma that we won't stop until we know why her husband died, and how his death is linked to Jade's disappearance, but it's Isla that greets us in the porch. If I was still in London, a fully trained family liaison officer would be in place. It's asking a lot of a brand-new constable to strike the delicate balance between collecting evidence and providing support. When I ask how Gemma's coping, she looks uncomfortable.

'Hazel went home to her kids, so Luke's taking care of her now,' she whispers. 'Shouldn't it be the other way round?'

Gemma is in the sitting room, where the pall of cigarette smoke is thicker than the mist outside. She's slumped on the settee, clutching Luke's hand. The young man appears so busy meeting his mother's needs, his own are being neglected. I still believe the reason for Minear's death could lie inside his family. The lad was pushed around for years, so he's a likely culprit, and Isla is keeping a close eye on him. She's been looking for signs he could have attacked his father, but so far nothing has come to light.

I drop to a crouching position in front of Minear's widow, forcing her to make eye contact.

'We're holding a meeting in the community hall, Gemma. Your friends all want to help. Is there anyone you'd like to see?'

She blots her face with a wad of tissues. 'Only Hazel. Keep the rest away, please.'

'Not even your mum? Maybe it's time to bury the hatchet.'

'She hated Scott. I bet she's crowing now, like all the rest.' She lurches forward suddenly, her hand on my wrist. 'Find Jade, please. I can't lose them both.'

'We're looking everywhere, I promise. Have you and Amy spoken about her dad yet?'

'Why would she care? I haven't seen her since she hooked up with that millionaire.'

'Her relationship's irrelevant, Gemma,' I reply. 'She's grieving for her dad.'

Luke looks up suddenly. 'I called her earlier. She's still too shocked to absorb it.'

'I don't need her crawling back here, now Scott's gone, after the names she called me.' The anger in Gemma's eyes shines even brighter than before. 'Do you know what makes me sick? The killer's an islander. Someone from my community took Jade, then killed my husband.'

'That's why I want you to try and remember who's clashed with Scott recently.'

'I wasn't his keeper,' she says, her face suddenly blank. 'Now Ethan's run off. Is he in danger too?'

'We'll bring him back. Do you mind if we search the house after the meeting?'

The question makes Luke look uncomfortable, as if he'd rather not allow strangers to touch his possessions, but he keeps his mouth shut.

'Do what you like,' Gemma says. 'Please just find the twins.' She removes her hand from my wrist at last, her bloodshot gaze drifting from my face.

Luke trudges down the hall behind me when I summon him to the kitchen. I probably looked the same at his age, hiding my fears behind a sullen mask, but the lad's reaction to his dad's death is so muted, my alarm bells keep ringing. I can't prove that he lured his father up to the Devil's Table without witnesses, yet I can see he's on the defensive. He keeps his arms folded tight across his chest.

'You'll get support, Luke, don't worry. How come your mum's so angry with your sister?'

'Amy told her to leave Dad. She said their marriage was toxic.'

'That's a powerful statement, from a daughter to a mother.'

'Mum doesn't forgive easily.'

'Do you have any questions, before we hold the meeting at the community hall?'

He shakes his head. 'Mum loved Dad, no matter what. She needs to see his body or she won't rest.' His voice sounds more authoritative than before – a man's tone instead of a boy's.

'He's at the hospital on St Mary's, I'll arrange it when it's safe to travel. Can I show you a couple of things, before you go back to your Mum?'

'Why now? She needs me with her.'

'It won't take long.'

When I pull the phone from my pocket, wrapped in its evidence bag, panic crosses his face.

'Is this your dad's, Luke?'

'I think so, but it looks broken. It won't work, will it?'

'The screen's shattered, but that won't matter. Do you know his password?'

'Dad never let me touch it.' The boy's arms remain folded, like he's struggling to hold himself together.

'It's okay, the network can open it for us.' I produce the ship in a bottle from my pocket, containing the exact replica of his father's boat. 'Have you seen this before? It was found at the murder scene.'

Luke peers at the model inside its plastic wrapping. The shock that passes across his face could be real or make-believe, depending on his acting skills. His voice is a hoarse whisper when he replies.

'Dad was proud of his boat. It was the most powerful launch on the islands. He could get to Tresco in five minutes.'

'So it mattered to him?'

'He had a tough upbringing, without any luxuries. That's why he gave himself presents now and then.'

I can't tell whether regret or guilt has reduced the lad to tears. He gets rid of them fast with an angry swipe of his thumb.

'Sorry, Luke. This is hard on you, isn't it?'

'Mum's hurting most – she'll never get over this. Gran's desperate to help, but she won't let her near. Once Mum makes a decision there's no changing it.'

Luke's reactions continue to trouble me; he's keeping his emotions under lock and key. Maybe he's too overloaded to make sense of his father's death, but he could be skilled at suppressing his emotions. The boy is already backing away, and I'm almost certain he's carrying a secret, even though he seems driven by his sense of duty. He heads back down the hallway, his mother's cries reeling him back to her side.

Eddie and I reach the community hall on the outskirts of Middletown ten minutes early. The building's red-brick structure is less attractive than the island's ancient cottages, but at least it's fit for purpose, and it's a testament to the islander's unity. They raised the money to build it, as well as the tiny observatory that lies in its grounds, which draws stargazers to the island every year. The hall is already warm and airless, the heaters rattling while the boiler cranks into gear. I've got a simple message for every family on the island: they're all at risk, until the killer's found. Everyone must follow a fixed curfew to avoid getting hurt.

'Jason Minear's still not answering his phone,' I tell Eddie. 'He's the one family member we haven't interviewed. Can you get transcripts of all the relatives' phone records, while I track him down?'

'Straight after the meeting, boss.'

'Scott's is the most urgent. Luke seemed twitchy about us finding it.'

'I'll do that first, Gemma might know his password.'

My deputy scribbles my instructions in his notebook, but there's no more time for discussion. Islanders are streaming through the doors, many of them straight from the fields, giving up their lunch breaks to hear our announcement. Over fifty people have shown up, two thirds of the island's current population, including Nina, who's standing at the edge of the crowd.

The only Minear family member present is Amy, who's being supported by Neil Kershaw. Her gaze fixes on me when I step onto the small stage. I feel certain that some of the island population have already heard the news, but there's still a collective gasp when I state that Scott Minear is dead, his body found on Chapel Down. I hold back the more bizarre details. If people knew that he was laid on the Devil's Table under a blanket of flowers, with his own knife planted in the middle of his chest, panic would take hold. I keep my voice steady when I speak again.

'I'm putting the island on lockdown. No one leaves St Martin's or travels here for the time being, and I'm imposing a curfew. I want you all indoors from ten p.m.

to seven a.m. until you hear different, please. If you know anything about why Scott was attacked or why Jade is missing, come and see us now. We'll be using the hall as our meeting place until the killer's found. Does anyone have questions?'

The crowd remains silent, their shoulders hunched as the meeting ends.

'One more thing, before you go.' I hold up one of the ships in a bottle, in its transparent evidence bag. 'We've found several of these, including one close to Scott's body. Please talk to us if you know anything about why someone's scattering ships in bottles across the island.'

No one says a word, as if the whole crowd has signed an oath of secrecy. They only start talking again as they file away, whispering speculations, but I feel certain someone on St Martin's knows why the Minears are being targeted. The vicious nature of the attack makes it seem like a revenge killing, and my best option is to maintain the lockdown while my investigation continues. I still need to know if Minear slept with the wrong man's wife, or broke up someone's business.

The community hall soon empties as pickers return to the fields, still discussing the murder in hushed tones. Only Amy Minear waits behind after I leave Eddie folding chairs away. The young woman stands on the path, hands deep in the pockets of an emerald-green coat, which clashes with her cascade of red hair. When she steps closer her eyes are swollen from crying. I can see panic in her expression, but no sign of grief, which reminds me of Luke. It strikes me again that the people with the most reason to hate Scott Minear may have been his own family, yet their involvement will be hard to prove.

'Please keep looking for Jade, Ethan can't cope without her.' Words gush from her mouth like water spurting from a tap.

'She's our highest priority, believe me.'

'It's not her fault our family's screwed up.'

'Gemma still seems angry towards you, Amy. Is that because of Neil?'

She shakes her head. 'Mum didn't get the life she wanted, and me leaving home felt disloyal, because Dad lashed out at her even more. Once Mum loses faith in you, you're history. She's even turning Gran away.' Amy's gaze drifts towards the table behind me. 'How come you've got flowers in that plastic bag?'

'I need to know what type they are.'

'I'd recognise them a mile off.' She releases a dull laugh. 'They're Grand Monarch jonquils, Dad's favourites. It's a hardy variety that fetches top prices. No one else grows them in Scilly.'

'Why not, if they're so valuable?'

'Dad wouldn't allow it, in case it spoiled his profit margin.' She stares back at me. 'Most of the islanders feared him. If you don't know that, you're talking to the wrong people.'

'How did you feel about him, Amy?'

'I was sick of his bullying, that's why I left.'

'Did Scott ever hit you?'

'Enough times to make me scared.' She takes a breath, her eyes welling again. 'He always said I asked for it; that's how he operated. Blame someone else, then attack, without warning. Luke got the worst of it. I thought it might break him.'

'Is that why you tried to row away at thirteen?'

'We got caught in the middle. Mum tried to leave, but he dragged her back, and they just carried on fighting. She's been drowning her sorrows ever since.'

'What happened after you were rescued from that boat?'

'My grandparents took me in for two months.' The odd smile that appears on her face unsettles me. 'I wanted to stay there, but Dad persuaded me to go home. He said everything was mended, which was a lie, of course. He always got his way, until now.'

Amy ends the conversation there, but she's given me plenty to consider. Scott Minear's corpse was hidden under a mound of expensive jonquils with an appropriate name. Minear behaved like a Grand Monarch all his life, and I can understand why his family hated his brutal regime. It's Jade's abduction that makes no sense, unless the killer plans to erase his entire bloodline.

26

Ethan is still trembling when he jogs along the side of a field with mud clinging to his shoes. He can see his father lying on Devil's Table whenever he shuts his eyes, so he keeps his gaze fixed on the ground. Shadow has vanished in the mist, but he must be nearby, his bark sounding every few minutes. There's only one place Ethan can go where safety is guaranteed. The boy follows the hedgerow back up May's Hill to his grandparents' house. Its tidy front garden and the holly sprigs decorating the porch make him feel calmer than before.

The boy twists the handle on the back door, but it's locked, for the first time ever. It's always left open so he and Jade can come and go as they please. His grandmother takes a long time to appear. He knows immediately that something is wrong, even though she looks the same. She's wearing a thick black jumper, her gold crucifix catching the light. Her lavender scent is unchanged, but her smile is missing when she glances past him, as if threats are waiting, just beyond the hedgerow.

'You can't come in today, love, I'm sorry. I'd walk you home myself, but I can't leave Grandad. He's having a bad day.'

Ethan's gran has never turned him away before; he wants to curl up in her kitchen, which always smells of freshly baked bread. His grandfather will be sitting on the sofa as usual, half asleep in front on the TV. When he looks at his grandma again, there's an ugly rash of bruises on her wrist, and suddenly he's afraid. The old woman tugs down her sleeve to cover the marks.

'I hate sending you away, sweetheart, but I want you safe.' She steps closer to peer down the lane once more. 'Wait here a minute. I've got something for you. Then promise to go home and play your music for a while. That always calms you, doesn't it?'

He gives a slow nod, and she returns with a paper bag full of shortbread. His grandmother points at the white cloud of fog, sending him back to the farmhouse, before the door clicks shut. Ethan remains there, uncertain what to do. He wants to carry on looking for Jade, but his mother will be angry if he stays out too long. Shadow bounds out of the mist suddenly, lifting his spirits. He gives the dog one of his grandmother's biscuits, then takes a bite himself, but its buttery taste offers little comfort.

27

Eddie and I return to Minear Farm straight after the meeting. I want to search for evidence to explain the farmer's death before it's lost, while he checks the family's phone records. I look inside Gemma's old-fashioned pantry for anything unusual lurking between the jam jars, sacks of potatoes, and bottles of wine. Scott Minear had plenty of money, yet his kitchen is twenty years out of date. The wooden units have withstood hard use, their surfaces scratched and dented. Everything is solid and functional, but there's no sense of celebration anywhere I look. The couple's difficulties seem to have tarnished their home life, yet Minear's widow is mourning him like her world has ended. Something about the atmosphere is out of key.

I head upstairs, leaving Eddie on the ground floor, searching Scott's office. There's nothing of interest in the attic, just empty suitcases and the mouldering furniture that was there when I rescued Ethan. The bedrooms appear unloved too, with several standing empty. No money has been spent on the place for years. The rose-print wallpaper in the master bedroom is peeling from the walls, curtains fading from red to pink. I can't imagine what drove Scott Minear to lavish thousands on the island's school yet spend so little on his own comfort.

Luke's room is the only one that's been modernised recently; the walls are a cheery yellow, floorboards newly varnished. It's so out of step with the rest of the house, I bet the young man decorated it himself. The clothes hanging in his wardrobe are too smart for a farm boy. They include a new suit, ideal for job inter-views. When I leaf through some papers on his desk, there's a letter bearing Plymouth Argyll Football Club's crest. It's an invitation to join their youth squad for a six-month trial in February, stapled to an unsigned job contract, dated two weeks ago. Why would a talented young footballer wait to accept such a golden oppor-tunity? Luke may be longing to escape the muddy, exhausting world of farming, and his sporting ambi-tions could have caused conflict with his father.

I'm about to leave the room when I spot something else on his desk. It's a ship in a bottle, palm-sized, like all the ones I've found. It contains a yellow lobster boat, like those used by local fishermen. It seems odd that such a simple object triggers my suspicions, but Luke could have gathered some of the boats left by Dave Carillian to use as part of a killing ritual. Disbelief almost pushes the idea from my mind. I can see why Luke might hate his father, but not his sister Jade, unless he resented her for being his dad's favourite. I'll need to find a way to get the truth, even though he's hiding his feelings.

Eddie is on his phone when I go downstairs to Scott's office. He's talking to the farmer's mobile provider, so deeply immersed he barely looks up. His face is flushed with success when the call finally ends.

'I hit the jackpot, boss. Here's a transcript of Scott's texts from the last three months; I've got his call log too.'

When I stand at his side, scrolling through texts, I'm struck by the number of abusive messages Scott sent to his wife. There are hundreds of them, deliberately cruel in tone, ridiculing everything from her appearance to her parenting skills.

Eddie's voice drops to a whisper. 'Why the hell did Gemma stay with him?'

'For the kids, probably, or maybe it was an addiction, like her drinking. Jason Minear still seems to be ignoring us; I need to get over to St Mary's and find him.'

I'd like to read the messages more closely, but the need to interview Scott's twin is more pressing. I want to hear why he left St Martin's last year, after a lifetime on the farm, and why he's been avoiding my calls. I'll have to sail over to Scilly's biggest island alone, ignoring the coastguards' advice. Eddie needs to remain here to check the transcripts and Isla is busy comforting Gemma.

*

The bowrider's engine gives a splutter of exhaust when I get down to the quay. It seems unwilling to brave the cloud of whiteness, taking three attempts to kick into life. There's no breeze to displace the mist, my journey almost soundless. It's foolhardy to set off in such dangerous conditions, with only a compass to guarantee my safety, but it's my only option. My eyes strain for familiar landmarks. If I run aground, rescue will be a long time coming. The lifeboat crew would set off from St Mary's if I sent out a mayday signal, but they'd struggle to find me in these conditions.

It's a relief when Hugh Town finally comes into view. I leave the bowrider tied to a mooring rope by the harbour's high-water mark then walk along the Strand. It's 3 p.m. and the afternoon light is already fading. Hugh Town looks like a distant relative of the crowded holiday destination it becomes in summer, with day-trippers jostling for space on the narrow lanes, admiring its pastel-coloured houses and hunting for souvenirs. The shops are all closed, apart from the Co-op, where a solitary assistant is sweeping the aisles.

I start my search for Jason Minear in the Atlantic, where a few old-timers are playing cards. Under normal circumstances they'd have a perfect view of the town's fishing boats and the off-islands in the distance, but today there's nothing. If any of the old men are bothered by the blankness outside, there's no sign of it. No one replies when I ask after Jason Minear, until the oldest man raises his head.

171

'He doesn't drink here anymore, thank God. They barred him for not paying his tab. Who wants to listen to all that misery? We're better off without him.'

The only other pub that remains open in winter is the Mermaid. I loved the place as a teenager, for its good beer and walls darkened by ancient tobacco smoke. It still feels like a smugglers' den nestled beside the quay, with hardly any light spilling through the windows, the walls smothered in nautical memorabilia. Jason Minear is at the bar, hunched over his pint. The man's resemblance to Scott is unsettling. His scruffy three-day stubble needs a shave and his gaze is bloodshot, but his bone structure's identical. He gives a wary nod when I pull up a stool and offer to buy him another drink.

'Ben Kitto, isn't it? Our deputy police chief. Where's that wolfdog of yours?'

'Avoiding me, right now. He prefers women and children.'

He gazes straight ahead. 'I had a Labrador like that once. My wife spoiled her rotten.'

'She'd get on well with Shadow.'

When Jason turns in my direction, I can tell he's not only drunk, but broken. This man looks like he'd travel a long way to avoid a fight. His melancholy expression only lightens when the bartender refills his glass, as if the amber liquid is his best medicine.

'If you're here about Scott, I've heard the news. It makes no difference to me if he's dead or alive. He

never contacted me all year, apart from the odd solicitor's letter.'

'Jade's still missing; we think she may have been
targeted by the same person that killed your brother.'

'How would I know about that?' Minear frowns into
his drink. 'Scott never showed his kids enough love. They
all suffered because of him, but Luke's too loyal to say.'

'I hear he's been offered a football trial.'

'I told him to go, but Scott would never have let him
leave. The farm was all he cared about.'

The man's reaction interests me. While Ethan is
heartbroken by Jade's absence, Jason almost seems glad
of his twin's death.

'Can you tell me more about Scott's personality?'

'He always had to be top dog. His wife and family
paid dearly for it.'

'Gemma's in pieces right now.'

'She was brainwashed, that's why.' He points at his
beer glass. 'We share the same problem. I saw her hitting the booze harder each year.'

I acknowledge the truth of it with a nod. 'Your
boat was seen in Highertown harbour the night Jade
went missing.'

'Someone's been lying. I'd never sail in such foul
weather.' He makes the claim in a steady voice, but
fails to meet my eye.

'Can your wife verify that?'

'Only if she's clairvoyant. Jean left me eighteen
months ago; she's in Falmouth with her new bloke.'

'I'm sorry to hear it, but you must have more information, Jason. The crimes are linked to the farm and the flowers grown there. You know more about Scott than anyone.'

He shakes his head vehemently. 'People expect all twins to be close, but that's bollocks. He saw me as competition right from the start. Scott used his fists to settle every argument. He'd sue me for talking like this; I've spent a fortune on lawyers over the years.'

'What was it like growing up together?'

'Tough, most days.' Jason swallows another mouthful of beer. 'The lifestyle was brutal. Our parents did everything the traditional way, using horses to plough the fields. If Mum wasn't looking after us, she was cooking or harvesting flowers. There was no time for any kind of tenderness. At least Dad was fair-minded when he realised I preferred sailing to the farm. He let me work on the trawlers half the year. Things got complicated after our parents died, within a year of each other.'

'How do you mean?'

'They left seventy per cent of the farm to Scott, the other thirty to me, but he got a lawyer to claim that I owed him money.'

'You didn't get half the value?'

'My parents knew I'd never be a farmer, but his reaction was the problem. He never paid me a penny. My brother wouldn't even let me live in the farm manager's cottage for free; I had to rent it off him.'

'That doesn't sound legal.'

'Do you think he gave a shit about laws?' Jason's tone is growing louder. 'Scott ran me off the fucking island, then threatened me with an injunction if I contacted his kids. He said I was a bad influence. I could call him every name under the sun, but there's no point now he's gone.'

'Scott can't have been all bad, surely?'

He barks out a laugh. 'Ninety per cent of him had no conscience at all, but some people on St Martin's saw him as a decent bloke, for investing in the school.'

'How did he treat his own kids?'

'They had to follow his orders, and Scott never minded using his fists. I thought Jade could take care of herself and Ethan was the vulnerable one, but I was wrong.' The sadness on Jason Minear's face deepens as he mentions the twins.

'Can you think of anywhere Jade might run?'

'I told the twins to come to me, if things got bad.'

'She couldn't do that in a storm, but you're fond of them, aren't you?'

Jason pulls his phone from his pocket to show me a selfie taken a few summers ago. He's wearing a carefree smile, with Ethan and Jade either side of him, sunbathing on Par Beach.

'No kids of your own, Jason?'

'That never mattered with the twins around. I was so close to them, they felt like mine.' The man studies the bar's marble surface like he's peering into the ocean's depths. 'I've been trying to stay off the booze, but it's not easy.'

'Where are you living these days?'

He looks embarrassed. 'On my boat, for now. I pay my overheads by catching lobster. I'll find somewhere permanent when tourist season starts.'

I lean forward to catch his eye. 'Do you realise how serious this is, Jason? Your brother's dead and everyone knows you didn't get along.'

'What's that got to do with finding Jade?'

'You tell me. If you've got information about your niece, I need it, before it's too late.'

My serious tone finally cuts through the haze of booze. 'I gave the twins a phone before I left St Martin's.'

'When was that?'

'September, when Scott was on the mainland. It's pay as you go, with plenty of credit. They promised to hide it from everyone.'

'Do they call you often?'

'Every week, to say hello, or any time they're upset. It was hard on them when I left. I kept in touch for their sake, as well as mine.'

'Give me the number, please.'

He fumbles his phone from his pocket, then texts me the number. It still strikes me as odd that he's shown more concern for Jade than his own twin, no matter how poor their relationship. I pull the ship in a bottle that I found in the flower field from my pocket.

'This was found where I think Jade was taken. Do you know anything about it?'

Jason looks at the bag dangling in front of his face, until his eyes turn glassy. 'That belonged to Scott when we were kids. He never let me play with it, even though I loved boats. Our grandfather gave it to him as a birthday present. Scott must have valued it, because he kept it somewhere I never found.'

The fisherman is halfway down his next pint, mumbling about the past when I say goodbye. His words may be slurred, but at least he's given me fresh information. Whoever has strewn the ships in bottles around St Martin's may have stolen the one I'm holding from Scott Minear, before murdering him. He would have noticed a prized possession going missing, yet the killer still managed to find it. Luke could easily have gone through his dad's things when his back was turned.

'One more thing before I go, Jason. How come the farmhouse is neglected, if Scott was so rich?'

'Can't you guess? He preferred to live in a pigsty than see Gemma happy.'

It's pitch dark when I leave Jason Minear to his regrets, even though it's only 5 p.m. The air smells of damp, cooking fat, and stale beer as I exit the pub. I can just make out Jason's fishing boat, the *Cornish Maid*, in the harbour, which raises another question. How could Saul Heligan be certain that the vessel in Highertown harbour was Jason's? The local fishing boats all share the same design, with high prows and covered fo'c'sles.

The landlord would have needed binoculars to read the name stencilled on its bow in faded paint.

I call Eddie before casting off, giving him the phone number Jason Minear provided. If Jade carried the mobile when she went missing, we may be able to trace it. I'll have to find out if Ethan's seen it recently. The lanterns on my boat make little difference as I motor through the harbour's mouth. Visibility is so poor I slow my speed down to a couple of knots. There's still no wind, but currents are pulling me off course. Twenty minutes pass before I realise the boat's drifting towards the Atlantic shipping lane, at the mercy of every passing tanker. The bowrider is so small by comparison, a container ship could slice my boat in two without the sailors onboard feeling the impact.

I'm about to steer west when a slab of rock veers from the water. I manage to avoid it, but the close shave confirms my location. The granite outcrop is a landmark called Ragged Island that lies half a mile east of St Martin's, surrounded by submerged rocks which have caused many shipwrecks. I'm still trying to guide the bowrider away when a length of wood floats past. It's a piece of elm lapping, the strakes still dovetailed together, making me stare back at Ragged Island. Something shifts in my chest when I see the outline of the *Galatea*, stranded on the rock's sharpest point. I can hear the moaning sound of wood being tested to the limit as the racing gig's hull cracks. My main concern is for Jade Minear. Whoever dragged the *Galatea* from the boatshed may have placed the girl inside. I'd like to sail closer and scale the rocks for a closer look, but conditions are against me. No one could have swum back to St Martin's in the freezing water, let alone an eleven-year-old child. Whoever sent the gig into a rising storm knew it would drift north. If the girl was trapped inside, she had no chance of rescue, her body breaking apart on the rocks, just like the *Galatea*.

28

Ethan has been alone since leaving his grandparents' house, but the hope of finding Jade prevents him from going home. The boy peers through the hedgerow at the farm, where a light burns in the kitchen window. He should go back inside, and accept his mother's blame for running away, but he can't face her angry stare, or the bitter smell that often lingers on her breath. It's more peaceful to stay in the deserted field, listening to an owl hooting and the wind rustling the elm trees' branches. He shifts into a comfortable position, kneeling on the muddy ground, where he can keep watch.

The boy can imagine his dad following his nightly routine of walking down to his fields to count how many furrows need harvesting tomorrow. But his father won't be coming back. He could rush indoors without any risk of getting hurt.

The chill has almost defeated his instinct to stay outside when Ethan hears twigs snapping behind him. He believes that Shadow has come back until it's too late. He's caught in a headlock, a stranger's breath hot against his skin.

'Stop following me,' a voice hisses in his ear. 'You don't want to end up like Scott.'

The pressure against Ethan's throat almost chokes him. He uses his elbows to jab at his attacker, but this time there's no escape. The arm squeezes tighter, making his vision blur.

'Stay out of it, do you hear? Or you won't see Jade again.'

The ordeal ends as fast as it began. Ethan lurches forward, spreadeagled on the mud, too terrified to move. He can't identify who hissed out the warning, their grip on his neck tight enough to burn. The fury reminded him of his father, but the voice was too quiet to tell whether it was a man or woman. The boy is still lying there when Shadow appears out of the mist, giving a low bark of greeting. Ethan is still shaking when the dog licks his face. He'd like to close his eyes and disappear, like Jade, but there will be no rest until she's found.

29

Eddie has turned the heaters down when I return to the community hall, but the atmosphere inside the barn-like space feels suffocating. The only blessing is that the air inside is clear, unlike the fog that's choking the islands. My deputy has found dozens of texts between Scott and Luke Minear. Their tone is even more abusive than the ones from Scott to his wife, as if the man was intent on breaking his oldest son's spirit. Luke's replies grow angrier too. His apologetic tone ended weeks ago, rejecting his father's criticisms in the same crude language. It underlines my sense that Gemma and Luke were both at snapping point. Scott's hateful messages could have triggered his killing. It interests me that Scott, Gemma and Luke were all at home when the first stone bearing the words 'Devil's Table' was lobbed through their window. It seemed like they were targeted by someone from outside, but it's possible that one of Scott's relatives persuaded another islander to throw it, to make themselves look innocent.

I expected Scott's phone to reveal a string of affairs, given his reputation, but there's no evidence yet. He may have emailed women instead, so we'll need an IT specialist from the mainland to unlock his account. Or he could have had a second phone that we haven't yet found. Gemma's call record seems much more innocent. The list only includes business contacts on the mainland, family members and Hazel Teague, proving how narrow her life has become. Her older children appear far more outward-looking. Luke and Amy have both made frequent calls to friends on neighbouring islands. I need to speak with Luke again, to find out whether his angry messages to Scott could have turned to violence, but Isla will be watching him carefully for any suspicious behaviour.

Scott Minear's phone gives no evidence that Dave Carillian contacted him, or lured him up to Devil's Table, but it's still possible that the old man saw him walk past late at night and decided to follow. The frustration of having so little evidence is making my head throb, yet Eddie seems undeterred. My deputy has moved on to checking the Minears' account books. The farm has been making a tidy profit, but spending little on upkeep, apart from forty thousand pounds set aside to pay for repairs to the cutting shed and two other barns. Scott and Gemma's only other big expenditures in the past year have been on the island's primary school, and maintaining the *Galatea*.

Eddie listens with his head on one side when I tell

him about seeing the gig on Ragged Island, beyond hope of salvage. His eyes are round with wonder when he studies the images on my phone, and I agree it's an odd spectacle. The racing boat is impaled on a spike of rock, defeated by the sea.

'I don't get it, boss. First his daughter's taken, then someone destroys his gig, before killing him. Could Dave Carillian have done all this? The bloke's obsessed by boats, isn't he?'

'I think it'll be someone closer to home. Jason Minear says the first ship in a bottle was Scott's favourite toy, that he kept hidden away. It must be someone with intimate knowledge of his favourite possessions, and his past, who could root through his things without being spotted. We don't have any hard evidence against Carillian, just circumstantial details. He leaves his ships around the island for local kids to find, so anyone could have picked them up.'

Eddie gives an exaggerated shudder. 'It's like the pied piper, luring kids inside a mountain, never to be seen again.'

'The killer's got a sense of drama, that's for sure. He's chucked rocks through windows, destroyed a racing gig, and scattered calling cards across the island. It feels like we're being taunted; the symbolism must have a meaning.'

'In what way?'

'The boats and flowers could be connected. Scott was the *Galatea*'s only sponsor, and his speedboat was his pride and joy. We've been told Jade was his favourite child, and the first ship in a bottle was his best toy, forty years ago. The Grand Monarch jonquils at the murder scene were his favourite flowers, because they fetch the highest price. It looks like the killer's destroying everything he valued most.'

'They must know him well to understand all that.' My deputy looks puzzled. 'We've still got twenty-three names on the suspect list. They can't provide alibis, but none of them have a police record.'

When I study the names again, Minear's closest relatives are still included. Gemma, Jason, Luke, and Amy all have reason to hate Scott. Another possible reason for his death is if he was having an affair with a woman on the island. I remember Suzie Felyer's disgust at being accused of a liaison, but the schoolteacher's name is still on our list because she lives alone and no one can vouch for her actions. A female killer would have struggled to overpower Scott alone, even with the element of surprise, but she could be working with an accomplice. Saul Heligan's name remains on the list too; we only have his word that he stayed indoors the night Minear died.

'Let's stay focused on the family,' I say. 'We know Scott had a sadistic side, he enjoyed making people suffer. Gemma, Luke, and Amy had the worst treatment.'

'You think his wife and kids did it?'

'They had a bad marriage, Amy hated her dad, and Luke's desperate to leave. Gemma could be faking her grief, couldn't she? We've seen that before.'

'She's one hell of an actor, if all that crying's a pretence.'

'If she hurt him, she'd be full of regret. The killer knew where to find Scott's harvest knife, his favourite flower, and his childhood toy. The killer managed to entice him outside in the middle of the night too. It has to be someone with intimate knowledge. The hitch is that Gemma, Luke and Amy had no reason to hurt Jade.'

'You think someone took her, then a second person attacked Scott?'

'We can't rule it out until there's proof it's a solitary killer.'

Eddie tells me that Isla's seen nothing to indicate that Scott's family were involved, despite staying vigilant.

'I want to give her a break from the farmhouse soon. The place is like a pressure cooker.'

'I don't mind staying there, boss.'

'We can divide shifts between us. Have there been any sightings of Ethan?'

'A woman from Lowertown saw him with Shadow on the beach an hour ago.'

'That's good news. We can't protect him from the weather, but Shadow won't let anyone hurt him. Have you had any luck with the phone Jason Minear gave the twins?'

Eddie passes me a transcript, but the calls are inconclusive. The twins rang their uncle, Amy and Luke, but no one else. The phone masts on the islands are too far apart to pinpoint the exact location of the mobile accurately, apart from telling us that it's on St Martin's.

I do a final call round to the island's families, telling them to lock their doors and observe the curfew. I can't rule out the possibility that someone is making random attacks, even though two members of the same family have been targeted. It's the killer's mindset I need to understand. Murder victims' bodies are often discarded like litter, but the Devil's Table was chosen for a specific reason, the killing highly ritualised. It might atone for an even greater crime committed by Scott himself.

'Run the names of any islander without an alibi through HOLMES 2, please, Eddie. Start with Carillian and Rob Paige, then the other lone males.'

It's common knowledge that most murders and child abductions are carried out by solitary, violent men, yet there are exceptions when women go on the attack. It's rare for a woman to act alone, but a tiny number solicit for male partners, like Myra Hindley, bringing children home for Ian Brady to kill. The idea makes my eyes blink shut, unwilling to imagine Jade Minear locked up somewhere, screaming for help.

'Are you okay, boss?' Eddie's voice brings me back to reality. 'You look tired.'

'Ethan needs his sister badly. We have to get answers soon.'

'How do you punish killers like that? We should dump them all on Samson with no food or water.'

Samson is the ghostliest island in Scilly. It was inhabited until two hundred years ago; the landscape still bears traces of an extinct community – a well that ran dry decades ago, and a dozen stone cottages slowly being dismantled by the Atlantic wind.

'Concentrate on finding who did it, Eddie. They must be on our list.'

I let my gaze wander over the names again, with Jason Minear's at the bottom. He's got a strong motive to kill his brother, after losing his home and family, even though he showed restraint when he was exiled from the farm. He claimed to be at home on St Mary's the night Scott died, but Saul Heligan has no clear reason to lie. The landlord's name remains on the list, and I still need to hear why he was so certain that it was Jason's boat he spotted that night. Rob and Felicity Paige are still persons of interest because of local rumours, which could have triggered her husband's violence. The list of potential suspects is full of people I've known all my life, but none can be ruled out until we have proof of innocence.

When I look up again the stone that was thrown through the window this morning catches my eye. It's wrapped in an evidence bag, and will be flown to the lab in Penzance once conditions permit. The words are written in crude black capitals, with gloss paint that stands out from the pebble's matt surface, but the childish script might be a cover. Any of the islanders could have collected it from a deserted beach, but they'd have to be fearless, and fit enough to escape, without being seen. Scott received exactly the same tribute before he was killed, and the idea dawns on me for the first time that Nina and I could be next on the killer's list, for getting in their way. I'll have to make sure she's fully protected and stay vigilant from now on.

I tap out a report for DCI Madron, hoping to avoid another accusatory phone call, but frustration nags at me. Eddie has begun inputting names into the HOLMES 2 programme, and the Home Office's software is notoriously slow. It can take hours to dredge up information on an individual, let alone a whole community. The Police National Computer holds details of every British citizen's encounters with the law, from verbal warnings to judicial sentences, but I can't just sit by the printer, waiting for it to spit out information.

'I'm going to check how Isla's doing, Eddie. I won't be long.'

My deputy says goodbye without looking up. I can tell he's in his element, typing names and dates of birth into the computer with a look of pure optimism on his face, like it's only a matter of time before it produces our killer's name.

I use my torch to follow the lane through the island's core. I keep expecting Shadow to materialise, like he does on my night-time strolls on Bryher, but there's no sign of him. I hope he's keeping Ethan Minear safe, as the fog worsens. My eyes are straining for better visibility when a figure barrels towards me out of the mist. This is the only occasion when my giant scale comes in useful; I can handle plenty of rough tackles on the rugby field without being toppled. When I take a step back, Neil Kershaw is clutching his shoulder like he's struck a brick wall, but the collision may turn out to my advantage. The man has been unable to provide a watertight alibi, with only Amy's word that he spent last night at home. Time spent with him could be more useful than catching up with Isla.

'You're in a hurry, Neil.'

He murmurs an apology. 'I need to see Hazel Teague. Amy's in a terrible state about her dad. I think she'll need tablets to help her sleep.'

'Maybe it's better to give her time to cry it out of her system.'

Kershaw's voice is strained. 'I hate seeing her suffer.'

'Taking pills will only delay it.'

Kershaw looks uncertain. 'You could be right; maybe I'll suggest she sees Hazel tomorrow.'

'Why don't I walk you back to yours? I've got some questions you might be able to answer.'

Neil Kershaw is quick to comply, as if he prefers following orders to giving them. He doesn't act like the owner of a successful vineyard, his manner tentative. When we reach his home he seems to relax, leaving his muddy trainers in the porch. Kershaw looks older than his years when he removes his woollen hat, with light-brown hair receding from a fine-boned face. The home he's shared with Amy for the past few months is so minimal, I can see little evidence of their personalities. The living room walls are painted white, with a leather three-piece suite that must feature in thousands of homes across the UK, a striped rug beside the hearth. The only unique thing I can see is the Siamese cat that's curled on an armchair. The creature gives me a look of contempt, before stalking away, leaving me to flick through Kershaw's record collection. His taste in vinyl ranges from Beethoven to Motown and Nineties Britpop. He's carrying two mugs of coffee when he finds me admiring a signed copy of an early Scott Matthews album.

'You've got good taste,' I tell him. 'I like everything here, except Harry Styles.'

'Not guilty. The recent stuff's Amy's.'

'That explains why you've got so much Billie Eilish.'

The man seems embarrassed. 'I know it looks bad, a middle-aged bloke, living with a seventeen-year-old.'

'It's legal, between consenting adults.'

'I never planned it this way, believe me.'

'No?'

'She kept dropping by, asking me about winemaking. We clicked, that's all. The age gap stopped mattering.'

'Have people given you a hard time?'

'Amy's parents disapproved, but the other islanders keep out of it. I couldn't believe her mum and dad were so bothered, especially when their own relationship was nothing to brag about.'

'How do you mean?'

'He cheated on her and she drowns her sorrows. Neither of them were ideal parents.'

Kershaw is describing a family at war, yet his tone remains neutral. He reminds me of a philosophy lecturer, explaining an ethical dilemma. There's something odd about his ability to keep his feelings detached from his words. The only time distress shows on his face is when footsteps rattle overhead.

'Poor Amy's pacing around. She loved her dad, even though he mistreated her.'

'She says people feared him. Do you think that's true?'

'I can't answer for anyone else, but he always had to take control. He acted like God after Amy and I got together, banishing us from his land, as if we were leaving the Garden of Eden. I'd hoped he'd soften, but he never did.' The man turns to face me. 'You know Saul Heligan wasn't his biggest fan, don't you?'

'How do you mean?'

'Me and Amy take a walk most nights, before going to bed. I've seen him hanging around near Minear Farm. He's been in love with Gemma for years, according to Amy.'

'I knew they had a relationship, but not that he was still interested.' I lean forward in my seat. 'What brought you to the Scillies, Neil? It's a remote place to open a vineyard.'

He hesitates before replying. 'I'd been working at one in Cornwall, then I inherited some money. The decision was simple.'

'But it's caused complications?'

'That's an understatement. Amy's family is like a soap opera.'

'Does she speak about her mum much?'

'Amy worries more about the twins, because of Gemma's drinking. She wishes Luke would get the hell out of there and make a life for himself.'

'It sounds like a minefield.'

'Or a Greek tragedy.' He gives a wry laugh. 'St Martin's seemed like the perfect place to make wine when I bought my land two years ago, and the business side's been great. We laid down two thousand litres of first reserve last autumn. I never thought a kid would go missing here, or someone would get killed.'

'There's other damage too. The *Galatea*'s breaking up on Ragged Island; it'll be gone with the next high tide.'

Neil Kershaw's jaw drops open when he peers at images of the broken gig on my phone. 'It looks like a Viking burial.'

'How come?'

'They put the bodies of their bravest warriors in longboats just like our gigs, then set them alight, believing their souls would be carried across the sea to Valhalla.'

When he hands the phone back I can see what he means. The *Galatea* has been lifted up, like an offering to the Gods, but my own boat would have foundered on the rocks if I'd sailed any closer. I may never find out if Jade Minear's body was trapped inside.

30

Ethan is still on the ground, weakened by shock and hunger. It feels easier to lie there, with his cheek pillowed against the mud. Dreams keep drifting through his mind. He pictures Jade, dancing in the mist, but after he opens his eyes, she's nowhere in sight. When he tries to call for Shadow, his mouth is so dry it feels like his tongue is coated in sand.

The boy is raising himself onto his knees when he hears someone on the lane, footsteps pounding on the tarmac, and the dog barks out a warning. Ethan remains hidden behind a hedgerow, but it's Luke who looms from the fog, his fists clenched at his sides. He's only seen his brother look so angry after his dad punished him. Maybe his mum said something to upset him? Luke is marching up May's Hill toward their grandparents' house.

Ethan is still wondering what put his brother in such a temper when he hears new footsteps behind him. They're lighter this time, but there's no way to escape. A torch beam sears his retinas, until it suddenly drops away.

'Sorry, I didn't mean to blind you.'

A tall woman stands over him, aiming her torch at the ground.

'My name's Nina,' she says quietly. 'And you're Ethan, aren't you? I've seen you before, with your sister.'

She kneels down, so their eyes are level. Ethan normally hates meeting strangers, but he's seen the woman buying food at the grocery store. She smiles at him and Jade whenever they pass her on the lane. He doesn't like people staring at him, but she's looking at the ground, her expression gentle. Her shiny brown hair is tucked neatly behind her ears, and she's keeping very still. The woman doesn't seem to mind his silence, and the dog has relaxed too. He's stopped barking, positioning himself at her side.

'Let's get you home, Ethan, it's cold out here. You don't have to say anything. Is that okay?'

The woman holds out her hand to help him up. Once he's back on his feet she releases his wrist, and he feels relieved. He hates being touched by people he doesn't know.

'Shadow led me to you,' she explains. 'He wouldn't stop barking till I followed him.'

The boy almost manages a smile, but their walk continues in silence until they reach the farmhouse. His mother rushes out once she spots him. A young policewoman is at her side, trying to sooth her. Ethan hates the tears rolling down her face, while Nina waits in silence, with Shadow at her side.

He's grateful when the policewoman leads him into the kitchen, then prepares him a plate of food. It's loaded with bread, cheese, and a slab of cake. His mum rushes to the phone in the hallway, her voice shrill, but Nina steps closer, settling on one of the stools.

'Do you want to keep Shadow here tonight, Ethan?' she asks.

When he nods she smiles in reply, then gestures for the dog to stay.

'He likes you, I can tell. Do you play that piccolo I can see in your pocket?'

The boy manages to nod his head again.

'I've got a special violin at home. Would you like to see it tomorrow?'

Ethan wants to say yes, but words dissolve in his mouth. When his mother returns to the kitchen Nina asks if it's okay to call by the next day. His mum agrees, but looks distracted. She mutters something about all her children letting her down. She says that Luke picked a fight, then stormed out. Nina says nothing, before placing her hand on his mum's shoulder for a moment, then stepping out into the dark.

31

I'm in sight of the community hall when Isla calls to say that Ethan has come home safe. Nina found him, hiding in the flower fields. I feel a sudden rush of relief. He may have been cowering outside all day, stunned by his father's death, alongside his fears for Jade.

Eddie is still working flat-out in the hall. He's gazing at his computer screen, wide-eyed, like it holds the answers to human existence.

'Have you ever heard gossip about Saul Heligan and Gemma Minear?' I ask.

'Not a word, boss. The bloke's been single for years. I thought he might be gay. He's pretty camp, isn't he?'

'I'd say theatrical. I need to know if he's been watching Minear Farm at night. When you go back to the pub, keep an eye on him for me. Even an actor would be feeling the strain, if he killed Scott.'

'Saul's so popular here, that's hard to believe.'

'Forget about preconceptions, Eddie. Killers often seem ordinary, decent folk, in my experience. Some are boringly normal. They've just snapped under pressure, or they're taking revenge.'

'You said it was most likely to be a family member.'

'We can't rule anyone out, unless there's an alibi. Get some rest, Eddie. You've been on duty twelve hours.'

'Not yet, boss. I'm waiting for HOLMES 2 to deliver.'

'You're out of luck. The Wi-Fi's down, because of the fog.'

My deputy lets out a stream of expletives, and I know how he feels. We need some good fortune, not an island-wide communication breakdown. I've never seen Eddie so disgruntled. He grabs his coat then marches away, like he's already fantasising about the pub's open fire and a nightcap before bedtime.

I scan the table once he leaves, considering the evidence from the murder scene. It doesn't amount to much – just some wilted flowers, a few ships in bottles, and Scott's damaged phone. I've placed the painted stone that was thrown through the window while Nina and I slept with the other items. Whoever broke my sleep may have followed me home from the pub, keeping tabs on the investigation. It strikes me again that they must hate my efforts to track them down, or they'd have settled for posting a note through our door, instead of the ugly din of glass shattering. The killer has to be physically strong to haul a fourteen-stone man onto the Devil's Table, unless they've recruited a helper.

Ideas about the murderer's identity are still churning through my mind when the door creaks open. People rarely knock or ring doorbells in Scilly; it's the custom to walk indoors while calling out a greeting, like you're part of the family. Rob and Felicity Paige have finally responded to my phone message requesting a meeting. Felicity's appearance is still angelic, while her husband looks like a vagabond smuggler from two centuries ago. I invite them to join me on the hall's uncomfortable wooden chairs.

'Sorry we're so late,' Felicity says, her voice breathless. 'You want to speak to me, don't you?'

'I'm just asking everyone the same questions, to understand why Scott Minear died.'

Rob is watching his wife like a hawk. There's hardly any space between them, and Felicity angles her shoulders towards him when I speak again, as if she's sheltering him from a harsh wind.

'How did you feel about Scott, Felicity?'

'He wasn't my favourite person.' Her face tenses, like she's swallowed something bitter. 'Gemma and the kids are great, but he didn't deserve them.'

'How do you mean?'

'Scott owned a stake in our business,' she says. 'He demanded payment on time every month. We only had to be a day late for him to come round and start bullying us.'

The woman's bitterness contrasts with her gentle appearance. I'm not sure how to continue; there's no easy way to question someone's fidelity in front of their partner.

'There are rumours about Scott having extramarital affairs. One of them concerns you, Felicity. People say he visited your house when Rob was away.'

'He never got what he wanted.' She gazes back at me, her expression hardening.

'How do you mean?'

'Scott came round a lot when Rob was away in hospital. He said he'd write off our debts if I slept with him on a regular basis, till Rob came back.'

'That must have increased your stress.'

'If someone thinks I went along with it, they've got a vivid imagination. I've been too busy to think, let alone sleep with a bully like him. I spend most of my time selling our jewellery to gift shops on the mainland. Rob handled that in the past, but we've swapped roles recently.'

'Why's that?'

'Can't you guess?' Her husband pulls down his eyepatch without warning. His wounded eye is milk white, with no pupil, most of his eyelid burned away. 'I've only been able to wear the patch since the wound's healed. If I pitched up for meetings like this, we'd get no business.'

I keep my expression neutral. 'People have much worse injuries. It wouldn't make any difference.'

'I agree.' Felicity's hand settles on her husband's wrist. 'It's an adjustment, that's all. He's been through four operations and never complained.'

'How did you get hurt, Rob?'

'By being an idiot.' He flicks the patch back into place. 'Some solder exploded in my face. If I'd worn a visor, it would have been fine.'

'Everyone respects you for carrying on regardless.'

'What else can I do? I can't let it beat me.'

The man lifts his chin like I've challenged him to a fight, rather than offering a compliment. He comes over as an alpha male like Scott Minear, passionate about his business, and his wife's devotion seems genuine. Felicity is clasping his hand. Instinct tells me she wouldn't cheat on a man who's been through hell, but gut reactions can be misleading.

'Where does Lauren go, when both of you are out?'

'To her boyfriend's normally.'

'That's Ivan Teague, isn't it?'

'They've been together six months,' says Rob. 'We worried about how keen they are at first, but she's so happy, we can't interfere.'

'He's a nice lad.'

Rob nods in reply. 'Luke Minear was her first boyfriend. We were glad when that ended. The family's so messed up, we didn't want her involved. It was tricky for a while, because Luke and Ivan had been so close. They were almost like brothers.'

The news takes me by surprise. I had no idea that Luke and Lauren had a relationship, but any ill-feeling between the two young men must have passed, or Ivan wouldn't have volunteered to help him in the cutting shed. I saw them working side by side in companionable

201

silence, so the two lads must have decided to forgive and forget.

The couple seem more relaxed as we say goodnight. They're still holding hands when they leave, but it's still possible they're telling lies. Rob could easily have dragged the gig down to the shore, under cover of darkness, as payback for Scott's bullying and the rumours about his wife. The physical pain he's suffered may have contributed, if he went on the attack after months of Scott's taunts. It frustrates the hell out of me that I have no access to forensic support. Gannick and her team would have crawled all over the Devil's Table until they found a hair, or a thread from the killer's coat, providing enough evidence to close the case.

It's 10 p.m. when I return to the Redmaynes' cottage. The only sign of this morning's visit from the killer is a piece of hardboard nailed over the broken window, until a glazier can travel over from St Mary's. Nina is curled up on the settee, reading *Dombey and Son*. She rises to her feet to kiss my cheek, her movements as graceful as Neil Kershaw's Siamese cat.

When I go through to the kitchen, a pot of minestrone soup stands on the hob. I help myself to a bowl before I've taken off my coat, suddenly aware that lunch consisted of an egg mayonnaise sandwich, nine hours ago. Nina and I have different approaches to food. She thinks mealtimes are sacred, true to her mother's Italian roots, whether she's eating alone or with friends. I only enjoy cooking at the weekends, when we've got spare time. We often compromise by going to my godmother's pub, the Rock on Bryher, for some of the best meals the islands can offer.

Nina appears in the kitchen as I'm finishing my meal. She pours apple juice into two glasses before settling on the bench opposite. She doesn't respond when I tell her the soup is delicious, as if perfect cuisine is guaranteed every time she lights the oven. I can feel her waiting for me to explain what's going on inside my head. I love everything about her, except her desire to work me out, like a crossword puzzle. She never accepts that I prefer actions to words. I'd rather put on my wetsuit and run into the ice-cold sea than face a difficult conversation. It's easier to plunge into freezing water, and let breakers crash over me, scouring away my bad mood.

'How did you find where Ethan Minear was hiding?'

'Shadow led me there,' she replies. 'The boy was in a field, covered in mud.'

'Did he say anything?'

'Not a word, but I didn't expect it. He's traumatised, and he's carrying his piccolo around like a talisman.'

'He knows more than anyone about the killer, but he won't even tell his mother.'

'Ethan needs psychological support; it was Jade that gave him stability. I can't guarantee that talking to me would help.'

'You're the only person on St Martin's that knows about trauma.'

'It could be weeks before he opens up.'

I lean closer, our faces almost touching. 'Don't make me beg.'

'Kids are fragile, Ben, and I'm not fully qualified. He needs a specialist child counsellor.'

'We can't get one till the fog clears.'

'That's emotional blackmail,' she says, drawing a long breath. 'Ethan's expecting me at the farmhouse tomorrow morning. I'll do an informal assessment, but that's my limit.'

'Remember not to go anywhere alone. That stone the killer chucked through our window is a calling card; he knows where both of us live.'

'You need to stay safe too, Ben.'

When I kiss her cheek she studies me intently, searching for chinks in my armour, like she's forgotten how to blink. I never imagined myself with someone so intense, but I've got no regrets. I dated a string of party-loving blondes in the past, which feels like a lifetime ago. Nina's changed everything, and there's no going back.

32

Wednesday 21 December

There's a break in the fog when I look out of the window at 8 a.m., so I call Isla and ask her to rouse Gemma and Luke. Soon a new band of cloud will settle over the islands, but the darkness is lifting, and this is their best chance to say goodbye to Scott before sailing is prohibited again. The bedroom is still dark when I pull back the curtains, because of the hardboard covering the broken glass, but Nina seems oblivious to the danger hanging over St Martin's, still so deeply asleep she doesn't stir.

Gemma Minear looks frailer than yesterday when I reach the farm, shattering my hopes of getting more detailed information about the days leading up to her husband's death. We need that conversation soon, but the circles under her eyes prove she hasn't slept. Luke seems far more in control, which still strikes me as unnatural. The pair appear to have given each other alibis for the night of Scott's death, but the growing tension between them shows in their body language. The lad is standing by the door, as if he'd like to run for the hills. Gemma tells me she's wary about leaving Ethan behind. I remind her that Isla can care for him and Nina will visit this morning, yet she still seems reluctant. She leans heavily on Luke's arm when we finally exit the farmhouse, placing too great a burden on her oldest son. There's a high chance she'll collapse when she sees Scott's body, given how she's reacted so far. The finality of a mortuary visit is always the worst type of goodbye.

Gemma huddles close to her son in the bow when my boat leaves Highertown Quay. The air is clear for once, the sky filled with early morning light that's so pale it could be high summer, if the temperature rose by twenty degrees. I turn my collar against the chill and head west for St Mary's, where Gareth Keillor is expecting us. The coroner wants a full autopsy, which will be completed once the family have signed the consent form. Gemma clings to her son as we cross St Mary's Sound, like he's her only chance of survival if the boat capsizes.

Time is unfolding at its usual slow pace in Hugh Town harbour. Most of the lobstermen are preparing to sail, a few old-timers loading their creels, tainting the air with seaweed and diesel, but Gemma seems oblivious as I moor the boat. When we set off for the hospital we keep bumping into people she knows, taking their dogs for walks, or enjoying the clear air. They all offer their sympathies for Scott's death, but I can tell she'd rather grieve in private. Gemma seems relieved to reach the top of the hill, leaving the town behind us.

St Mary's Hospital is just big enough to serve Scilly's permanent population of around two thousand souls, with a couple of small wards and an out-patients clinic. The mortuary is tucked away behind the main building. I can almost taste the bleach from the freshly swabbed floor when we walk inside, the smell of ammonia lingering in my airways. Gemma and her son remain in the corridor while I enter Gareth Keillor's domain. The pathologist looks relaxed while he fills out forms, even though Scott Minear's corpse is his only companion. Keillor tucks his clipboard under his arm then slips away through the fire exit, so the relatives can say goodbye in private.

Gemma looks ready to bolt when I lead her to the body. Luke has to take the parental role again, telling her she'll feel better once the visit's over. Gemma mutters under her breath when she sees her husband's corpse covered by a white sheet. Her eyes are screwed shut when I draw it back, exposing Scott's face to the light. The pathologist has cleaned his wounds, his skull wrapped in bandages to hide the damage, the smell of formaldehyde filling the room. There's no trace of the man's charisma or his cruelty now, his expression peaceful. It's Gemma and Luke's reactions that surprise me. Her face is calm, but the lad's skin is ashen, his eyes starting to roll.

I have to leave Gemma staring down at her husband's body, now that Luke needs my full attention. He's on the verge of collapse, suddenly a child again, without anyone to support him. I haul him out to the corridor and lower him onto a bench, his tears splashing onto the lino. Instinct makes me put my hand between his shoulder blades and leave it there for a few seconds. I need to find out if he snapped under the weight of Scott's cruelty, but I can't help pitying him.

'It doesn't seem real,' he says, swiping away tears with the back of his hand. 'Dad's been murdered and Mum's going through hell.'

'You must be suffering too.'

'I just wanted him to be proud of me.'

'He wasn't an easy man to impress. The texts he sent you were vicious. You didn't want us to read them, did you?'

'Only because they show how fucked up my family is. I never wanted this to happen.'

'I know, Luke. It's okay.' I've seen him as a young man until now, fuelled by years of psychological abuse, but his body language is like a kid, mourning something he never had. 'What hurt you most about him?'

He's gazing down at his feet. 'The way he treated Ethan. Dad slapped him when he was six, hard enough to break his eardrum. He turned mute after that. Ethan would only talk to Jade, and Mum told the doctor he fell off his bike.'

'I wish I'd known that at the time; we'd have put

some protection in place.' It takes me a moment to accept that Scott's violence caused Ethan's muteness.

'He hurt us all in different ways, but his opinion still mattered. That's what I don't get.'

'He was your dad, no matter what. I saw that letter in your room. Did he stop you taking that football trial in Plymouth?'

'Dad laughed about it.'

'Why?'

'He said I'd never make it as a professional.'

'You look pretty skilled whenever I watch you play.'

He almost manages a smile. 'I'll never leave now. Mum can't run the farm alone, anyone can see that.'

'I lost my dad early, so I know how it feels. It's not all on you, Luke. Other people will help.'

'Only Hazel gives a shit about Mum now, even Gran's giving up on her. I asked her for help yesterday, to get Mum to stop drinking, but she's keeping out of it.' He shoots a glance in my direction. 'What happened, after your dad died?'

'Mum got stronger over time, with help from friends and neighbours.'

'Mine won't cope alone; she's too damaged,' he says, his tone angry. 'Dad's still hurting her, even now.'

'Were you planning to go to the mainland, till this happened?'

'I'd booked a ferry ticket for January. I split up with my girlfriend six months ago, so it felt like the right time.'

'You were seeing Lauren Paige?'

He gives a slow nod. 'I'm over it now. Me and Ivan have been mates since nursery; I couldn't stay pissed off for long.'

'That sounds like a mature decision.' I lean forward to catch his eye. 'We'll find out who killed your dad, Luke. A forensics team will come over, once the fog clears. They never miss a thing.'

The boy's face registers panic for a moment, then he gives a rapid nod, to end our conversation. I watch him stride away to confront his demons, leaving me divided. Luke is carrying enough anger to damage anyone within touching distance, but his football dream has been shattered by his father's death. Only his sense of duty is keeping him pinned to his mother's side. Would he really have killed his father, knowing that his mum would become his responsibility?

Gemma is kneeling down in the mortuary, her face level with her husband's, whispering a message too quiet to hear. She looks exhausted, and Luke's anger still shows in his frown. I can't tell whether he's furious with the situation, or because he revealed his feelings to a stranger, but it's the wrong time for questions. I advise the pair to wait for me at the police station, then see them out. They can keep warm without facing well-meaning acquaintances, and Lawrie Deane will make them welcome, until we sail back to St Martin's. My next task is to watch the post-mortem, which is never my favourite activity.

Gareth Keillor wastes little time before starting work. The man's style is always methodical: he begins by walking round the body in a slow circle, then he examines Minear's hands and fingernails. The pathologist speaks to the microphone that hangs over the gurney. Words like 'oedema' and 'cyanosis' fly over my head, but I stay quiet. Keillor hates distractions, as if one badly timed comment could corrupt vital evidence.

When I study Scott Minear's body again, he could be any middle-aged farmer. His arms are muscular, his barrel chest showing his strength, the man's paunch proving he enjoyed his beer. There's a narrow wound in the centre of his chest, but Keillor removed the blade that ended his life before the relatives arrived, to save them any more trauma. The pathologist is examining it under an intense light, while I deal with a fresh bout of nausea. I saw plenty of corpses during my time undercover with the Murder Squad, but it never became second nature. The autopsies I attended were often on vicious criminals. There's something far more unsettling about confronting the physical remains of someone you know.

Keillor's tone changes when he rolls Minear onto his side then unwinds the bandages to study the chasm at the back of his skull. I'd rather not stare at a gaping head wound before breakfast, but the pathologist pores over every detail. It's a relief when he finally strips off his gloves to scour his hands clean at the sink.

'Do you want the cause of death now, Ben? There's no need to stay for the dissection. I can see you're turning green.'

'Is it that obvious?'

'Even giants like you are affected by such terrible injuries. The man had a bad death.'

'How do you mean?'

'There are multiple head wounds, but the stab wound to his chest didn't kill him. I'd say that was purely symbolic.'

'How do you know?'

'The knife penetrated between his fifth and six ribs. The blade would have entered his heart, causing catastrophic blood loss if he'd been alive, but there's very little swelling. It's likely the chest wound came after his heart stopped beating.'

'You think he died from being struck on the head?'

'The attack was vicious enough to kill anyone. There are multiple wounds to his skull, from different weapons. One was a blunt instrument like a mallet, with a two-inch square head, but the other could have been a standard domestic hammer.'

'Someone beat him with a mallet and a hammer simultaneously, then planted a knife in his chest for good measure?'

'It must have been frenzied to cause that much damage.' He raises both fists in the air, like he's clutching two weapons, beating out a furious rhythm. 'X-rays will help identify how many blows to the skull. I've counted eleven so far, but there may be more. Scott's assailant had no intention of letting him live.'

'I'll need another golf lesson soon to wipe it from my mind.'

'Happy to oblige. I'd like to see how your drive's coming along.'

Keillor is putting on fresh surgical gloves when I reach for my coat, like he can't wait to get back to work. It amazes me that the man can spend all morning cutting up a body then eat a relaxed lunch with his wife, but he's given me plenty to consider while I walk back to Hugh Town. Scott Minear upset many people on St Martin's, but someone hated him enough to attack him from behind with two weapons, beating out a savage tattoo. It's an odd mixture of ferocity and premeditation. They were calm enough to lob a stone through the window, leading me to his body. It strikes me again that we could be dealing with two attackers. One of them is clear-headed and methodical, the other fuelled by so much anger, they're out of control.

Hugh Town's crescent-shaped harbour stretches out at the bottom of the hill. It looks picturesque enough for a holiday brochure, with the quay's long arm protecting a flotilla of small boats from the high tide, but the impression of safety is deceiving. We need to return to St Martin's fast, before the fog thickens again.

Gemma is in tears when I reach the police station, her face concealed behind a wad of tissues, despite remaining calm through her ordeal at the hospital. Luke's expression is so blank I can tell he's overloaded, and I know how he feels. Minear had plenty of enemies, but no one on the island has a history of violence. I'm about to escort the pair back to the quay when DCI Madron opens his office door, summoning me inside with a jerk of his head. He looks immaculate as usual, his white shirt bleached to perfection, with razor sharp creases in each arm. Noise travels easily through the building's paper-thin walls, so he addresses me in a stage whisper.

'This is an unholy mess, Kitto. The girl's still missing and her father's been slaughtered, like a pagan sacrifice. What do I tell the Chief Super?'

'The truth, boss. We're pursuing all the evidence.'

'She wants an arrest today. How hard can it be with less than a hundred people on the island?'

'Minear's death doesn't explain Jade's abduction.'

My boss's face is grim when he steps towards me. 'Use your brain, Kitto. There must be some logic to it.'

'Feel free to help, sir. I need one team member for family liaison, so it's just me and Eddie doing all the leg work.'

'Deane and I have four other islands to police, remember?'

'How could I forget?'

Madron's grey eyes assess me for signs of disrespect. 'Don't delay, that's all I'm saying. The super wants a conference call at two o'clock.'

'Noted, sir.'

'Be on time, for once.'

I can't help wishing that my boss was more like Gareth Keillor, with his casual disdain for hierarchies. The pathologist balances his work and home life with ease, while Madron exists for his job alone.

Gemma seems relieved to return to the harbour. She's stopped crying, but her face tenses again when she spots Jason Minear's boat moored next to mine. He's unloading bait boxes onto the quay, and an ice crate full of lobsters. Luke walks ahead to greet his uncle, while his mother comes to a halt. I can tell she'd prefer to avoid her brother-in-law, but there's no time to waste; I want to get back to St Martin's without navigating through a wall of fog.

Jason Minear's face is hangover-grey. The man must have a strong constitution to brave the Atlantic cold after a night on the booze. His gaze is downcast when he addresses his sister-in-law.

'I'm sorry for your loss, Gemma.'

'Liar,' she hisses. 'You must be thrilled he's gone.'

'Let's forget the past, please. I only want to help.'

'Was it you, Jason? I bet you had something to do with it.' She lashes out before I can stop her, striking his face with a resounding slap. 'Keep away from us, you bastard.'

I catch hold of Gemma's wrist before she can hit him again. The last thing she needs is an assault charge before her husband's funeral, but the constraint only worsens the situation. There's a mad look in her eye when she jabs her finger at my chest.

'You should arrest him. He hated Scott's guts.'

Jason is still rooted to the spot, his cheek a livid red, but there's no evidence to support Gemma's accusation, even though the man had reason to attack his twin. I cast off once my two passengers are seated in the bow, still shocked by Gemma's behaviour. Her form is so slender it looks like the first strong wind could carry her away, yet she attacked her brother-in-law like a prize fighter. Her husband enjoyed using his fists too – I can imagine her and Scott trading blows, as well as insults. It worries me that she could be giving the same rough justice to her kids. I'll have to get one of the island's two part-time social workers to do a safety assessment, once the dust settles. Gemma keeps her thoughts private when we leave the harbour's protection, her eyes fixed on the horizon.

33

It's 11 a.m. by the time I walk Gemma and Luke home, my phone buzzing with messages. I listen to my voice-mail after saying goodbye; the most urgent one is from the island's nurse, Hazel Teague. It's a request to visit her house immediately, which gives me an excuse for a fifteen-minute walk to the other end of the island. I'm hoping the nurse has found some useful information about Scott's death, the case lingering in my mind as I follow St Martin's only tarmacked road to Lowertown. She may be able to cast light on Gemma's behaviour, after their long friendship. The angry words Gemma threw at Jason may have slipped out because her mental balance is upset by grief, but I have no solid proof that he was on St Martin's the night Scott died. I can't tell whether Gemma loved her husband obsessively or is trying to displace my suspicions.

I stop to take a breath when Lowertown fills the horizon. Hazel Teague's house stands near the Karma Hotel, with a direct view of uninhabited islands sprinkled across the ocean. The outlines of Tean, Men-a-Vaur and St Helen's are veiled by the encroaching fog. I reach the small end terrace, where a Christmas tree glows in the front window. When Polly opens the front door the hall looks festive too. Bunting hangs from the ceiling, with homemade paper stars over every doorway, but the young girl looks unhappy. She barely speaks before leading me to the living room, where Hazel stands over her son like a prison guard. I've only seen her smiling until now, like it's her duty to raise people's spirits. Ivan is keeping his head down, clearly sick of rebukes. I looked the same at seventeen – tall, with a raw-boned face, keeping my feelings hidden. There's no trace now of the upbeat young man who shadowed me at work last summer.

'Thanks for coming, Ben,' Hazel says. 'Ivan broke your curfew last night; he didn't come in until 2 a.m. I was going out of my mind with a killer out there. I thought you should know he broke the curfew.'

'It was safety advice, not a question of legality, Hazel.'

I'm shocked that she summoned me here in the middle of a murder hunt just to discipline her son.

'Explain what you did, Ivan,' Hazel snaps. 'You're wasting Ben's time.'

The lad's cheeks are scarlet with embarrassment. 'I went to meet my girlfriend, that's all. Sorry it's caused trouble.'

'Couldn't you see her during the day?' I ask.

'Lauren left me a note, saying she'd be on the beach.'

'She put a message through your door?'

He shakes his head. 'There's a hollow tree, halfway up May's Hill. We used to leave messages there as kids; the younger ones still do. She drops stuff for me there sometimes, for a laugh. She prefers it to texting.'

'Because her parents check her phone?'

The lad shrugs, but doesn't reply, making his mother tut under her breath.

'I can't believe you went out in the middle of the night,' Hazel snaps. 'There's a killer out there, for God's sake. I hope you walked Lauren home safely.'

'Of course I did,' Ivan replies. 'We're adults, Mum; we can take care of ourselves. It's your life that's a mess, not mine.'

Suddenly the boy's on his feet. He marches from the room, with his sister following in his wake, visibly upset. When I face Hazel again, her cheeks are a livid red. I can't tell whether she's angry or embarrassed.

'I'm sorry you had to see all that, Ben. I'm at my wit's end.'

'Are you angry about the curfew, or that he's got a girlfriend?'

'Ivan put them both at risk, that's what shocks me.'

'I can't lock him up for having fun. Kids will be kids, after all.' My gaze lands on a packet of cigarettes and a bottle of brandy on her work surface. 'I didn't know you smoked, Hazel.'

'I never have. I confiscated those from Ivan just now; he'd hidden them in the shed.' The anger in her voice is giving way to exhaustion.

'Keep him indoors till tomorrow, with no fags, no booze, and no girlfriend. He'll soon see the error of his ways.'

'What he needs is a father figure to keep him on the straight and narrow.'

'Doesn't his dad keep in contact?'

A bitter look appears on her face. 'You're having a laugh. I was still in my teens when I fell pregnant – his dad told me to get a termination.'

'On the mainland now, is he?'

'Ivan's never met him,' she says, looking away. 'At least Polly's dad sends letters and birthday cards.'

'You're doing a good job on your own. They both seem like great kids.'

She presses her hands to her face. 'Ivan's always tried to help me, since he was small. Now he's going off the rails.'

'Come on, you're overreacting. Teenagers love testing boundaries.'

She gives a weak laugh. 'You're right, I should cut him some slack. He's running on hormones, isn't he?'

'It'll be Polly next. Lads will be texting every five minutes.'

'No way, she's staying indoors till she's twenty-one.'

'Can I ask about something else while I'm here?'

'Of course.'

'Do you think Scott Minear was having an affair?'

I see conflicting emotions on her face before she answers. 'The way he treated Gemma appalled me, to be honest. He had flings, but she was in too deep to notice. He even tried flirting with me once, after the pub, but I told him where to get off. Scott only cared about himself.'

'Most people agree with you.'

'It's Gemma I pity now.'

'It's lucky you give her so much support.'

'She'd do the same – we're more like sisters than friends.'

The nurse's smile has revived when she closes the door, but no doubt her son will remain in the doghouse, his antics casting a shadow over Christmas. Teenagers need privacy to explore their feelings, but it's in short supply on a small island. I think about the note Lauren Paige left for Ivan inside the hollow oak. The killer could have left a message for the twins there, then waited to intercept them in the field, but that doesn't explain why they were targeted.

There's little good news waiting for me at the community hall. No one has reported any fresh information about Scott Minear's death, and Ethan is refusing to leave his room. When I look outside the fog has thickened again, and it's starting to feel like Groundhog Day. If I was alone I'd kick a few walls to release some frustration, but Eddie is ploughing through a pile of evidence reports, his face bright with excitement after a good night's sleep. At least DCI Madron can't sail through the fog to cast his shadow over the investigation.

34

Ethan is lying on his bed, face to the wall. He's heard the adults talking and knows that Luke and his mum have been to see his father's body. He gazes straight ahead until shapes crawl from the wallpaper, grotesque faces glaring at him between the flowers. The dog is lying at his feet, half-asleep. He almost jumps out of his skin when someone pushes the door open. His tension fades when Luke appears, even though his brother looks tense when he leans down to stroke Shadow's fur.

'Beautiful creature, isn't he?'

The dog rolls over, letting Luke rub his belly, but Ethan can see worry in his brother's eyes. When Luke speaks again, his voice is a slow whisper.

'Dad can't hurt either of us again, but it's not over yet. Stay indoors tonight. Promise me?' Ethan nods in reply. 'It's not safe out there.'

Luke soon walks away, leaving Ethan more confused. He should be outside, looking for Jade, despite his promise. Soon exhaustion makes his eyes close, and for once his dreams are peaceful: his sister is with him again, and the sun is blazing down on Par Beach.

Ethan is woken by a quiet tap on the door. When he pulls himself upright Nina is on the landing, standing perfectly still. Frustration has been building in his chest all morning. He's desperate to spit out what he knows, but words desert him as usual.

'I wanted to see how you and Shadow are doing,' she says.

He feels calmer when she enters the room. Nina settles on a floor cushion, glancing around like every object fascinates her. She only speaks again when the dog settles at her side, his muzzle resting on her knee.

'My violin's downstairs. I can show you later, but right now I'm starving. Can I nick one of your sandwiches?'

Ethan follows her example, but it's like chewing cotton wool. Nina talks quietly as he forces down another mouthful, her voice soothing, as if she's reading a story. The way he feels is natural, she says. Her kindness makes him desperate to speak. He'd love to tell her everything, from the note he found in the hollow tree, to the way his mum scares him sometimes, but only a hiss of air escapes from his mouth.

'It's okay, Ethan, don't force it. You can talk to me anytime. Let's pop out for a minute, and give Shadow some freedom.'

Mist is still drifting past, the world too blurred to make sense.

'We can just smell the air, then come back indoors, I promise,' Nina says.

The boy would rather stay put, but now there's no choice. Shadow is already alert, tail wagging, forcing him onto his feet.

35

I go searching for the hollow oak at midday. Kids used the same method on Bryher when I was young, even though neighbours were so close by it would have been easier to post envelopes through their doors. It was more fun leaving notes for girls I fancied, and for my best mate Zoe, between the bricks of an abandoned well, like members of a secret society. It's the only way kids can communicate on St Martin's, because most of the youngest ones don't have phones, apart from Ethan and Jade. The oak tree lies opposite the Minears' top field, where pickers are once again gathering flowers. The community has rallied round, bringing in the harvest without Scott cracking his whip.

The tree stands halfway up May's Hill. It's still growing, despite a deep fissure running through its core. I can't see anything inside the opening until I spot something small and glossy that I grasp with an evidence bag. Another ship in a bottle rests in the palm of my hand. This time it's a luxury yacht like the ones millionaires cruise around the Caribbean in, with dozens of portholes and a wide sundeck. Scott Minear's suspicions about Dave Carillian may be true after all. His house stands just fifty metres away. He can watch the kids leaving messages from his top window all day long. The old man could easily have left an anonymous note for the Minear twins, inviting them outside at midnight. I walk straight to his front door and ring the bell, but this time there's no answer.

I keep the glass bottle in my pocket until I reach the community hall, where Eddie looks triumphant, as if he's cracked the case single-handed.

'Results are coming through from the PNC, boss. I've been doing some calling round too. Do you want an update?' His eyes gleam brighter when he sees the miniature yacht. 'The desk sergeant in Mousehole remembered Dave Carillian's name. He got into trouble, apparently. The bloke hung round the children's playground so often the parents complained.'

'Was he charged?'

'Just a verbal warning – it didn't even get logged as a caution, but locals spray-painted his car. They wrote "paedo" on his front door, and the rest is history. He flogged his mum's house and moved here.'

'He may have been escaping his demons.'

'I meant to tell you, boss, Elspeth Hicks rang earlier. She remembers seeing Carillian hanging round by the hollow tree, the evening the girl disappeared.

Maybe Scott had a reason to give the old boy a black eye after all.'

Eddie's statement makes me feel like punching the air. 'Track Carillian down for me, please, we've got enough evidence to arrest him. I've looked round his house already, but I'll get a full search warrant from the CPS. I can set that up after my conference call.'

I log on to Skype at exactly 2 p.m., as Madron ordered. I'm expecting more criticisms when his face appears on my screen, but he keeps quiet when Chief Superintendent Naomi Gibbs opens the meeting. She's in her late fifties, with short grey hair, giving me a no-nonsense stare. I've been in the force long enough to understand that women at the top have to be tougher than their male counterparts, after smashing a dozen glass ceilings. Gibbs is no exception, but her approach is more supportive than Madron's. She offers to send five officers from the mainland when transport's running again. She looks relieved that I'll be arresting a suspect this afternoon.

'That's strong progress, Kitto. I'm afraid the news websites are all over this; nasty crimes on small islands always fascinate people.'

'I know, ma'am. It's happened before.'

The murder of a wealthy islander is ideal fodder for the tabloids, making me glad of the fog's existence for once. Journalists can't travel here in bad weather, and drones can't take pictures, so there will be no interference while it lasts. The Skype conference ends before Madron can air his view.

It's half past two when Dave Carillian finally reports to the community hall. The wound on his face looks worse than before, the bruises on his temple and jaw darkening to midnight blue, yet his appearance is hard to interpret. He might just be an assault victim, or he could be a murderer. The old man looks like the TV image of a child killer, out of shape and badly dressed, his ashen face full of suspicion. I take my time explaining the terms of his arrest. The old man's hands are shaking as he listens to the formalities, and realises he must remain in the community hall until further notice. It's fortunate that he waives his right to legal representation, because it could take hours for a solicitor to brave the weather conditions and sail over from St Mary's.

'I found another of your model ships in the old tree where kids leave messages. Did you put it there, Mr Carillian?' When I pass him the object, he seems reluctant to take it, but eventually raises it to the light, still wrapped in its evidence bag.

'This isn't mine. Someone left it by my front door, so I took it down to the tree, for the children to find.'

I stare back at him. 'You're saying three different people on St Martin's make ships in bottles? The first was made decades ago, then yours, and now this.'

'There are dreadful errors of scale here.' He hands the bottle back, with a look of distaste. 'It's a crude beginner's attempt. I keep a log of the models I build in a notebook at home.'

'Maybe you rushed this one out. How about Scott Minear's speedboat? Have you ever copied it?'

'I'm afraid not. I think someone's trying to shift the blame.' Carillian sits straight-backed in his chair, his voice reedy. 'I told you last time that I left some of my models around the island every summer, for the children.'

'Like an Easter Egg hunt, without any rules?' Eddie asks.

'Is generosity a crime these days?'

'Why did you sell your house in Mousehole, Mr Carillian?' I ask.

'I had no choice.' There's panic in the old man's gaze when he looks at me again. 'It was a witch hunt, and it's happening again.'

'Give us the full story, please.'

'I sat on a park bench, feeding the birds. What's wrong with that? I took my mother to the same park in her wheelchair every day when she was alive. No one complained then. Once she died, they came after me, mob-handed.'

'Where's Jade Minear, Mr Carillian? I'll bet you've watched other kids leaving messages. You could have written an anonymous one yourself, then lied about seeing Jade and Ethan in the field late at night. Were you waiting for them there?'

'I would never hurt a child.' The old man's voice quavers when he speaks again. 'Go ahead and search my house from top to bottom. I've got nothing to hide.'

'We will, once this interview ends.'

I carry on questioning Carillian for ten more minutes, but the shutters have come down, and I can't help
pitying him, even though he may be lying through his
teeth. The man has remained on the island all year.
He's had no visitors, his life hermetically sealed behind
an invisible wall, like one of his boats. When I bring
the interview to a close he stays silent, keeping his gaze
fixed on the wall.

36

Ethan feels better once he's outside, with his piccolo tucked inside his jacket. Pop music drifts from the cutting shed, and the pickers' voices sound happy, like nothing bad has happened. He feels safe near the house, but too afraid to walk beyond its gates after his brother's warning. The boy can still remember being dragged through the hedgerow with someone's hand smothering his mouth. Nina's presence is reassuring, but words are building up inside his chest, until he can hardly breathe. Shadow is sniffing the ground, while Nina keeps her hands warm in the pockets of her jeans. He wishes his Mum would relax like that, but it's been months since he's heard her laugh. Ethan closes his eyes, trying to picture Jade's face, but all he can see is the Devil's Table, scattered with flowers, and his dad staring up at the sky. An ugly noise spills from his mouth, between a cry and a moan.

'Let's take Shadow back indoors,' Nina says, her tone gentle.

Ethan's glad to return to the living room, his panic subsiding. The atmosphere is peaceful, with Shadow stretched out at his feet, the dog's eyes closing for a nap. Nina points at a narrow case that's leaning against her chair.

'That's my violin, Ethan. It was made a hundred and fifty years ago, in Italy, from a special kind of wood called spruce. I carry it everywhere I go, like you with your piccolo.'

The boy edges closer, eager to see it. The instrument rests on its satin lining, the neck glossy from decades of handling, its curved body gleaming in the winter light. Nina hands him the bow first.

'They used to string these with horsehair, but that stopped years ago. They're all synthetic now.'

Ethan is surprised that the fibres feel as soft as human hair.

'Can I see your piccolo, in exchange?'

Ethan rarely lets anyone handle it, but Nina's smile encourages him to hand it over. It feels strange to touch the violin's smooth wood, the surface as supple as skin. He rests the instrument on his lap, touching the delicate scrolls carved on its frame.

'Some piccolos are made of solid silver, for the resonance, aren't they?' Nina runs her fingers across each key. 'Would you play a few notes for me?'

The boy hates performing for anyone except Jade, but instinct makes him reach for his instrument. He plays scales first, until memories overtake him. He closes his eyes and suddenly he's playing in time with the mist whispering in his ears, Jade's scream, and his own pounding heartbeat as he raced back to the farm. It's only when his eyes reopen that he sees the concern on Nina's face.

'I can hear you, Ethan. You're trying to explain what

231

happened, aren't you? But you're not quite ready. Remember that music's a safe place to go, if you ever feel scared.' Her eyes are still level with his. 'I think you saw something bad, the night Jade left. It might help to write it down, if that's easier than speaking, but there's no rush.'

Nina places a notepad and pencil on the arm of his chair. The paper's white expanse is blank and terrifying, like the fog outside. He wants to write the truth, but his hand freezes. His pencil traces ghost words in the air, before it slips from his grasp.

37

I don't get far on my return journey to Dave Carillian's house before my first interruption. They're a fact of life in Scilly; the islands are so small that you bump into your neighbours every day, which can be a blessing or a curse. There's little chance of arriving anywhere on time, but people always step up if you need help. Saul Heligan is heading in my direction, carrying supplies from the island's only shop in Highertown. His theatrical past is easy to spot. He's wearing a worn leather jacket, a bandana knotted around his throat, cowboy boots visible under his jeans. I can tell from his expression that he's longing for gossip, yet Neil Kershaw's claim that he hangs around Minear Farm at night lingers in my mind. The landlord's bloodshot eyes assess me from head to toe, like he's reading the state of play from my body language. Heligan's avid interest in the case seems to grow stronger by the day.

'Dave Carillian's been charged, hasn't he? I heard you're keeping him at the community hall.'

'We're making progress,' I say, with a professional smile. 'The investigation's going well.'

'Funny old bugger, isn't he? I spoke to him on the ferry, the day he arrived. We were quite chummy until he turned into a hermit. He gave me one of his model boats; the quality blew me away. The guy's talented, whatever he's done. I collected them for a while, so I know a thing or two. I told him to leave some outside for the local kids.'

'You encouraged him to scatter his models round the island?'

Heligan beams. 'Sweet idea, isn't it? I bought a big one off him for the pub too; people often admire it.'

'I've been meaning to ask something, Saul. How could you tell that the fishing boat in the harbour was Jason Minear's that night? They all have the same design; you couldn't have recognised it from the lane in the dark.'

'Jason's boat's distinctive, with that red stripe down its side,' the landlord replies. 'I know all the local fishing vessels by sight. There's something cosy about seeing them all lined up inside the harbour in winter.'

'You must have amazing night vision.'

'So the optician tells me.' His voice falls to a stage whisper. 'By the way, I've got some information. Come to the pub tonight for the full lowdown.'

'Why not tell me now?'

'I have to get back.'

'Okay, I'll try to call by later.'

I'm still processing the fact that Heligan told the island's oddball to leave his glass-bound ships around the island. It's a reminder that anyone with a keen eye could have gathered them, not just the island's children, including the landlord himself. The murderer could have built up a collection, but I still need to find out if Dave Carillian is guilty or innocent.

I use the old man's key to enter his house. Unlike the locals, he's left his property secure, the mortice lock clicking as I twist the key. The place still feels cold, as if fog has found its way inside, leaving its damp breath on the walls. It sounds like I'm not alone, a door slamming in the distance, but it must be the draft rattling his windows, because all the rooms are empty. The man's possessions are sparse, and his loneliness is on full display. A pair of binoculars lie on the window ledge in his lounge, enabling him to observe the island's human population, as well as its birds. His kitchen is unchanged, his magnifying glass still on the table, beside an array of matchsticks, pins, and scraps of canvas. I find an ancient laptop in a cupboard, but the man's claims not to own a mobile phone or have internet connection appear true when I check his household bills. Carillian's landline rarely gets used, his monthly charge little more than the cost of line rental. There's nothing in his outbuilding except trowels, spades, and bags of compost.

The man's strangeness is even clearer when I go upstairs. One bedroom stands empty, apart from the ancient carpet that flows through his house. The next contains a single bed, with a faded patchwork quilt, and a book about naval history on the bedside table. The wardrobe contains old-fashioned suits, ties, and lace-up shoes. But it's the final room that stops me in my tracks. Apart from another narrow bed, the space is filled from floor to ceiling with an armada of ships in bottles. One is two feet long, containing a perfectly realised submarine, its black glass portholes reflecting the overhead light. The man's obsession extends from galleons and tea clippers to modern catamarans. I pull out my phone to photograph them. It reminds me of a butterfly collection; each brightly painted vessel is vacuum-sealed in place, like exotic species pinned behind glass.

Frustration nags at me when I go back downstairs. There's no evidence that Carillian's harmed either Jade or Scott Minear, despite being spotted by the hollow tree. I promised Ethan to bring his sister home, but my claim may not be realised. My spirits are low when I go back into the kitchen for a final look around. It's only when I get down on my hands and knees that I see a faint stain on the worn lino, near his table, the smell of bleach overpowering. The mark is almost a foot wide, and I remember the county forensics chief saying that bloodstains are almost impossible to remove from synthetic surfaces. I wish Liz Gannick was here to wave her UV torch over it and confirm my suspicions.

When I photograph the mark it's too pale to register, but it's still incriminating. Carillian's mild demeanour almost had me fooled, and maybe I was trying too hard not to pigeonhole him. It's so easy to imagine a young girl's wounded body lying on his floor, I have to blink to dislodge the image from my mind.

38

I walk to the top of May's Hill after the search. It reminds me of growing up on Bryher, where the poor phone signal often forced me to climb Gweal Hill to call friends, and little has changed. The line takes ages to connect when I ring Eddie, my deputy's voice crackling with static. He's using the small office inside the community hall to keep Dave Carillian confined, so he won't overhear conversations about the case. I can't prove yet that the stain on the old man's floor is from Jade Minear's blood, but offender behaviour is often cyclical. Carillian's daily habit of watching kids play spooked his neighbours on the mainland. He's continued the pattern on St Martin's, and this time his intent may have been much more sinister.

'He's begun asking for a lawyer, boss,' Eddie says.

'Tell him we'll get one once the fog clears.'

The sergeant releases a quick laugh. 'Sometime next year.'

'There's a stain in his kitchen that wasn't there

yesterday. We'll have to wait for forensics, but he's staying in custody.'

'I've found something else, boss. Cornwall only has a handful of vineyards. I've called them all, and no one remembers Neil Kershaw.'

'Why would he lie about places he's worked?' I fall silent while ideas slot into place. 'Contact the Serious Fraud Office, Eddie. The vineyard must have cost a fortune, try and find out where he got his money.'

I remain standing when the call ends, watching mist roll in with the tide, its return as predictable as clockwork. Neil Kershaw's lie is harder to understand. Secrets are easily exposed in such a small place, but darker ones may lie below the surface. Kershaw has chosen one of the youngest women on the island, but his appetite may extend to children like Jade. There's an outside chance Kershaw took the route favoured by many violent sex offenders, of killing his victim to avoid punishment. He would have needed to murder Scott Minear too, if the man guessed his daughter's fate, but I can't let my imagination run wild. I've been hunting for clues ever since Jade disappeared, frustration getting the better of me, but another visit to Kershaw's home might put him in the clear.

I'm still running through scenarios when I reach the vineyard. The land Kershaw bought is sheltered by Chapel Down, with a view of the Eastern Isles scattered across Crow Sound. It may be peaceful now, but the calm atmosphere will vanish when I question

Kershaw about his past. My old work partner in London taught me there's no place for emotion on a murder case. All that counts is the evidence, but it's hard to remain neutral when a child goes missing. The few murderers I've interviewed about killing juveniles are often just like Kershaw – softly spoken, plausible, and easy to miss.

It's dark by the time I reach his front door, with few lights glowing inside the property. There's no answer to my knock, so I walk down the side passage to the kitchen where Neil is too busy to notice my arrival. His knife flies at a hectic pace as he chops herbs. I wait until he's transferred them to his saucepan, before tapping on the window. The man almost jumps out of his skin, and I can understand why. My appearance would spook anyone. No one welcomes a visit from an out-sized cop with a thuggish face, especially if they've done something wrong. The man's smile slowly regroups when he beckons me inside, but the knife remains in his hand.

'Abandon your weapon, please. I come in peace.'

He manages a laugh before laying it on his chopping board. 'It's good to see you, Ben. Would you like some wine? I just opened some for this casserole.'

'I'm on duty so I'll pass, thanks. It smells good though, whatever you're making.'

'It's from a recipe. I'm hopeless without instructions.' He gestures for me to sit at the breakfast bar, then drops onto the stool opposite.

'Is Amy here, Neil?'

'She's at the farm, trying to patch things up with her mum.'

'That's a good idea.'

'I hope it works out, Amy wants it so badly.'

There's a mismatch between Kershaw's mild voice and his tense expression. I know my next question will sour our conversation, but there's no alternative.

'We've been doing some fact-checking. Your professional background doesn't quite stack up, so there could have been a mistake. Can you tell me the name of the vineyard you worked at before coming to Scilly?'

Kershaw recoils in his seat. 'Are you saying I'm a suspect?'

'Someone on the island killed Scott Minear. Everyone's under suspicion until the case is solved.'

'Don't I get legal advice first?'

'I'm just gathering information. Sorry if that's uncomfortable, but Jade's been missing for three days, and none of the vineyards in Cornwall remember you.'

He gives a slow nod. 'I didn't stay long. I mainly did temporary jobs when I was back in the UK, seeing my folks.'

'Where do your family live?'

'My parents both passed away recently.' By now he's squirming in his seat.

'Sorry to hear it, but I'd like your CV, bank details, and passport number.'

'Why? I've done nothing wrong.' He stares back at me.

'Your current girlfriend is less than half your age, her sister's missing, and you've been telling lies.'

'Why in God's name would I attack Amy's sister?'

'You tell me.'

Kershaw raises his hands like a gun's pointing at his chest. 'All I've done is start a business here. I pay my taxes like everyone else.'

'Your national insurance number would help us too. You can let me have it tomorrow, if you don't remember.'

The man is still scowling when he tears a sheet from a notebook, scribbles out a few lines then thrusts it at me. 'That's the last three places where I worked. I'll have to check my records before you get the rest. Please leave now, so I can finish cooking dinner.'

I can see genuine emotions on his face at last: fury, mixed with humiliation at being caught out. He's still edgy when the front door slams, and footsteps clatter down the hallway. Amy Minear is too upset to notice the atmosphere between us when she rushes into the kitchen. I can tell immediately that she and Gemma have failed to mend their rift. She hurls herself into her boyfriend's arms, face hidden against his chest, even though he may be a total fraud. Neil Kershaw continues giving me a hostile stare while she sobs, then drops a kiss on the crown of her head. Something about the gesture makes my stomach crawl. He's holding her just like a doting father, comforting his child.

39

It's 7 p.m. and Ethan is in his room with Shadow. The dog stayed at his side when Nina left, but the boy's anxiety is rising again, as well as his guilt. He should be looking for Jade, but Luke told him not to leave the farm tonight. Ethan picks up the pad Nina left for him, then hunts for a pen. He wants to record everything that's happened, from finding the mysterious invitation in the hollow tree, to Jade vanishing in the fog. He should tell the police about being followed too, and the attacker grabbing him, while he hid in the hedgerow. Ethan forces the pen down onto the page, but the mist outside seems to enter his mind. He can't think clearly, only a black scribble of lines appearing on the blank sheet, making him admit defeat. He tries to draw the field instead, with its long furrows, but he lacks Jade's art skills, soon tearing out the page and throwing it away.

A memory arrives of his grandmother teaching him and Jade to pray. She showed them how to kneel bedside their beds, thanking God for his mercy, but the stories his gran read from the Bible no longer convince him. If God was real, Jade would be at home, perfectly safe. He'd like to say a prayer, in case someone's listening, but his voice still won't work.

When the boy sits on the floor again, Shadow gazes at him expectantly, like he's waiting for something, and a familiar noise has started again. His mother is in her room, her voice drifting across the landing. She's trying to keep her voice down while she makes a phone call, but her bitter tone reminds him of her rows with his father. Ethan glances around the room, looking for anything to silence the noise. When he rummages through his box of treasures his hand settles on his ship in a bottle. He places it on his bedside table, close to his pillow, then lifts the piccolo to his lips, but the instrument's quiet song is too soft to block out his mother's anger.

40

My visit to the vineyard has raised so many questions, I decide to visit Amy's grandparents again before returning to the community hall. Elspeth Hicks will have views on my potential suspects. She's lived here all her life and is so straight-talking, it could help to fill in the gaps.

The air cloys in my mouth as I walk uphill. It feels like I'm ascending into the clouds, visibility dropping with each stride. Dense whiteness surrounds me as I walk, wishing the conditions would improve just long enough for me to enlist help from the mainland. Like Neil Kershaw, Elspeth is in the middle of cooking dinner, an apron tied around her waist. The old woman shakes her head vehemently when I apologise for disturbing her, then ushers me inside, determined to be hospitable.

Stan is slumped in front of the TV when I glance through the living-room door, too focused on the flickering screen to notice my arrival. It's a reminder that even though the man has retained his physical strength, his world has shrunk beyond recognition. He must sleep in the hospital-issue bed that's pressed against the wall, and he's too confused to leave the house alone. Elspeth leads me through to her kitchen, following the island tradition of offering hospitality too forcefully to refuse.

'There's a shepherd's pie in the oven, Ben. You'll stay and eat with us.'

'Thanks, but . . .'

'. . . you must, because I bet you've had nothing decent all day. You can give us your news about Jade.'

I accept her invitation before noticing that the table is already laid for three. 'Who's your other visitor, Elspeth?'

Her eyes blink rapidly. 'Luke said he might drop by soon, but we often have visitors. Plenty of kids have run here over the years.'

'Why's that?'

'I like to help, and so did Stan. If we don't encourage the youngsters, they'll fly away and leave us behind.'

'How's Stan been, the last few days?'

'I can't tell how much he understands, but I know he's afraid. He won't even leave the house for a walk most days. The panic in his eyes upsets me more than anything. It's like he's lost himself. Can you imagine how terrifying it must be, if the world suddenly stopped making sense?'

Elspeth's face looks strained, the burden of nursing her husband finally taking its toll.

'I'm sorry it's so hard on you both.'

She relaxes slightly when I lend a hand tidying up, letting me wash a few pots and pans. Elspeth claims that Neil Kershaw treats Amy well, removing her doubts about the age gap. He seems like a force for good, employing three islanders to tend his vines, and paying them decent wages. She seems to have no idea that Kershaw has lied about his background, so I turn my attention to her relatives instead.

'Have you spoken to Gemma much since Scott died?'

'Only once, and now she's blocking my calls,' Elspeth says, looking flustered. 'She loved that man so much, but he drove a wedge between us.'

'Neither of you have said why you fell out.'

'I don't like talking about it, to be honest, even though it's been going on for years. She was so unhappy with Scott, she stopped taking care of herself. I threatened to report her to Social Services if she didn't get help with her drinking.' Elspeth is clutching the crucifix round her neck like she's hoping for divine intervention. 'Scott persuaded me and Stan to sign over our land years ago, to avoid death duties. He never consulted us after that, even though Stan's family owned those fields for generations. Gemma had to watch him flirting with other women straight after their wedding. He only married her to get our land. That's clear as day, even if she can't see it.'

'Gemma left him for a while, didn't she?'

'Luke and Amy were babies when she ran off to

Falmouth, to live with Saul Heligan. If she'd stayed there she'd be a damn sight happier now.'

I stare back at her. 'I didn't know Saul was involved.'

Elspeth's expression softens. 'He's a kinder man, I wish she'd stayed with him, but Scott had a weird power over her. He lured her back here easily, but he didn't do it out of love. He wanted the land, and knew it would be lost if they divorced. Gemma came round here raving drunk in the middle of the day, begging for help to leave him once and for all. But she lost the courage, once she sobered up. Stan had his stroke a few days later. I'm convinced the strain of all that drama broke his health in the end.'

Elspeth's statement clashes with her daughter's. Gemma may be erratic enough to lash out, especially when drunk, but a premeditated murder would have involved planning, and her behaviour appears too chaotic for that much forethought. I can't blurt out my suspicions to her mother, so I shift the conversation to an easier topic.

'Do you think Saul might be involved in Scott's death?'

She appears shocked. 'Lord, no. That man wouldn't hurt a fly.'

I catch sight of a few circular bruises on her neck, fading from blue to brown, reminding me of Dave Carillian's injuries. I've seen victims of strangulation lying on mortuary slabs with exactly the same injuries.

'Your neck looks sore, Elspeth. Did Scott hurt you, before he died?'

Her hand flies up to her collar. 'He was cruel, but not stupid. I'd have reported him straight away.'

'Who attacked you then? Those bruises are from finger marks.'

Elspeth's eyes glisten and she's slow to reply. 'Stan's personality changed after his stroke, that's what I tried to explain. There are days when he doesn't even recognise me, and losing his independence has broken his spirit. It's not surprising he's frustrated and scared. He keeps himself in the living room, day and night, even though he can walk to Top Rock Hill if I coax him outside.'

'How much rehab is Stan getting?'

'Hazel's been wonderful. She comes here every week in her spare time, and Ivan pops round too. She does exercises with him, and tries to help him speak, and the boy keeps him company, to give me a break. Hazel and I are the only ones that can get him out for exercise and fresh air. He loves her visits, but there's nothing else on offer.' Elspeth blinks moisture from her eyes. 'I'm more worried about Jade. None of us can rest easy till she's home.'

She still looks distressed, but I need her opinion on one more suspect.

'Dave Carillian's your nearest neighbour, isn't he? Do you know him well?'

'That man's not keen on human beings. We tried everything at first: I took food round, then plants, and bottles of wine. Stan fixed his generator when it packed up, but he prefers his own company.'

'Do the twins ever visit him?'

'I doubt it. They want friends their own age, not that dry old fossil.'

Stan is lumbering down the hall, in time for dinner. He gives me a suspicious look as he sits down and Elspeth's tough situation hits home. We pass a strange mealtime, with his wife keeping up a stream of chatter, while Stan fixes me with a fierce scowl. His face only lightens for a moment when his wife mentions my father.

'Stan and your dad used to have a pint together sometimes, at the Mermaid. You're the spitting image,' she says. 'You remember Mark Kitto, don't you, Stan? He was a pal of yours.'

The old man says nothing, only the glint in his eyes proving he's listening.

'It's tragic what happened,' Elspeth murmurs. 'I remember that boat going down like it was yesterday. A storm blew up out of nowhere; five good men taken in a blink. It affected the community for years.'

Stan doesn't react at first. Elspeth is still talking about my father's boat capsizing when he grabs a tumbler then hurls it at the wall, the noise silencing her. She tries to pacify him but he leaves the room, without looking back. Elspeth appears shaken, but not surprised. I make a mental note to ask one of the islands' two social workers to do a safety assessment on Elspeth's home situation, as well as her daughter's.

*

Dave Carillian is locked in the small office on my return to the community hall. I'd like to know immediately if the stain at his home is blood, but my boss's cautious approach is to blame. He refuses to keep testing kits at the station, including luminol sprays, convinced that chemical agents should only be used by trained forensics officers. It's frustrating to still have no hard evidence that Carillian hurt Jade. There's panic on his face when I explain the terms of his arrest for the murder of Scott Minear, and Jade's abduction. A forensics officer will be flown over from the mainland, to analyse evidence from his home.

'You need to tell me about the stain on your kitchen floor, Mr Carillian. It wasn't there the first time I called round.'

The old man looks flustered. 'I spilled some paint and scrubbed it away. The lino's so old, it shows every mark.'

'It looks like a bloodstain, so we need it analysed, I'm afraid. You'll be taken to the holding cells on St Mary's when the fog lifts.'

'You can't hold me against my will.'

'I've told you your rights already, but I can repeat them: you do not have to say anything, but it may harm your defence if you do not mention, when questioned, something which you later rely on in court.'

I can see years of resentment on Carillian's face. It bothers me that the evidence for his arrest is all circumstantial, but it can't be ignored. The old man has aroused suspicion before, and he's found a new way to interact with the island's kids, through his model boats. He was seen hanging around the hollow tree, so he could easily have lured the twins outside, but the investigation must go on regardless, in case Carillian turns out to be innocent. I need to find out if any other islanders make ships in bottles, but it's too late to conduct more house-to-house visits. Tomorrow I can phone Neil Kershaw's past employers, to find out his real background, and talk to Saul Heligan, but we have no absolute proof that either man is involved. The case is making such slow progress, I feel like a sailor on one of Carillian's boats, trapped inside a glass bubble, with no wind to carry us forward.

41

Isla arrives for our final meeting of the day at the community hall. I can tell from her expression that forty-eight hours at Minear Farm have taken their toll. Her face is blank with tiredness, black hair plastered to her skull by the damp outside. She thanks me for asking one of Gemma's friends from Middletown to take her place until tomorrow morning, to give her a break. The young constable reports that Gemma's volatile moods are affecting her sons. The grief we both witnessed on the day of her husband's death has been replaced by anger, and her drinking is getting worse. The woman's frail mental state is one of the saddest parts of the case, making me keener than ever to wrap it up fast, but Scilly's isolation isn't helping. I can't even get Dave Carillian ferried across to St Mary's to spend the night in a holding cell, instead of locked in an office that isn't fit for purpose.

Scott Minear's death reminds me of reading Shakespeare at school, even though King Lear gave his treasures away, instead of hoarding them. The farmer committed errors on the same grand scale, banishing his teenage daughter, then burdening his oldest son with too much responsibility, and abusing his wife. It's still possible that my first assumption is correct, and a member of his own family reached the end of their tether, but Minear's death wasn't a crime of passion. The killer's staging was elaborate, from the flowers strewn across his body, to the model boats placed at the crime scenes. The murderer may have intended to frame Dave Carillian, aware that he's seen as an outcast.

Isla tells us that Gemma's anger is often focused on her oldest son. Luke is working tirelessly to bring in the harvest, yet his mother never thanks him.

'She was at his throat again today,' Isla says. 'Whenever I leave the room she starts yelling, but Luke just takes it. She goes quiet when I'm around, but it must be terrible on top of losing his dad. Gemma keeps phoning Scott's brother too. She's convinced Jason had something to do with his death.'

'You've spent enough time up there, Isla. I'll speak to her again tomorrow,' I reply.

'Nina did us a favour today – Ethan calms down whenever she's around.'

'That's good to know.' The news that Nina fulfilled her promise fills me with relief, but I can see my two officers starting to tire. 'Get yourselves back to the pub, you deserve a rest. Thanks for your hard work today.'

Eddie remains at the table. 'Do you think Jade's

still alive? She's been gone a long time.' His gaze shifts to the window, as if the young girl might be hiding in the dark.

'We'll find her quicker if you get some sleep. Walk back to the pub together; I need to stay here and guard Carillian tonight.'

My deputy shakes his head. 'I can camp here, boss. There are mattresses and blankets the scouts use in the store cupboards. I'll make sure he's comfortable.'

I do my best to dissuade him, but Eddie claims he won't sleep, with his mind so full of the case. He's rummaging through the hall's store room for pillows when I thank him, then say goodnight.

Isla seems subdued as we head for the Seven Stones. I felt the same pressure when I worked undercover on a case involving child trafficking. Most officers became too emotionally involved, because we knew how much the victims suffered. Isla says goodnight immediately when we reach the pub at 9 p.m., disappearing up to her room.

Saul Heligan is busy chatting to a customer when I enter the bar, too immersed to look up, giving me the chance to observe him more closely. He's dressed in a flamboyant turquoise shirt, recounting a long story, his gestures theatrical. It bothers me that he never mentioned Gemma living with him, making it sound like a brief love affair. It's feasible that he attacked the twins, then killed their father the following night out of jealousy, yet he looks perfectly relaxed.

A few locals are hunkered by the fire, and two old boys are gossiping in the corner, the other tables empty. Heligan is playing old Christmas pop songs, with Chris Rea claiming that he'll be driving home for Christmas as I take off my coat.

My gaze catches on the large ship in a bottle taking pride of place above the bar. It's a model of Saul's own dayboat, its red sail billowing, with the words 'Scilly Boy', emblazoned on its prow. It's only when I look closer that I see him at the tiller, dressed in a sailor's uniform. Carillian seems to have got under the island's skin, despite avoiding its inhabitants. He's forging a different type of intimacy by observing them and their boats so accurately.

Saul gives a broad smile when he spots me at last. He pulls us both a pint before beckoning me closer. I follow him through a gloomy corridor, then upstairs to his living quarters. His lounge is almost as spartan as Dave Carillian's. The landlord works such long hours, he hasn't bothered to personalise the space, even though the bar is packed with Christmas decorations. The room has a worn out three-piece suite and old-fashioned curtains. His bookshelf is full of vintage crime novels by Len Deighton and Reginald Hill, which might explain why he's so keen to know about the investigation, despite keeping his secrets hidden. The landlord's theatrical persona fades now we're in private, as if his regular punters are the one audience he craves.

'The local kids are feeling it worst,' he says. 'They're used to running around, day and night, perfectly safe.'

'What's this news you've got for me, Saul?'

'It's about Suzie Felyer.' The landlord's eyes glitter with excitement. 'Her and Scott were definitely having a fling. A girl at Island Travel says they flew over to the mainland several times, on the same flight, last summer. It doesn't take rocket science to work that one out. Penzance is full of cheap hotels, isn't it?'

'I've been on the same plane as Suzie myself a few times. She's got family there, hasn't she?'

He gives a grating laugh. 'I saw Scott coming out of her house myself, wearing a big fat smile.'

'What are you saying, exactly?'

'Maybe Suzie was heartbroken that he'd moved on to Felicity Paige.' He looks irritated, like I'm a slow pupil, failing to keep up.

'You've just accused the island's schoolteacher of being a murderer, Saul. What makes you so sure the killer's female?'

'Scott treated women like dirt. The ones he abandoned must hate his guts.' Heligan turns his head away, visibly annoyed. 'It's a no-brainer, isn't it?'

'I'll be following up every suggestion, but I'd like to know more about your past. It can't have been easy when Scott took your place with Gemma. Why didn't you say that you lived with her and the kids, the year she left Scott?'

The man's bonhomie suddenly evaporates. 'That

was years ago, for God's sake. Luke and Amy were just babies. I was teaching acting at Falmouth uni, to support us all. I came home one afternoon and Gemma had taken them back here. She didn't even leave me a note.'

'Yet you moved back too, by yourself.'

'Two years later, when I was over it. I was born here, remember? It's my island too.'

'I'm not disputing your right to live here, but many islanders had a reason to kill Scott, including you, potentially. We're all connected in a place this small.'

The landlord's face is sombre. Heligan's unwillingness to mention his past with Gemma has moved his name higher up my list of suspects.

'You've been seen hanging around Minear Farm late at night, Saul. I've got to say that bothers me.'

'I told you, I like to stretch my legs, and this place is open long hours. Evenings are my only chance to exercise.'

The landlord snatches up my empty glass and struts back to his bar, but my question hit a raw nerve. His friendly manner has vanished for once. Saul barely raises his head when I say goodnight.

42

Ethan heard his mother and Luke going to bed an hour ago. The farmhouse has been quiet ever since, apart from seabirds bawling as they wing inland, looking for shelter. The boy is drifting into sleep when a sound wakes him. Someone's crossing the landing, their movements slow and measured, like they're trying not to be heard. Shadow is alert too, ears pricked as the noise continues.

When Ethan opens his door by a fraction, Luke is on the landing, almost hidden by the dark. Ethan knows something's wrong, because his brother is fully dressed, in a sweatshirt, jeans, and trainers, even though no one's supposed to go outside. Luke is tiptoeing across the floor, trying not to make a sound.

Once Luke is gone, Ethan looks out of his window. His brother is heading across the yard to the cutting shed, where a light flickers behind the window, then suddenly dies. A new wave of panic lurches in his chest. The policeman told them all to stay indoors at night, but Luke is breaking the rules. Ethan listens carefully, making sure no one else is awake, then grabs his clothes. When he glances outside again his brother is nowhere to be seen, and panic surges in his chest. Jade disappeared because he didn't help her. He grabs his torch then opens the window and drops onto the flat roof, with Shadow following. The creature leaps to the ground a few seconds later, tongue lolling with excitement, like they're going on a big adventure.

The boy soon reaches the cutting shed. He peers through a crack in the door, but the only source of light is from a torch rolling across the dirt floor. He's about to enter when the door flies open, knocking him off his feet, while Shadow growls. Ethan hears his brother's voice inside the barn, calling for help, almost too weak to hear. Whoever threw the door open is still inside. He looks back at the farmhouse, but instinct pulls him in another direction to get help, and Shadow seems to agree. The dog runs at his side as Ethan sprints away at his quickest pace.

43

I'm too wired to sleep, even though it's midnight. Nina is keeping me company, the pair of us sitting by the hearth in her temporary home. The fire is so low in the grate we should cover the embers and go to bed, but my head's pounding with information.

'How's Ethan doing?' I ask.

'He's still very fragile. I called a child trauma specialist at the Maudsley Hospital today, for advice. She says victims can stay silent for months. Ethan may know who took Jade, but be unable to access that memory. The psychologist talked about a syndrome called "forced recall". If a child is pushed to remember something painful it can damage them for years. Ethan's best chance is to let him recover at his own pace.'

'Keep working with him, please. It could unlock the whole story.'

'Aren't you listening to me, Ben? Ethan's trapped in his own world. We can't just wrench him out of it.' There's an undertone of controlled anger in her voice.

'What's happening with his mum?'

'That's a neat change of subject. She's furious, but it's natural for her to feel that way.'

'How do you mean?'

'Grief comes in stages: shock and denial, pain and guilt, anger and bargaining, followed by depression. It can take a long time to reach acceptance, hope, and reconstruction. Some people get stuck in the middle phase. I think Gemma's grieving could be complex and long-term.'

'How come?'

'Her relationship with Scott was based on conflict, from the sound of it. People with no regrets suffer the least. If you love someone deeply, your grieving's painful, but at least there's no guilt.'

'Like when you lost Simon?'

'Maybe, but it's still taken me three years to get this far.'

'Where's that, exactly?'

'On the verge of falling for another man.'

'Why not just let it happen?'

'It's not like diving into a swimming pool, Ben. Teenagers often get stuck in a grieving phase, if they don't get counselling.'

'We're not back on my past, are we?'

'Losing a parent is the worst pain imaginable. I think you locked down your emotions out of guilt or sadness.'

'Why would I do that?'

'I'm not trying to counsel you, but I see it, every day.'

She turns in my direction, her amber-coloured eyes reflecting the dying fire. 'Maybe it's time to let it go.'

My mind flicks back to my father exiting the house for the last time. I can see myself by the kitchen window, watching him leave, but the memory soon vanishes. I made a conscious choice not to revisit it years ago.

'Why do you keep making me look back? Isn't that forced recall?'

'I think you remember it every day,' she says, her hand settling on mine. 'Because it hurts so much.'

'That's not true. I've forgotten most of it.'

'It never really goes away though, does it?'

This is the point when my relationships sour. Everything's fine until my past raises its ugly head, and I back off at full speed. But there's no curiosity in Nina's expression, just sympathy. This time there's nowhere to hide.

'You'll be the first person I tell, if I do remember.'

'We have progress then.'

I'm about to speak again when a noise comes from outside. It's the high scream of a wolf baying at the moon, Shadow's call instantly recognisable. But when I open the door there's no sign of him. His next call is so high and strained I'm afraid he's picked up another injury.

'Where the hell is he?' I pull on my trainers, almost falling over in my hurry to get outside.

'I'll come with you.'

Nina reaches for her coat, and there's no time to

insist she stays behind. White tendrils of mist hang on the air as I listen for Shadow's next call, but nothing comes. All we can do is wait until he bays again. When it comes, the sound is further away, but at least we're going in the right direction. Five minutes pass before I see him up ahead and anger surges through me. The figure at his side is Ethan Minear, his mother failing to keep him safe indoors. At least Shadow's with him, but Gemma took her eye off the ball. I told her to lock every door and window till morning, but she must have forgotten to hide the keys.

We're both out of breath when the pair head for the farmhouse, and the boy's speed is increasing. He glances over his shoulder, checking that we're following, with Shadow chasing ahead. When we reach Highertown, the pair follow the track to Minear Farm. They stop by the cutting shed, then Ethan races inside. I should have grabbed my torch from the hall table, because the lights aren't working when I press the switch: the kid is close by, but I have to grope towards him through the dark.

A narrow circle of light shows me where he's standing, his expression terrified.

'It's okay, Ethan, let me just take a look around. There's nothing wrong.'

I realise my mistake when the citrus scent of flowers hits me, then something darker and more pungent. The kid's hands must be shaking because his torch beam is bouncing from the walls, falling on crates and packing materials, then on the cutting table itself. Nina cries out, but I block the sound from my mind.

I ask the boy for his torch before approaching the table. Luke Minear is lying there, with Grand Monarch flowers littered across his body. When the picture comes into focus, Nina is at his side already. She did three years medical training, so she may be able to save him, but it could be too late. For the second time in three days the crime scene looks like an ancient sacrifice, with another victim prepared for the Gods.

PART 3

44

Thursday 22 December

When I press two fingers against Luke Minear's neck, his pulse is weak but regular. Nina is busy examining him. I can't risk Ethan escaping again, when the killer may still be watching us, so I let him keep Shadow at his side to calm him down. Gemma rushes into the barn in her dressing gown. She says that she was woken by noise from outside, but I leave Nina to explain what's happened. It's more important to get help for the wounded boy. I warn them to keep Ethan safe, then hurry down to the farm manager's cottage with the kid's torch still clutched in my hand.

Will appears seconds after I hammer on his door. He's fully dressed even though it's past midnight, his gaze unblinking.

'What's the trouble, Ben?'

'Luke Minear's hurt. Has Maria got any medical kit?'

He looks startled before running upstairs. The

couple both grab torches from the hall table, then we run the hundred metres back to the farm.

Maria joins Nina in the barn, while Will and I check the lights. Someone has cut the cables that feed electricity to the wood-framed building, which explains more about the killer's mindset. He or she has used the same modus operandi, with detailed staging, and they're prepared to take risks. I can't tell what time they approached the farmhouse, with a sack of freshly picked flowers, then severed the wires. Luke must have been lured outside, so I'll need to check his phone to see if he's received any recent texts or calls.

Maria has taken over caring for him when I go back into the barn.

'Did he recognise the attacker?' I ask her.

'He's not able to talk much yet. There's a nasty bump on his head, and a stab wound on his upper arm, but the tourniquet's stopped the blood flow,' Maria says. 'Luke fought hard, I think. One of his hands is quite badly cut. We can care for him here, but I'd rather he was in hospital.'

'There's no chance of sailing in this fog. Can we carry him inside?'

'Take care how you lift him. He's pretty dazed, so we'll have to watch him tonight, in case of concussion. You should let him rest till morning.'

Nina is busy comforting the new victim. He keeps trying to sit up, but she makes him wait until he feels stronger. Gemma's face is blank with shock when Will and I carry her oldest son upstairs. I can tell the latest attack on her family has pushed her closer to the edge. She's standing in her kitchen when I come back downstairs, her face ashen. I keep my voice low when I speak to her again.

'I'll make you a hot drink, then we can talk. Okay?'

Her eyes are glassy when she drops onto a chair, ignoring the coffee I place in front of her.

'There's safety in numbers, Gemma. I think Amy should stay here, until the threat's over.'

'No way. We've hardly spoken since she ran off.'

'Your family will be safer if you're together and the farmhouse is locked down.'

'What if I refuse?' She gives me a hostile stare, making me question why she still blames her daughter for leaving home, after months of separation, and all the recent violence.

'This is to protect your kids. I'm afraid you don't get a choice.'

'I can't talk now. I should be with Luke.'

'Go ahead. I'll stand guard here tonight.'

'Do what you like. I can't stop you, can I?'

Gemma pushes her untouched drink away then marches upstairs, leaving me alone in her neglected kitchen. The Minears' home still seems on the brink of destruction, while they continue tearing each other apart, and it amazes me that Saul Heligan remains in love with a woman whose mood fluctuates between sadness and fury.

I'm still looking around for clues to explain why Luke ventured outside when Will taps on the door. My old friend looks concerned when he crosses the threshold.

'I fixed the outdoor light,' he says. 'Is Luke okay?'

'Nina's monitoring him, but he's recovering. Maria's helped us so much.'

'Amazing, isn't she?' He appears so dazzled by his wife's virtues, he's lost in his own world, until his expression focuses again. He fishes something from his pocket, then passes it to me, bundled inside a cotton handkerchief. 'I found these on the cutting table.'

The parcel contains a wooden-handled knife, and another ship trapped inside a bottle, but I can't help wishing he'd left the items in situ. When forensic help does finally arrive, his fingertips will be smeared all over them. I swallow a surge of anger at the sight of Luke Minear's initials carved on the knife's handle. The young man is lucky to be alive. Maybe he fought so hard, the killer got hurt too, escaping from the scene wounded when Ethan disturbed him. When I study the bottle more closely, it contains a replica of the police launch, including its fluorescent marking, and the deep gash on its fibreglass hull that's been there all year. One of the islanders has copied our boat with complete accuracy. The killer might be shifting his anger towards my team, for defending the Minears. The tiny vessel looks vulnerable when I hold it up to the light, its balsa-wood structure too flimsy to last five minutes on the open sea.

45

Ethan peers out from a crack in his bedroom door, with Shadow motionless at his side. His mother stands by Luke's bed while the other two women take care of him. Nina is wiping blood from his shoulder, while Maria unfolds a bandage, his brother's face as pale as the bedsheets.

The boy feels queasy when he spots some used dressings in a bowl on the floor, crimson with blood. Jade's pulse is still there when he touches his chest, tapping out a faint echo, but there's no chance of looking for her tonight. His mother turns round suddenly, her cold gaze connecting with his. She makes a shooing motion with her hands, ordering him back to bed. Loneliness overwhelms him when he returns to the darkened room.

Ethan lifts the loose floorboard beside his bed, pulling out the phone he rarely uses. The battery is almost dead, but tonight he's desperate for reassurance. His Uncle Jason takes a long time to answer, with the sea's low roar behind his voice. The boy wants to explain what's happened but the words never arrive.

'It's okay, Ethan, I know it's you.'

His uncle must be on his boat, the engine's throb almost drowning his speech.

'Struggling to sleep, are you? I'm not surprised, after what's happened. But you're safe now, I won't let anyone hurt you; I might even come and live on St Martin's again, without your dad chasing me away. You'd like that, wouldn't you?'

Uncle Jason's upbeat tone confuses Ethan. His father died a few days ago, yet his uncle sounds happy, and why is he sailing so late at night? It's a relief when the call ends. Ethan slips the phone back under the floorboard, still too tense to go back to bed.

46

I wake at seven thirty after a few hours of fitful sleep. The Minears' sofa is a foot too short, my feet hanging over the armrest until I haul myself upright. The fog outside looks innocent in the early light, as soft as cotton wool, unlike the choking air that's smothered the investigation from the start. I'd like to run off the adrenaline that's swilling round my system after Luke's attack, but outdoor exercise isn't an option until the killer's found. I drop to the floor and make myself do enough press-ups, squats, and lunges to make my muscles burn. I learned years ago that exercise is a personal necessity, like a carthorse ploughing a field. My energy soon turns negative if it's not put to good use.

My head's clearing by the time I use the Minears' downstairs shower, then dress in yesterday's clothes. My first duty of the day is to fire off an email to the CPS, requesting a warrant to search Saul Heligan's property. I know it's unlikely the man has harmed any of the Minear family, but his desire to know about the case and his keenness to be involved make him a person of interest.

I'll need to keep the entire family at home until the killer's found, yet they seem reluctant to stay indoors. A member of my team must stand guard permanently, because the killer's campaign is growing more intense.

When I walk upstairs, it's Nina beside Luke's bed rather than his mother. It surprises me that Gemma is keeping her distance. He looks childlike in sleep, the burdens his father placed on him finally stripped away. His wounded arm lies on top of the sheets, right hand heavily bandaged, reminding me of his lucky escape. Nina tiptoes outside to join me on the landing.

'How's he doing?' I ask.

'Okay, I think. His speech is normal, and there's no nausea or double vision. The wound on his hand needs stitches, but the cuts on his arm are superficial. Maria will come up soon to keep an eye on him, until we can get him to hospital.'

'Has he mentioned the attack?'

'Give him time to recover first.' She puts her hand on my arm. 'The one thing he's worried about is his phone. He had it on him last night, and now it's gone.'

'I'll look for it now. I don't want you spending time alone today. The killer hates the Minears; he may target anyone that's helping them. Can you look after Ethan here? You're still my best chance of getting him to talk.'

'You want me to stay with him all day?'

'Text Lauren Paige, if you need a break. She volunteered to help.'

Nina's expression is solemn when she agrees to care for the boy. She insists on being her own boss under normal circumstances, so I'm glad she's prepared to help me until the family are safe.

I head out to check the barn again as the sky fills with light, scanning the ground for anything the attacker could have dropped. All I find are dead flowers and discarded ribbon, dropped by the pickers. When I use a broom to sweep the flowers away, there's no new evidence, apart from a dried patch of blood on the cutting table. I use an old piece of black oilcloth to cover it and the place looks clean again. The killer did a neat job, just like at Devil's Table, leaving few visible traces behind.

Amy protests long and hard about coming home when I make my call, but she finally agrees, when I stress that it's for her safety. She grumbles loudly when I advise her to pack a bag, because she may be staying several days. I'm so concerned about her being at risk that I insist Neil accompanies her to the farmhouse, despite my misgivings; the killer seems to hate the Minears so much, she might be next on his list.

When I go into Scott's office on the ground floor, Gemma's voice drifts through the wall. It sounds like she's on the phone, misery reducing her voice to a lifeless drone. The woman's reactions have bothered me right from the start. She can move from vulnerability to aggression in seconds: Gemma may have been so incensed by her husband's infidelities that she launched a frenzied attack, then drove his own harvest knife into his chest. But why would a mother abduct her own daughter, or assault her own son, leaving him with serious injuries?

I cast my gaze around Scott Minear's workspace again. It contains a desk, a worn-out swivel chair, and two filing cabinets with loose documents stacked on top. Eddie has examined the farm's records with a fine-tooth comb, but I'm looking for evidence of the dead man's secrets. The walls are grubby beige, a roller-blind half covering the window, even though the view outside is the only thing of beauty. Scott and Gemma's land unrolls into the distance, still glittering with the yellow flowers the farmer prized so highly. None of the objects on his desk carry an emotional value: a stapler, a jar filled with pens, and a desk diary with a black cover. The pages only contain dates for ploughing, sowing and harvest, as if the man's essence lies buried in his farm.

I'm about to leave when I find a manila folder at the back of the desk drawer. It contains solicitor's letters and legal documents from three years ago, and Jason Minear's bitterness finally makes sense. The letters prove that Scott fought hard for every field and building, claiming that Jason spent all his time at sea, until he won almost the entire estate. His empire extended even further after he married Gemma, acquiring her family's land too, so long as their marriage lasted. I still can't understand how the farmer became so bitter and manipulative, the sadistic side of his personality worsening over time.

Neil Kershaw's grudge about our last conversation still shows when he appears at the back door. The man scowls at me as Amy kisses him goodbye. He leaves immediately, like the air inside the farmhouse might poison him. The place feels even more like a tinderbox when Amy dumps her holdall on the floor, and her mother's only welcome is a grudging nod.

'How long do I have to stay?' the girl asks. 'Why didn't anyone tell me last night about Luke getting hurt?'

'There was no need to worry you. I'm holding a meeting at eight a.m., but you can get settled first.'

She sighs loudly before disappearing upstairs. Gemma is standing by the window, gripping the work surface like a lifeline. She's dry-eyed after days of weeping yet she seems even more brittle, as if the next challenge might break her in two.

The meeting starts on time, with all of us seated round the Minears' kitchen table. Eddie has arrived from the community hall, leaving Isla guarding Dave Carillian. Gemma and Amy sit at opposite ends of the table, and Luke is still asleep upstairs, with Nina keeping Ethan occupied in the living room.

'All of you need protection,' I say. 'Your family's under attack, and my priority is to find out what's happened to Jade and why Luke was attacked, to lead us to the killer. I need you all indoors until the threat's over.'

Gemma stares back at me. 'We can't just sit here – the flowers are spoiling.'

'Will Austell's volunteered to run the harvest, with help from your most experienced pickers.'

'The next shipment needs delivering tomorrow.'

'He's aware of that, but it's your lives that matter now, Gemma. We'll keep a police officer here round the clock, and the only people we'll let inside are trusted helpers. Think long and hard about which islander could be targeting you. I want to hear about anyone the family's clashed with recently.'

'It's a no-brainer, isn't it?' Gemma snaps. 'Amy's bloke hated Scott's guts from day one.'

Amy stands up so fast her glass tips over, splashing water over the table. I have to block her way before she can reach the back door. The meeting falls apart while the table's wiped dry and the girl is persuaded to stay.

'Dad was a bully, and you're no better,' Amy says, spitting out the words. 'Are you surprised I left? Neil's so much kinder than you.'

'He'll soon get sick of you. Then where will you be?' Gemma hisses.

I hold up my hands. 'Put your grudges aside. We can't safeguard you at separate locations, so you're here, till this ends. Make the best of it, please. Do you understand?'

Neither woman speaks, so I take silence for assent and explain the arrangements. I'll take turns on guard duty with Eddie and Isla, in twelve-hour shifts. Our priority will be to chase every piece of information the community provides; in a place this small, someone must know the killer's identity.

The atmosphere remains hostile when the meeting ends. Gemma and her daughter retreat to separate rooms, leaving me free to check on Luke. He's alone when I go upstairs, sitting up in bed. He still looks unnaturally pale, but seems aware of his good fortune. I can tell he'd rather be left alone to recover, but I've given him time to recover. It's my job to ask difficult questions and I can see him squirming when I try and find out why he went outside last night.

'I heard noises in the yard, then someone set on me, the minute I went into the barn.'

'Did you see who it was?'

'I dropped my torch. Someone punched me in the gut, then I was on the floor. I tried to hit back, but he kicked my head, while I was down.'

'You're certain it was a man?'

He nods vigorously. 'He had me in a chokehold, on the ground. A woman couldn't have done that.'

'Can you guess who it was, from how they moved, or their voice, or even their smell?'

The lad looks even more uncomfortable. 'I didn't hear him speak, the whole time. I must have dropped my phone when it happened. I haven't seen it since.'

'Well done, remembering that much. You should rest, until you feel strong enough to get over to the hospital for that head X-ray.'

'I'm fine, there's no need.'

'Go anyway. Better safe than sorry.'

I'm about to leave Luke to rest when footsteps pound up the stairs and Ivan Teague appears on the landing. The lad's too preoccupied to say hello, muttering that he's only just heard about the attack. He hesitates before entering the room, but Luke appears relieved to see him. They've been playmates since birth, the only lads of roughly the same age on St Martin's. Island friendships are sometimes born from necessity instead of a genuine connection, but I can tell Luke's glad to see someone he trusts, instead of being quizzed by a police officer. He's faced so much trauma, he's probably desperate to offload to his friend. The young men's conversation follows me down the stairs. Ivan is only offering his support, but their voices are hushed, as if they're exchanging secrets.

47

It's 9.30 a.m. when I decide to set Dave Carillian free. He can't have carried out the attack on Luke last night, and we have no hard proof the man's involved. Our only evidence against him is the stain on his kitchen floor, which could be from a paint spill, just as he claimed. I'll get it checked by the forensics team when help finally arrives, but it's not a good enough reason to subject an elderly man to another day of confinement. Isla's voice is flat with disappointment when I call her, but I can't waste an officer's time guarding Carillian all day. We've all questioned him, but there's been no fresh information.

I spot a new email on my phone just as I ring off, from the Serious Fraud Office. They've run Neil Kershaw's name through their records, and the truth is interesting. The vineyard owner made millions from working in finance, then became a venture capitalist, asset-stripping businesses for big returns. He changed his name by deed poll after travelling abroad.

I already knew he'd lied about his past, now I need to find out why.

The harvest is in full swing outside the kitchen window. Pickers loom from the fog-bound air, bearing sheaves of flowers, destined to adorn Christmas tables on the mainland. When I go inside the cutting shed, Maria Austell is hard at work, even though she's been awake most of the night. She cuts broken stems from each bloom, her movements deft, like she's been handling flowers all her life. Her smile is dazzling when I thank her for taking care of Luke, giving me the impression that she would gladly help anyone in a crisis.

Will's voice drifts from the field, telling the pickers which furrows to reap. It surprises me that after many years away, he's prepared to help the Minears, potentially putting himself in danger while they're under attack. Plenty of people would have withdrawn from the threat, but him and his wife seem fearless after their time in warzones.

The atmosphere inside the farmhouse feels like a battlefield too. There's an uneasy truce between Gemma and Amy, who looks braced for the next attack. I'm guessing the teenager missed breakfast, because it's only mid-morning yet she's loading a plate with bread, cheese, and fruit. She makes no attempt at conversation before bolting back upstairs to the room she occupied until a few months ago. I'd like to question her about Neil, but not until she's cooled down.

I find Eddie hunched over the sash window in the

living room. He's using an electric nail-gun to secure it, so it can't be opened from the outside.

'Neat work, Eddie. Don't any of the windows have locks?'

'None at all, but I'm not surprised, boss, mine are the same at home. Has there ever been a burglary in Scilly?'

'Not in living memory. Have you spoken to Gemma this morning?'

'She clams up whenever I go near; the only person she trusts is Hazel Teague.'

I hear a new sound while his words register. Nina's violin is playing an old pop song, with a piccolo echoing the melody. Ethan Minear's playing matches his delicate appearance, the notes faltering, yet perfectly in tune. I'm glad Nina has gained the kid's trust, but there's no guarantee he'll talk. I leave Eddie making the place secure, glad he's enjoying the task. He seems happier with practical work after the frustrations of multiple interviews that led nowhere.

I'd like a catch-up meeting with Isla, but she's patrolling the island now that Carillian's free, reminding the islanders to stay safe indoors after the latest attack. She'll check their whereabouts last night too, finding out who could have attacked Luke Minear. It takes me several minutes to find Gemma in the boot room, sweeping mud from the floor.

'Can we have a word?'

She jumps out of her skin, like I've fired a starter pistol. 'Jesus, I didn't see you there.'

'Sorry to scare you.'

She rises to her feet slowly. 'I can't sit still, so I'm doing some tidying. I hadn't noticed the place is filthy . . .' Her voice fades to silence.

'It looks fine to me. We can talk here, if you like?'

'Outside's better, I need a fag break.'

I follow her down a pathway, where she drops onto a low stone wall, then offers me a cigarette.

'No thanks, I quit in my twenties.'

'Me and Hazel gave up last year, but now I'm half-way through Scott's supply.'

'How are you doing, Gemma? You've had to handle so much.'

The gentle approach breaks down her defences. Her head drops onto my shoulder, fresh tears rising to the surface. There's little I can do except wait for her sobbing to end. Her eyes are red and swollen when she looks up at me again.

'Sorry I've been such a bitch, I just can't make sense of it. Scott was arrogant sometimes, but he wasn't a monster, and Jade's just a kid. She never hurt anyone.'

'We're making progress. I should have news soon.'

She sits upright again, dragging in another mouthful of smoke. 'I loved the old bastard, that's the trouble. I can't imagine life without him.'

'I know you're in pain, but why are you so mad at Amy?'

'Neil's a bloody cradle snatcher, yet she acts like he's God's gift. I can't make her see sense.'

'She's scared right now, just like you.'

'What can I do about it?' She gazes at the muddy ground. 'Amy wanted me to leave Scott and start a new life, and maybe she was right. I haven't been much of a mother, always working, never listening.'

'Do you think someone could be targeting you, not Scott? I've heard Saul Heligan's still got feelings for you.'

Gemma gives a slow laugh. 'Saul's the one person on this island that would never hurt me.'

I study her again. 'Scott did sometimes, didn't he? You wanted to leave, but couldn't get away.'

'He almost broke me, but he could be the sweetest man on earth.'

Gemma speaks about her husband in a fierce whisper. Her feelings are still so raw, her face is alight with emotion, but it doesn't reassure me. I've seen that look on killers' faces too. It's a blend of reverence and hatred for the life they've destroyed.

'Tell me more about Saul. You were together for a while, weren't you?'

'He called me his soulmate when we were teenagers, but he was a dreamer. Saul expected me to wait while he went off to drama school, then he begged me to leave Scott. He rented a house for us all in Falmouth, but I didn't love him enough to stay.'

'That must have been tough to accept,' I reply. 'Did you know he collects ships in bottles?'

'He gave me one as a present years ago. Saul's always loved the sea, that's why he came back to Scilly. The

Seven Stones' terrace is the best place to watch the tide come in, on a clear day.' She gazes down at her hands. 'Scott was the opposite of Saul. My husband didn't have a romantic bone in his body. He thought it was a joke that another bloke cared about me.'

'I'm sorry to ask, but do you think your husband had any affairs during your marriage?'

Her shoulders jerk with tension. 'The gossips chattered about it, but my husband loved me, even though we struggled. His flings never lasted more than five minutes.'

My question has touched a raw nerve. Gemma drops her cigarette on the ground, her body crumpling forward, her tears silent this time. She looks more fragile than ever, yet I can still imagine her lashing out at anyone that threatened her life with Scott. There could be someone on the island that hates her even more than they despised her husband.

48

Ethan is still with Nina and Shadow when afternoon comes. The dog is asleep by the fire in the living room, not even stirring when Ethan rubs his fur. Nina is sitting on the floor, watching the flames.

'What do you feel like doing now, Ethan?' she asks.

The boy rises to his feet immediately, pointing at the door.

'I'm afraid we have to stay inside today, but is there a game you'd like to play?'

Ethan walks to the bookshelves, where rows of farmers' almanacs and seed catalogues stand in rows. He selects a photo album and places it on the floor. Nina moves closer, so they can look at the pictures together. Dozens of family photos are contained inside. The first shows Ethan and Jade in their room upstairs, when they were still at nursery. They're surrounded by a sea of Lego, jigsaws, and toy cars. Ethan runs his finger over the image then shuts his eyes. He can almost feel the summer heat, and the rug's coarse fabric under his knees, inhaling the floral scent of his sister's hair.

'Pictures tell stories, just like words.' Nina's voice draws him back to the present. 'Do you want to show me what you saw, the night Jade left?'

Ethan glances at her face, but her gaze is steady, like there's nothing to fear. He takes time selecting the first image. It's of him and Jade last summer, leaning against a drystone wall, their body language identical, with sandy hair touching their shoulders, wearing matching smiles.

'Two peas in a pod, aren't you?' Nina whispers, like it's a joke between them. 'You were together when she ran away, weren't you? Can you show me what happened next?'

Ethan flicks through the pages, until he finds a picture of the top field before last winter's harvest, the land a dazzling gold.

'You went into the field together that night?'

He nods just once before flicking through the album's pages again. His childhood unfolds before him, a stream of open skies and shorelines, the ocean a long gash of blue. Suddenly his hands freeze in mid-air, then he slams the book shut. He caught a glimpse of his attacker's face, the sight so terrifying he can't open his eyes.

'What did you see, Ethan?'

The boy brings his knees up to his chest, his body rocking from side to side.

Nina's hand skims across his shoulders. 'You made a good start, Ethan, it's okay. I won't let anyone harm you. I'm going to play you some music, then you can go up and rest for a while.'

The sound of her violin fills the air, low and soothing, while his thoughts race.

49

The search warrant for Heligan's living quarters above the Seven Stones has arrived at last, the emailed document appearing on my phone. I leave a voice message for Neil Kershaw, asking him to come to the farmhouse this afternoon. I'm interested to hear the excuse for his lies, but not until I've searched Heligan's property. Isla is waiting for me on the lane when I arrive. The constable is peering at her phone, her expression puzzled when she finally looks up.

'I've visited nine families,' she says. 'They gave me tea and biscuits, on their best behaviour, like I'm an outsider.'

'What did you expect?'

'Honesty would be nice. Plenty of them hated Scott's guts, but it's like they've signed the Official Secrets Act.'

'It's often that way, remember? No one lives on a speck of rock in the Atlantic unless they enjoy their own company, and islanders hate giving up secrets. Did they give you anything useful?'

She scans her notes again. 'Elspeth Hicks was very upset about Luke's attack. I told her to stay at the farmhouse with the rest of the family, but she's worried about upsetting Stan's routine. He's agitated by all this, even though he doesn't understand most of it.'

'I'll call by later, to make sure they're okay. The only thing that matters now is finding out who's targeting the family.'

'Could it really be Saul? The bloke always seems so laid-back.'

'He trained at Bristol Old Vic – I bet Saul can act any part he chooses. We know he lived with Gemma on the mainland for a year, looking after Luke and Amy when they were babies, and he told me he collected ships in bottles. If he never got over Gemma rejecting him, he may still want to punish her.'

Isla looks uncertain, even when she hears more about the man's long infatuation. Saul may seem good-humoured, but he's been too interested in the investigation from the start, and the killer's calling cards bother me too. The young constable looks glad to have a change of task when I ask her to help me pay a visit to the pub.

The landlord is polishing the bar when we walk inside. He's dressed in an emerald-green shirt, with a crimson scarf round his neck, his cowboy boots polished to a high shine. It takes imagination to picture a middle-aged dandy like him waiting in the dark to attack an eighteen-year-old boy, but the killer's theatrical flourishes match his larger-than-life personality.

'Good afternoon to you,' he says. 'The weather may be cold, but my inn is always warm. What can I get you?'

'We're not drinking, thanks. It's just a few questions, if you don't mind.'

'I'm always glad to help.' He gestures for us both to sit at the bar.

'I still need to know more about your relationship with the Minear family.'

'Haven't we exhausted that subject?' He puffs out a breath of air. 'I get on fine with all of them. A publican can't afford enemies.'

'Did you ever fall out with Scott?'

'I never barred him from my pub, if that's what you mean.'

'People say you've never got over Gemma. Is that true?'

Saul frowns back at me. 'It took me a while, I freely admit. I hate seeing her unhappy, like any old pal, but our romance ended years ago.'

'Can we see your collection of ships in bottles, please, Saul?'

He looks startled by the change in direction. 'I took them to a charity shop years ago, but I still love the craftsmanship. That's why I bought one for the bar from Dave Carillian.'

'How come you got rid of your whole collection?'

'I don't need models to remind me of the sea these days. The ocean's right outside my window, just like when I was a kid.'

'Your parents farmed here, didn't they?'

His smile fades. 'Until they grew too old. My mother passed years ago; Dad's in a care home now, in Penzance.'

Heligan's statement echoes the facts of life here: island existence becomes harder as you age. There's only one nursing home in Scilly, so plenty of families have to visit their elders on the mainland, when the burden of care becomes too much.

Isla looks up from her notebook. 'Scott Minear bought your parents' farm, didn't he? It's the land above Highertown Bay. Their farmhouse is a holiday cottage now, isn't it?'

'I sold it for a fair price. The capital helped me to buy this place.'

'It must have been painful, losing your family's land.'

'Can you see me wading through boggy fields?' he replies, in a light voice. 'I swanned off to drama school with no intention of growing flowers. I expected to be a TV star, but ended up doing voiceover work and pantomimes. My only regret is that I chased the dream for too long before coming home.'

'You came back to St Martin's to keep an eye on Gemma, didn't you?'

He hesitates before replying. 'I was born here; I had a right to come home. The islands are in my DNA.'

The landlord's friendly attitude dies when he hears about our search warrant, but Isla is enjoying herself, after the disappointment of releasing Carillian. Her eyes glitter, as if she expects to find enough incriminating evidence to arrest the man immediately. We do a rapid search of the bar first, looking for anything to link him to the crime scenes. The carpet is threadbare, the ceiling yellowed by years of smoke from the inglenook fire, but the place still has a raffish charm. Velvet curtains cover the entrance doors as a draught excluder, but they also turn the bar into a theatre set, with villains and heroes waiting in the wings. Heligan's mood worsens when we set off to search his living quarters upstairs. He makes a show of reading a newspaper in the bar, but I can tell he's rattled.

Isla works at lightning speed while I scan the lounge again. I'm looking for anything to reveal Heligan's motives, but it still seems like the domain of a man whose entire life is played out behind the bar of his pub. Isla is ferreting through kitchen drawers, as if secrets lie hidden between his knives and forks, yet the facts are simple. Gemma never fully returned his affection, and Scott snapped up his family farm, increasing his monopoly over the island's farmland.

It's only when I leaf through the postcards and bills stacked on his mantelpiece that the landlord's old romance resurfaces. There's a monochrome photo of two teenagers with arms entwined, standing in the flower fields. Gemma Minear looks beautiful, with blonde hair pulled back from her heart-shaped face. Heligan is dressed in faded jeans and a leather jacket, like a young movie star. When I turn the photo over the words 'me and you' are scribbled in ink that turned sepia years ago. Could the man's feelings for his old girlfriend really make him kill her husband and attack her kids? It runs through my mind that he and Gemma could have hatched a plan to kill Scott together, but the idea is so far-fetched, I dismiss it immediately.

I go on searching among Heligan's old-fashioned furniture, under chairs and rugs, for another hour. I can't find any ships in bottles, and it's possible that he told the truth about giving his collection away. There's nothing of interest in the two bedrooms, apart from old theatrical posters tacked to the walls, advertising shows that closed years ago, and the dry smell of loneliness.

50

I leave Isla to complete the search alone so I can speak to Neil Kershaw, who has arrived at the farmhouse. Another layer of fog is swirling inland, cocooning me in a world where sounds are muffled and sightlines reduced to zero. I'm walking too fast when I hear someone approaching from the other direction. Nina and I come to a halt, our bodies almost touching. The case may be spinning in circles but the sight of her lowers my stress levels instantly. She looks tall and elegant, even though she's wearing everyday clothes; a waterproof coat, faded jeans and wellingtons, her chocolate-brown hair caught in a ponytail. It's her eyes that make the biggest impact. They're such a clear amber they seem to look straight through me.

'Why aren't you indoors, keeping safe?' I ask.

'You weren't answering your phone, so I had no choice. Ethan's at crisis point. I can't keep pushing him, Ben.'

'He needs Jade at home, that's why. I'm certain he knows what happened.'

'Ethan can't tell us anything yet. I won't be responsible for hurting a vulnerable child.'

'He needs you supporting him. Can't you see that?'

Anger swirls in her eyes, like the ever-present fog. 'I'd never neglect a vulnerable child, and you're not my supervisor, remember?' She turns on her heel, about to march away, until I grab her arm.

'What the hell's wrong?'

'You don't listen to me. That's a problem for us going forwards.'

'We'll have to talk about this later. I need to work.'

She raises her hands like I'm a lost cause. 'You never see the gap between us. It's getting wider all the time.'

'I'm running a murder investigation, Nina.'

'That makes no difference. You're always out of reach.'

'Why didn't you say if you've been upset?'

'I've tried often enough. I hoped we'd grow closer, but it never happens.'

'Is this about my past?'

She frowns at me. 'I make mistakes too. Why stay together if we can't communicate?'

'We'll discuss it tonight, I promise. Let me walk you back to the farm.'

The pair of us march down the lane in silent lock-step, until we reach Minear Farm. I'm about to speak again when she vanishes indoors, too angry to say goodbye, and I'm left floundering. I can't explain why it's so hard to express my emotions, to her or anyone, but that's irrelevant now. I have to forget the conversation and focus on the case.

Neil Kershaw is waiting with Amy when Eddie and I enter the Minears' living room. The girl's flame-red hair looks wilder than ever today, her image contrasting with Kershaw's show of clean-cut respectability. He could be a teacher, counselling a sixth former, yet she's clinging to his arm. Amy gives me a look of dislike before leaving the room, and the man's hostility last night has been replaced by rigid politeness when he sits opposite us and begins to speak. The guy's record of lying makes me glad to have Eddie at my side to witness his statement.

'I haven't been completely open, I hope you'll forgive me for that. My past is nothing sinister, I promise.'

'Go ahead, I'd like to hear what you have to say.'

Kershaw's hands are clasped tightly in his lap. 'My background's in finance, not winemaking, but the stress of bond trading exhausted me, so I went travelling for two years. When I came home I did a course on winemaking, but no one would take a novice seriously, so I pretended to have experience. The rest is just beginner's luck.'

'Why did you change your name?'

'For a fresh start.'

'You said you inherited the cash to buy your land.'

He squirms in his seat. 'I'd made enough myself, from stocks and shares.'

'How stupid do you think we are, Neil?' I lean

297

forward to eyeball him again. 'The SFO are checking your finances right now. You've been dodging the taxman for years, haven't you? That could land you in prison.'

'I never broke any laws.' Kershaw's face remains calm, but there's panic in his voice.

'I bet you know every loophole. Your whole life story's make-believe, but it hurt you when Scott and Gemma criticised your relationship. Do you hate Amy's family enough to go after them?'

His mouth flaps open. 'I came to St Martin's for a fresh start. That's not a crime, is it?'

'Stay here, until further notice. Don't go anywhere without our permission.'

Kershaw's body language is tranquil, but the look in his eyes is like a trapped fox, hunting for an escape route.

51

Ethan is alone in the safety of his room with Shadow dozing at his side, paws in the air, taking an afternoon nap. The dog wakes immediately when footsteps tap upstairs, and someone knocks on the door.

When Lauren Paige appears, Ethan feels glad. She's pretty, with a cloud of curly hair and a gentle smile. She used to babysit for him and Jade, and still calls at school to see them each week. He remembers playing Frisbee with her on the beach, and going on beachcombing expeditions, but Shadow seems upset. The dog barks at full volume until Ethan grabs his collar.

'Dogs never like me,' she says. 'Which is weird, because I'd love one.'

Shadow calms slightly, until Lauren steps closer, making him bark even louder. He only quietens when she sits down at the far side of the room, leaning her back against the wall, her expression watchful.

'I thought we could hang out for a bit, if you like. I brought a pack of cards.'

Ethan likes Lauren's soothing voice, and the tangle of

friendship bracelets on her wrist, the same as Jade's, but she looks on edge.

'I'm sorry about your dad, Ethan. You must be feeling so sad right now.'

The boy blinks in surprise. Lauren is talking like he's a grown-up, her serious tone forcing him to listen.

'It'll hurt less after a while, I promise. The thing I wanted to say is that you can choose what kind of person to be. I only just real-ised that. You can be good or bad, kind or cruel. It comes down to making good choices. Your dad made some big mistakes.'

Ethan is uncertain how to react. He feared his father while he was alive, but loved him too. It bothers him that Lauren seems upset, her light-blue eyes glossy with tears.

'He hurt innocent people, but you don't have to be the same. Do you get what I'm saying?'

The boy nods, even though he doesn't understand. She hesitates before talking again, like an actor with stage fright.

'Your dad behaved like a monster sometimes. I overheard him bullying Mum to sleep with him when my Dad was in hospital. She refused, of course, and Dad only found out after he came home.' She pauses, then shakes her head. 'I probably shouldn't say any of this. You're too young to understand; Ivan's the only person that really gets it.'

Ethan tries to smile, even though he's confused.

'We've all done bad things, but your dad did worse. He got what he deserved, Ethan. You'll realise that one day.'

Lauren moves closer, with the pack of cards in her hand, but the sudden movement upsets Shadow again. The dog snarls at her, releasing a low growl as she backs away.

52

Instinct tells me to remain at the farmhouse as darkness arrives, and keep my two officers safe indoors too, now that Isla has returned. My first action is to tell them that Neil Kershaw has joined the growing tally of people we need to keep at the farmhouse. He'll have to co-exist with Gemma, until all his secrets are exposed. Black air presses against the window when I return to the kitchen, the atmosphere outside almost as oppressive as Amy's stare. We're alone in the room, but she doesn't bother to say hello, her movements jittery. The girl's red hair spills over her shoulders, make-up circling her eyes in dark smudges. I'm expecting a torrent of teenage fury, but her voice is level when she finally speaks.

'Why are you bullying Neil?' she says, stepping closer. 'He's got nothing to do with it.'

'It's my duty to report anything illegal. Surely you can see that?'

'Neil's the gentlest man alive,' she says, distress

registering on her face. 'It was my father that punched him, not the other way round. Dad cared about me and Luke when we were small, but that changed as we grew up. He expected us to work every spare moment.'

'Is that why you took the boat out that night?'

'I could handle long hours in the fields, but not the cruelty and humiliation. Mum just swallowed it. I didn't want to be a doormat like her after he started hitting me, and Jade's got the same mindset.'

'Your father abused you all, psychologically and physically.'

'It kept us on our toes, that's for sure.' The girl is fiddling with her hair, unable to keep still. 'Neil's so kind, I don't care about his past.'

'That's irrelevant while your family's under attack.'

Her voice drops to a whisper. 'The person with the biggest reason to kill Dad is Mum, isn't it? She's self-destructive, and addicted to booze. It made her accept all the shit he doled out. I remember them dancing together at parties, madly in love, but I was tiny then. They attacked each other for years.'

The girl falls silent when her mother appears out of nowhere. Gemma looks ghostly in her grey tracksuit, her eyes haunted, and the effect on Amy is powerful. She struts away, as if some law of physics prevents them from occupying the same room. Amy may be keeping out of her mother's way because the threat of violence still exists.

It's the first time I've ever heard a daughter accuse

her own mother of cold-blooded murder, but Gemma's appearance seems to prove Amy's point. Scott's widow looks like a prisoner already. The light in her eyes is missing, her drab clothes suitable for a lifer on kitchen duty. Gemma ignores my presence once we're alone. Her movements are slow and deliberate as she prepares the evening meal for her divided family. When she lifts a packet of spaghetti from the work surface, her gestures are so mechanical, it's like she's in a trance.

53

Ethan carries a tray of food up to his brother's room with Shadow at his heels, both glad to escape the tense atmosphere downstairs. Luke is propped up in bed listening to the radio, his face lighting up at the sight of them.

'That dog's crazy about you, Ethan.'

Luke hauls himself upright, resting the tray on his lap. Ethan can tell that every movement hurts, a trace of blood visible on his bandaged hand.

'It looks worse than it is,' his brother says. 'Stay here for a bit, can you? Keep me company.'

Ethan settles on a chair, surprised when Shadow leaps onto the bed, curling up by Luke's feet.

'Great looking dog, isn't he? He's like one of those Siberian huskies that run for miles through the snow.'

Ethan studies Shadow again, imagining him in an icy forest, dragging a sled. Luke doesn't seem interested in his bowl of pasta, only swallowing a few mouthfuls before pushing the plate away.

'Can you do me a favour, mate?' he asks. 'The police can't

find my phone but it must be in the yard somewhere. Find it for me, can you? I need to speak to Ivan again and Mum wants me to rest. She won't lend me hers.'

Luke's face is serious, as if Ethan's help is a matter of life and death.

'Don't leave it too late, bro. It's not safe out there, remember?'

Ethan gets to his feet immediately, his brother's murmured thanks following him across the landing. Luckily there's no one in the kitchen when he peers at the dark outside, then twists the door handle. He tries again, but it refuses to budge. He's still standing by the door when the young policewoman appears. She doesn't look much older than Luke and Amy, with black hair and a thin, intelligent face.

'We have to stay indoors, Ethan,' she says. 'Why not come and watch TV with me and your mum?'

The boy does as he's told, but Luke has never asked for a favour before. Ethan's determined to do as he asked, because he can't help Jade. But he'll have to wait until everyone's asleep.

54

I reach Nina's cottage later than intended, after a call from DCI Madron. My boss likes things to happen with split-second precision, but murder investigations take time, particularly in a community that hates interference. I'm still mulling over details when Nina opens the door. If she's nursing a grievance about this afternoon's tense conversation, there's no sign of it. She reaches up to kiss my cheek, then leads me into the kitchen. I'm grateful she's prepared another meal. Nina's passion for food is always a bonus, and the fish pie smells amazing. I pour us both a glass of wine, but she waits until we're seated before mentioning the case.

'Sorry if I overreacted earlier. I can't counsel Ethan, but I'm happy to spend time with him. He's got real musical talent. He could make a career out of it one day.'

'Maybe he'll find a way to talk to you, if he relaxes.'

'I won't force him.'

I change the subject, to avoid covering old ground.

Nina looks great, as usual, that sweep of dark hair framing her oval face. One of her best talents is her ability to surprise. She can make me laugh, then prick my conscience moments later. She keeps me guessing with no effort at all, and it helps that the attraction between us never seems to fade.

'Want to finish your wine by the fire?' she asks.

Nina curls up in an armchair, while I take the sofa. It looks like she's giving me a reprieve, prepared to tackle our differences another day, but her expression has changed. I can hear the sea hammering the shore, even though the windows are closed, and the stakes have risen. I could lose her if I put a foot wrong.

'Ask me whatever you like, Nina. I'll do my best to answer.'

She gives a measured smile. 'Or you could volunteer information for once, without me dragging it out of you.'

'Where do I start?'

'Tell me a secret, from the past. Something that changed your life.'

I put down my wine, focusing my gaze on the fire, letting my mind wander. 'The islands felt like paradise as a kid. I was always outdoors with Ian or Zoe, swimming, or beachcombing. Our parents were happy too. Dad was big like me, slow to anger, keen on books. He loved his job, but he knew the risks.'

'Was he like Ray?'

'Three years younger, and more outgoing.'

'And you loved him?'

'Of course.'

'Say the words, if you like. It won't kill you.'

'I loved him, yeah. We were similar, I suppose.'

My speech runs out suddenly. I've reached this point before, almost finishing the story, until my conscience trips me up. I knock back another mouthful of wine. Nina looks serene while I'm floundering.

'It's okay, Ben, take your time.'

'My father took risks at sea. I only found out years later that he was famous for it. Mum didn't earn much as a part-time teacher, so he sailed out to the Atlantic Strait in bad conditions, just to buy us football boots and send us on school trips. I didn't even thank him for it. I just assumed he'd come home safe every time.'

'Most kids would feel the same.'

'I let him down in a big way. Dad had to fight so hard to buy his own trawler; he hoped me or my brother would join him at sea, but neither of us wanted to fish.'

'You had to follow your own paths.'

'The sea was in his blood, I know it hurt him. Dad worked on his father's trawler for the first time at fourteen, and he asked me to give it a try at the same age. I agreed to go along, then got cold feet; I didn't fancy wasting five days of my summer holiday in that stinking hold, gutting fish. I had a rugby match to play and Zoe was throwing a party.' The words catch in my throat, reducing my voice to a whisper.

'What happened when you refused?'

'A guy from Tresco took my place. He was twenty-three, married, with a one-year-old. Dad was so pissed off he didn't say goodbye to me the morning he left. I was at Zoe's party the night his boat went missing. He sent out a mayday, but it was too late. All five crew members missing, presumed drowned.' I don't want to see Nina's expression, so I keep my gaze fixed on the hearth. 'I expected to get the blame, for a man dying in my place, but no one said a word. The bloke that stood in for me was called Steven Yarrow. His wife left the islands with their baby soon after his funeral, too broken to stay. I'd have preferred a stretch in prison to all that controlled misery.'

'A storm took that boat, remember. It wasn't your fault.'

'Logic's fine, but the facts don't change. Steve Yarrow would still be here if I'd honoured my promise.' I blink my eyes shut for a second. 'That's enough stories for one night. Maybe I'll open another bottle. How come you're not drinking?'

'I'm not in the mood. It's your turn to ask me for a secret.'

'Go on then, surprise me.'

'It's a big one. Do you promise not to share it?' she asks, leaning forward in her chair.

'I'll do my best. Are you a spy, or a genuine Italian princess?'

'It's nothing that daft, I promise.'

'What then?'

'I'm ten weeks pregnant.'

I stare back at her, open-mouthed. 'You can't be, you've been taking the pill.'

'Remember that stomach bug I had? It must have happened then.'

I let the idea register before speaking again. 'So we'll be parents by next summer?'

'It looks that way, if you agree.'

My thoughts spin back to Stephen Yarrow's child, and the apology I never gave his family. Relief mixed with happiness must show on my face, because Nina's smile has returned. I understand now why her wine glass stands untouched on the coffee table, and why she reacted so powerfully to the idea of me keeping secrets. She needs to trust the father of her child one hundred per cent. I want to pick her up and whirl her round the room, but it's the wrong time. I choose a long embrace instead, with my face buried in her hair.

55

Ethan hears the house fall quiet. Amy has stopped pacing across her room next door, his mother is in bed, and the policewoman is in the living room. When he looks up from his pillow, moonlight shifts across the ceiling, like a torch beam flicking back and forth. His body can't relax, even though Shadow is sleeping peacefully. The dog barely stirs when he gets up. He hates letting Luke down, but there was no chance of escape with the policewoman watching, and now he's afraid to go outside. Whoever attacked Luke in the cutting shed may have come back. He must wait until morning to search for his brother's phone.

The fog has returned. When he looks outside, it's even thicker than before. The cutting shed is thirty metres away, but he can't see its roofline, the entire building hidden from view. It reminds him of running to school with Jade in winter, their breath condensing into clouds, but this is different. Fog has smothered the farmhouse for days, making it hard to breathe.

Ethan's about to go back to bed when his heart kicks

against his ribcage like a snare drum. Jade is nearby, her pulse thudding at the base of his throat. He leans closer to the window, hands pressed against the glass. The boy stands there for a long time, but the whiteness never shifts. He only sees the bright flash of colour from the corner of his eye. Now the echoed heartbeat matches his own, its rhythm fast but steady. Jade's crimson scarf appears again, just for a second.

He's in a blind panic, ramming his feet into boots then grabbing his windcheater. Shadow is awake too, whining for attention, but he shakes his head. Jade is out there, waiting, and nothing can get in his way. Ethan crosses the landing without making a sound, but panic hits him again downstairs. Every window is nailed shut, and someone is bound to hear him soon. He rummages through coats hanging from a row of hooks until he finds his mother's keys. He sighs with relief. Ethan slides back the bolt, then sprints into the dark. His promise to find Luke's phone is forgotten as he scans the horizon for another splash of red.

56

It's 2 a.m. but my mind's still on overdrive. I'm sitting by the hearth in my dressing gown, imagining the future, while Nina sleeps. My house on Bryher is worse than shabby. It needs a complete overhaul, starting with converting the box room into a nursery. It's easier to list DIY chores than imagine being a dad. I need to talk to someone I trust, before the case swallows me again.

I feel no guilt about skyping Zoe in the middle of the night. We made an agreement in our teens to contact each other if we ever needed help, and the promise stands. She takes ages to answer, her peroxide blonde hair sticking up in spikes. My old friend looks younger and more vulnerable without make-up, her face blank with sleep.

'You complete bastard,' she mutters. 'I was having a beautiful dream about me and Dev, in a jacuzzi.'

'I need to talk.'

'At two in the morning, for fuck's sake? Is it about the case?'

'Not at all.'

She peers at me more closely. 'I need my beauty sleep, babe. Tell me what's up, pronto.'

'I was trying but you never let me speak.'

'So?'

'Nina's three months pregnant.'

'Why the hell didn't you say?' Her face splits into a neon smile, then the picture shakes from side to side.

'Stop jumping about and tell me what you think.'

'He'll be drop-dead gorgeous, a surfer dude that loves books. Oh my God, he'll be adorable.' Her voice is a breathless rush of enthusiasm.

'What if it's a girl?'

'She'll be even better,' Zoe replies. 'How do you feel?'

'Pretty good, but my house is a disgrace. The generator's buggered, and the kitchen hasn't been decorated since 1992.'

'Stop overthinking. You're having a baby, and you're so bloody lucky. I bet it just happened, with no effort at all.' Zoe's smile suddenly ebbs away.

'Have you and Dev been trying?'

'I'm on my second round of IVF, but let's not talk about that now. Congratulations, sweetheart, and smile, for God's sake. You'll be the world's best dad.' Her expression changes again. 'I don't want to put a dampener on things, but I tried calling you today. Do you know about the row between Will Austell's family and the Minears?'

'He never said anything.'

'I called Mum yesterday and mentioned Will was back. She was amazed, after so much bad blood between the families.'

'How do you mean?'

'Scott let the Austells rent a field for their caravan for years, then gave them only a few weeks' notice to clear off. He wanted to grow Grand Monarch flowers on the land. Will's parents were heartbroken. They tried taking him to court but ran out of money.'

'Will would have come back sooner, if he wanted revenge.'

'I know you two were close, but the guy's changed, Ben. Part of him's missing, isn't it? Before he started voluntary work, I heard he was fighting IS in Syria, volunteering on the front line.' The idea churns through my mind while she speaks.

The signal breaks down before I can reply. Zoe's delight about the baby is reassuring, but her point about Will Austell stays in my mind, even though he's helped the Minears ever since he came back to Scilly. I'm still considering the possibility that he's involved when my phone buzzes at my side. Isla is speaking too fast when she explains that Ethan has escaped again, leaving the back door open. I can hear Shadow howling at top volume, unhappy to be separated from the child.

Nina rouses from sleep when I grab my clothes, her eyes barely open when I tell her what's happened.

'He'll be looking for Jade,' she murmurs. 'Want me to come too?'

I make her promise to stay indoors then drop a good-bye kiss on her cheek.

The weather is working against me when I follow the path to Highertown, a new wave of sea mist rolling in like the tide. Ethan Minear has chosen a bad night to put himself in harm's way.

Isla looks edgy when I greet her in the kitchen, even though the situation isn't her fault. Shadow is still barking in the room above, the sound almost drowning out our conversation.

'Gemma's in a bad way, boss. Ethan going outside again could be the final straw.'

'Wait a second, I'll let the dog out. That row's making matters worse.'

Shadow exits the house like a speeding bullet when I open the back door, just as Eddie arrives. My deputy looks ready for action, despite his lack of sleep, and by now the entire household is awake. Luke and Amy are talking upstairs, their mother crying in the living room until Eddie goes to comfort her, his soothing voice drifting down the hallway.

Ethan's vulnerability lingers in my head when I step into the farmyard. He's attached to his sister by an invisible thread, unable to rest until he knows the truth. I look for his footprints but can only see dead flowers dropped by the pickers mingling with fallen leaves, until something shiny catches my eye. I hiss out a few expletives when I pick up the killer's latest offering. The vessel inside is a red Wayfarer dinghy, just like the one I saw Luke and Amy using a few years ago. The killer has left us a model of a boat owned by the latest victim's family, but I feel certain it wasn't made by Dave Carillian this time. The paintwork is patchy, the tiller off-centre, yet the craftsmanship matters less than the message. How did he lure Ethan outside, into the drenching fog?

The killer has left us different gifts each time. I'm still looking at the boat when my thoughts suddenly click into place. What if the message is so simple a child could understand? The killer may simply be announcing that he, or she, uses a boat to complete the abductions. Few mariners would be crazy enough to sail into dense fog, unless it's someone with local knowledge. When I look up again, Isla is close by, her face expectant.

'Let's check the harbour,' I say. 'We may have missed something obvious.'

I need to search the island's only bay where boats can moor, before the chance is lost. Isla pulls away as we run downhill; she'd beat me hands down in a sprint race, and is metres ahead when we reach the harbour. Disappointment hits home as I scan the handful of dinghies, skiffs, and cruisers. They all belong to people from St Martin's, until I catch sight of Jason Minear's fishing boat. He must intend to stay till morning, because it's on a long mooring line, rising and falling with the tide. Isla helps me haul it to the jetty. There's no one aboard, but it looks in decent order. The bait barrel stands by the fo'c'sle and its deck has been scrubbed clean recently.

'Hang on to the rope, Isla. I'll take a look onboard.'

The small craft rocks under my weight. Jason Minear's chaotic lifestyle hasn't affected his boat, which surprises me. Ropes are neatly coiled, the hydraulic hauling kit in good order, but I need to know why he's made the voyage. Any sane fisherman would stay in bed on a night like this. I switch on the light in the wheelhouse, scanning his navigation instruments and the tide table pasted to the wall, looking for anything that could link him to the crimes.

Jason's reduced lifestyle shows when I enter his cabin. He's been living here since Scott drove him away, the confined space smelling of booze and cigarettes. Clothes are piled in boxes, but there are few other personal possessions. The space is so tight I can't even stand up straight. It must have hurt to plummet from a comfortable lifestyle to a cabin with a single porthole.

Something catches my eye as I turn away. It looks like an old rag dropped in the corner, but on closer inspection it's a child's red bomber jacket, just like the one Jade wore the night she ran away.

57

Ethan wishes Shadow was with him for company. It's been ages since that quick flash of red shone in the dark; it looked like Jade, running through the farmyard, expecting him to follow. He wanders through the fog, eyes straining for another glimpse.

The boy is glad to reach Highertown. The lights are out in the Post Office and all the houses have their curtains closed, but he could find shelter in any one of them, even though he's not ready to abandon his search. Instinct makes him jog downhill towards the harbour. He takes a shortcut through the vineyard. Grapevines reach from the black earth like the gnarled claws of monsters buried underground, making him quicken his pace.

Ethan spots a light once he reaches Middletown. It's coming from the back of the Seven Stones pub, yellow light bleeding from a gap in the curtains. He catches sight of Saul Heligan when he peers inside. The man is fully dressed, an empty bottle of wine at his elbow. He's gazing at his computer like nothing else exists. Ethan's sure the pictures are of his mother, when she was young. Something scary in the man's expression makes him back away, sending a garden spade clattering to the ground. He's scrambling to his feet when Heligan appears, his face empty.

'What are you doing here, Ethan? The police want us all to stay safe indoors.'

The boy stands still, unable to respond.

'Come inside, I'll call your mum.' The landlord gives him an odd smile. 'Did you know that I wanted to marry her, once upon a time? But she had other plans. I've worked hard lately to make her change her mind.'

Heligan's tone sours when Ethan stays rooted to the spot. 'You can't just leave, without saying goodbye.'

The landlord reaches for his arm. Panic makes the boy kick out until he's free again, racing through brambles, with sharp thorns tugging at his clothes.

58

Friday 22 December

I can't guess where Jason Minear has gone. The only house with a light on is Suzie Felyer's, beside the school-house. The teacher may have left it burning by mistake, but the property has a direct view of the harbour, so there's a chance she saw the boat arrive. Isla and I hold a murmured conversation as we walk back uphill, aware the killer could be hiding in the fog, listening to every word.

'What do you know about Jason Minear?' I ask.

Isla lives on St Mary's, and despite being the most heavily populated island in Scilly, with over a thousand souls, it's still hard to keep secrets.

'Not much, boss. Only that he goes to Alcoholics Anonymous most weeks.'

The news surprises me. He seemed on a downwards path when I saw him at the Mermaid, using booze to drown his bitterness. His struggles must be common knowledge, because the islands' only AA meeting happens every Wednesday night at St Andrew's Church Hall, a handful of addicts filing inside, like penitents to confession.

The dim light strengthens as we approach the teacher's home. People rarely bother to draw their downstairs curtains in such a tiny community, and Suzie Felyer's private life is on full display tonight. The island's well-respected schoolteacher is holding hands with Jason Minear on the settee, their heads bowed close. Isla and me exchange looks of amazement. Why would such a pillar of the community choose one of the islands' most troubled souls?

Suzie looks tense when she finally answers her doorbell. It takes me a full minute to persuade her to admit us, her resistance only crumbling when I make an ultimatum.

'We can talk to you here, or at the community hall. It's your choice.'

The smell of Christmas hits me again when we enter her home; sugar, spices, and the cloying smell of dried fruit. It's another reminder that life has carried on regardless, while my team hunts for a missing child. I can tell Minear is sober when we finally meet. His face is pallid, and there's a sheen of sweat on his forehead. I'm braced for a full-on attack, like Scott would deal out, but he's retreating into his shell.

'Sit down, both of you, please,' I tell them. 'I had no idea you two were a couple.'

Jason looks embarrassed. 'We won't go public until my drinking's under control – right now people would lay bets on us breaking up. Gossip's the one thing we both hate about island life.'

'That's your choice, but you didn't give me the full picture about Jade.' I pull his niece's jacket from inside my coat, wrapped in an evidence bag. 'She was wearing this the night she disappeared. We found it on your boat.'

Suzie Felyer touches his shoulder. 'Explain properly, like you told me just now.'

'I sailed here late on Saturday night,' he says, his voice hesitant. 'Suzie lets me stay if I'm tempted to drink. I'd been doing okay, till all this – I didn't touch any booze for three months. Jade appeared around midnight, while I was mooring up. She said her and Ethan had been attacked. Someone almost caught her, but she managed to escape. She never saw the person's face.'

'Why didn't you say so in the pub?'

'I thought you'd arrest me,' he replies, his voice shaky. 'My brother took me to court for plenty of stuff I never did.'

'You should have walked Jade home.'

'I would have done, once she calmed down.' He stares at his hands. 'She was sick of Scott's punishments and Ethan was suffering too. Jade begged me to talk to her parents in the morning, but I said her dad would never listen. She vanished, when my back was turned, because I let her down. She left her jacket behind. I thought she'd run straight home. If she's been killed, it's down to me, for not chasing after her.'

I turn to the schoolteacher. 'Is all this true?'

'Jason told me tonight, like he said.'

'I should arrest you both for obstruction, but there's no time. Ethan's run off again. His life's in danger.'

'Let me join the search, please,' Jason murmurs, as fear registers on his face. 'Gemma keeps phoning me with accusations, but I'd never harm the twins.'

The misery in his eyes tips the balance. He chose the path most islanders would pick, without recourse to the law, hoping the situation would right itself. I'm almost certain he tried to help his niece, but the killer's campaign is escalating.

'Stay here, both of you, till Ethan's found.'

Suzie Felyer is clutching Jason's hand. Maybe she sees him as another wayward child to nurture, but the couple's bond seems genuine. Saul Heligan must have seen Jason entering her house at night, not Scott. Anyone could make the same mistake, the twins would look identical from a distance. The teacher's distress about Scott's death makes more sense too. She knew her boyfriend would never get any form of reconciliation with his twin. Jason still appears tense as we leave, as if his fears for Ethan have flooded his mind.

We're no nearer finding the truth. I suspect the killer has been keeping watch on the farmhouse, but something about Jason Minear's story strikes me as odd. The killer failed to catch Ethan or his sister, yet they overpowered Scott Minear and lifted his body onto the Devil's Table with no trouble, then launched a vicious attack on Luke.

Grabbing the twins should have been easy compared to hurting two fully grown men, yet they both escaped.

'Do you think Jade's still alive?' Isla asks, once we're back on the lane.

'If she is, there are only two possibilities. Her abductor caught her, second time around, or she's staying away from home voluntarily. If she's a free agent, I bet she's been hanging around the farm, out of sight, keeping watch over Ethan.'

'But her dad was her only threat. Why not just go home?'

'Maybe her mum scares her too, or she doesn't know Scott's dead.'

My thoughts stall when we return to Minear Farm. The first property Jade would have seen if she ran inland is the old farm manager's cottage, where Will and Maria Austell are staying. I've never considered them as suspects, assuming they had no reason to hate the Minears, but Zoe's words echo in my head. What better reason to attack a family than to avenge your own? Will has had the ideal opportunity to track the Minears' movements since he arrived. I don't want to believe my old friend is involved, and Zoe's ideas are no more than a hunch, but I still want to question him about his feelings towards the family.

The fog is thinning, giving me a better view of the terrain, the land still thick with flowers. I feel uncomfortable about hammering on the door at this time but my nagging suspicion can't be ignored. Maria Austell is wrapped in a thick bathrobe, her gaze flicking from my face to Isla's like she's prepared for bad news.

'Sorry to wake you again,' I say. 'Can we see you and Will together, please?'

Maria hesitates before allowing us inside. She stands by the doorway, unsmiling, hands fiddling with the belt of her towelling robe.

'Will's not here, is he?'

'The bed was empty when I woke up just now.' She drops onto the seat opposite. 'He copes with his night-mares by going for a walk, to clear his mind. I thought he was recovering, but he's had a tough few days.'

'Why did he come back here? He must have bad memories of St Martin's.'

Maria looks confused. 'Maybe he needs closure, on the pain of leaving, and his life as a soldier.'

My friend seemed fine the last time we met, his past almost forgotten, but he was wrenched from familiar soil overnight, due to Scott Minear's greed. The atroc-ities he witnessed in the army and in Syria may have added insult to injury, and he's been trained to kill. He's young and fit enough to overpower a man like Minear, if his stored anger is finally erupting.

'Call him for us, please, Maria. We need to see him urgently.'

Her hands shake when she rings Will. I can hear the dialling tone at the end of the line, but no one picks up. When she puts the mobile back in her pocket, her face is white with panic.

59

Ethan is calm again now he's escaped from Saul Heligan. He's alone in the woodland behind Par Beach, able to breathe more freely as the fog clears. The island's beauty is visible at last, the sea floodlit by the moon, while wind gusts inland. When he lifts his head again Shadow is calling him. The dog must have escaped and be heading closer. Ethan's torch battery is fading, but he scans the trees for signs of Jade. Instinct makes him come to a halt, trying to feel her presence, his eyes closed in concentration.

When Ethan scans the woods again, there's another flash of red in the distance, and this time he knows it's real. Jade is a hundred metres away. He wants to call out but his voice is a dry whisper. All he can do is give chase, to find out where she's leading him, but she's running too fast. He scrambles over fallen branches, feet skidding on wet ground. He's breathless when he reaches the lane. His grandparents' house lies at the top of the hill. He can't understand why the place scares him, after many happy days there, but the feeling won't shift. He's crouching by the hedgerow when a new sound startles him.

Someone is close by, twigs snapping underfoot, their tread stealthy. If it was Jade, she'd call out his name.

There's nowhere to hide, until his gaze falls on Dave Carillian's house, where a light shines from a downstairs window. The footsteps behind him are gathering pace. He puts two fingers between his lips and releases a whistle, hoping Shadow will hear, then runs to the property. Ethan peers through a downstairs window into the old man's kitchen, where an overhead light glares. The room is empty, the other windows in darkness. He's certain someone's watching him, the skin crawling on the back of his neck. Now the footsteps are so loud he's afraid to look back. Instinct forces him to sprint into the dark, his pace fuelled by adrenaline and panic.

60

Maria Austell is blank-faced when she gives us permission to search her rented house. I scan the ground-floor rooms for anything to place my old friend at the crime scenes, while Isla checks upstairs. The property's emptiness proves that the Austells returned from their travels with few possessions, except their laptops, phones, and cameras. The two-hundred-year-old cottage appears to hold nothing incriminating, until I discover two ships in bottles on their mantelpiece, hidden behind some postcards. One is a British warship, the other a pewter-grey naval submarine. The sight of them increases my discomfort. Could my old friend be the one that's leaving the models at every crime scene? It takes a stretch of my imagination to believe such a gentle soul is involved, but he wouldn't be the first soldier to come home brutalised.

When Isla calls me upstairs she's flicking through a leather-bound sketchbook. It triggers memories of Will claiming that he'd be an artist one day, with pictures hanging in famous galleries.

'Take a look at these, boss.'

Will seems to have used the book as a visual diary. The charcoal sketches look beautiful at first, showing the Minears' flower fields. It's only when I look closer that they fragment into battle scenes. Soldiers lie wounded in the furrows, their bodies blown apart, almost hidden among knee-high blooms. My old friend must be going through hell, remembering so much carnage.

'He goes to Porth Seal sometimes, to clear his head. I'll ask Maria to contact us if he comes home. Let's go there now.'

Isla remains silent when we follow the lane along St Martin's northern coast. This is only her second murder hunt, and I can feel her excitement. She keeps pace as we pass Turfy Hill Point, then the empty beach at Frenchman's Graves, with Top Rock Hill lowering over us. The night is fading from black to grey, revealing ancient graves carved into the hilltop. We need the spirits with us tonight, to find Will at his favourite lookout point. The horseshoe bay is sheltered from the wind, with the far outlines of St Helen's rising from the sea. I can't see anyone until Isla points at the shoreline.

'That's him, isn't it?'

My old friend is hunkered by a boulder, his back turned. 'Wait here, can you, Isla? I've known him since we were kids, he might open up to me.'

Will looks startled when I clamber across the boulders, his expression defensive. 'Did Maria send you? There was no need to panic. I don't sleep well, that's all.'

'Ethan Minear's run away. I thought you might know why.'

'I haven't seen him since yesterday,' he says, staring out at the sea. 'I loved it here as a kid, but the place has changed, Ben.'

'Tell me more about what happened after you left St Martin's. You only gave me a few details.'

Will leans back against the rock. 'Dad scarpered, then Mum got sick. I spent my seventeenth birthday admitting her to a psychiatric ward.'

'That sounds hellish.'

'She stayed there for months, and the army seemed like my best option. It was a thousand times worse than I imagined. I heard a mate screaming like a baby, buried under a collapsed building in Helmand.'

'Didn't you speak to anyone when you left?'

'What's the point? Maria's helped me, but the past doesn't go away. If we'd stayed here I'd have trained as an artist, then come back to paint these landscapes, but anger's pointless. It only weakens you.'

'How did you feel about Scott, after he made you leave?'

He releases a hollow laugh. 'I wanted to beat the crap out of him for years, but the guy seemed to regret sending us away. Maybe he only wanted me and Maria for cheap labour, but it suited us to stay for a while.'

I'm not convinced by his story. Scott Minear was too

macho for benevolent gestures, apart from rare acts of generosity, like supporting the school. Will's body language is growing agitated, his movements jittery.

'Come to the community hall with us, Will.'

His eyes flare open suddenly. 'You're arresting me?'

'I'd just like you to give Isla some more details; she'll take your statement. You have reasons to hate Scott Minear, after the pain he caused your family. I can't rule you out until we have the full story of where you've been over the past three days.'

'Do you seriously think I'd hurt a young girl, then kill her dad? I may be screwed up, but I'm not evil.'

'Let's get moving, Will. It's warmer in the hall.'

He mutters curses as I lead him inland. My old friend's life collapsed because of Scott Minear's greed, starting a chain of events that cost his mother her sanity, but he's suffered too. The brutal violence he's witnessed may have left him unable to tell right from wrong.

61

No one answers when Ethan reaches Nina's cottage. He taps on her door again, praying she's at home. Shadow's barking has stopped. He can only hear the breeze rustling through the bushes. When he looks back down the lane no one is in sight, moonlight glistening on the surrounding fields, yet he doesn't feel safe.

The boy's system floods with relief when Nina finally appears. She's dressed in leggings and a T-shirt, her face puffy with sleep.

'It's late to pay me a visit, Ethan. Are you okay?' She reaches out to press a switch on the wall. 'A fuse must have blown. Come inside, you can help me fix it.'

Ethan is crossing the threshold when someone rushes out of the dark. He's bundled into the house, then shoved aside. The boy's head hits the wall with a sudden jolt. Nina cries out, then everything vanishes, as if the island's fog has conquered him at last, erasing every thought.

62

Will barely speaks when we escort him to the community hall. It feels uncomfortable leaving him there, but I can see how much he's changed. He was a wild spirit in our teens, hungry for adventures, with a quick smile, but his manner is taciturn when I ask him to describe his actions since Jade went missing to Isla. The young constable looks disappointed to be left behind, but someone neutral should interview him. I can't allow my past friendship to prejudice me, and I need to find Ethan before the killer can target another member of the Minear family.

Full daylight is still a few hours away when I follow the lane east. The sky is mid-grey and the landscape clearly visible at last, a mosaic of fields rolling down to the sea, while the high ridge of Turfy Hill rises to my left. On a normal day I'd stop to admire the island's beauty in the moonlight, but it gives me little comfort today. I still feel sure the cause of the violence lies inside the family. One of them knows the reason, but no one is willing to explain.

I've almost reached the farm turning when I hear Shadow calling at top volume. The incessant howling is close by, making me swear under my breath. Trust him to distract me when my sole focus should be on the killer. I yell his name, but the noise increases. It's possible that he's hunting for Ethan, after spending the past two days with him, so I set off at a jog. His baying gets louder as I run up May's Hill, but my dog only comes into sight when I reach Dave Carillian's house. He's sitting by the old man's porch, howling at full volume.

'Come here, you mongrel,' I hiss, but it makes no difference. The creature's attention is so fixed on the house, he doesn't even glance at me, and he's woken the owner. I can see a human shape moving behind the drawn curtains.

'Shut up, can you? I can't think straight.'

Shadow whines softly when he comes to my side, then runs back to Carillian's door, with ears pressed flat, as if he's chasing prey. I'm about to walk away when a figure looms out of the dark. Elspeth Hicks isn't carrying a torch, so familiar with the island's terrain she needs no illumination. The old woman is normally so calm, her panicked expression surprises me.

'What are you doing here, Elspeth? Everyone should be indoors.'

'Amy texted me,' she replies, her tone hesitant. 'Ethan's run off again, hasn't he? I'm afraid he'll get hurt.'

'I'll find him. Go home, please, and keep your doors locked.'

'I can't sit around waiting. I'm sick of this mess.'

The old woman's face crumples and I can guess why she's afraid.

'You're looking for Stan, aren't you? That's why you're here.'

Elspeth doesn't reply, still rooted to the spot, her face averted.

'Sit down for a minute and tell me what's happened.'

The old woman is slow to join me on a drystone wall; she's gazing back up May's Hill, where her house shines like a beacon. 'I've lied to you, Ben. I should have explained after Jade went missing, but it felt disloyal.'

'Keep going, Elspeth. I need to hear.'

'Stan refuses to go outside during the day. He hates bumping into people, when he can't speak or remember who they are, but it's a different story at night. I hear him leave sometimes, from my room upstairs.'

'You think he's involved.'

She presses her fingers to her lips, like she's trying to contain the words, but they bubble out anyway. 'His temper can snap at any moment, and he's so angry. Hazel says it's a common side effect when a stroke affects the frontal lobe of the brain. The tranquillisers make no difference. Normally it only lasts a few months, but Stan's mood gets darker every day . . .' Her voice tails into silence.

'He's hit you, so you're afraid he's attacking other members of your family?'

'Stan feels so locked out, I can see it in his eyes. For a man who loved to communicate, it must be agony.'

'You should have told me all this before.'

Tears leak from her eyes, but her voice is steady. 'I'm sorry, Ben. He was a wonderful husband, and now I barely recognise him.'

Elspeth's reluctance to give up searching for her husband and grandson shows in her slow gait when she trudges back uphill, but her presence soon leaves my mind. Shadow is still making frantic attempts to grab my attention. He quietens when I approach Carillian's house, as if I'm finally on the right track. I peer into the old man's lounge and kitchen, then shine my torch through his letterbox, catching sight of something on the stairs that makes my breath catch in my throat. It's possible that Elspeth was wrong. Her husband may have had nothing to do with the attacks, and my original suspicions about Dave Carillian were probably correct after all. Jade Minear is smart enough to leave a trail of possessions in her wake, because a child's bright-red glove lies abandoned on the bottom step.

63

When Ethan comes round he's lying on his back. His head rests on a carpeted floor, hands tied in front of him, his eyes blindfolded. He can't tell how much time has passed since reaching Nina's cottage. An overpowering smell fills his senses. He'd recognise it anywhere; it's the scent of jonquils, sweet and heavy. Ethan blinks his eyes, but only a needle of light pierces the darkness. Someone is whispering, the sound almost too quiet to hear. When he concentrates hard he recognises Nina's voice. It's so low and calm, it sounds like she's sharing secrets with an old friend, but she's talking to the attacker. Ethan hears someone move closer, the floor creaking a few metres away.

'Let us go, please,' Nina says. 'Neither of us saw your face. Untie us and leave, before Ben finds you.'

'Shut up, and let me think.'

The new voice is so strained Ethan can't recognise it. Silence floods the room, and his sister's presence overwhelms him. She's closer than ever. The sensation is so real, he can almost feel her warm breath on his face.

'Jade.' Her name emerges in a whisper, but there's no reply.

A long time passes before Nina speaks to the killer again. 'Something went wrong in your life, didn't it? Scott Minear hurt you so badly, you could never forgive him.'

'Don't tell me how to feel.'

'What did he take from you? Was it something precious?'

'I told you to keep quiet, you stupid bitch.'

Ethan hears Nina cry out in pain. Someone is kicking her, over and over. He can hear the thud of someone's boot striking her body as she calls for help. If the attack lasts much longer, she won't survive. The boy finds his voice at last. His wailing builds to a scream. He needs to distract the killer so Nina won't get hurt again, and suddenly he's the new victim. The first blow lands on his back, each impact worse than the last. Only Jade can save him now. She must be waiting somewhere in the dark, just out of reach.

64

'What have you done with her, Mr Carillian? Did you bring Ethan here, too?'

The old man blinks at me when he opens the door, as if my torch is blinding him. 'I've done nothing wrong.'

'I should never have let you go.' I barge past, then brandish the child's glove at him, his expression terrified. 'Was she here tonight?'

'I didn't lay a finger on her, I promise. Jade asked me for help.'

'If she's dead, tell me where you put her body.' Something snaps inside me when I march him to his kitchen, then force him into a chair. 'Tell me right now, or I'll beat the living shit out of you.'

'Let me go, please.' He tries to squirm away. 'Jade's been staying here, since she ran away. I knew the risk was high, but I couldn't refuse.'

'Why not?'

'I got hounded out of one community for no reason. I can't let the past stop me doing the right thing.'

'You should have brought her to me.'

'I tried, but she refused. She's afraid to face her mother. Jade thinks Gemma killed Scott, because they fought all the time. She was terrified of what might happen. The child missed her brother terribly, but couldn't bring herself to go home.'

I gape at him, and suddenly small details make sense, like the door slamming when I searched the place before. Jade must have hidden outside until I left. 'If that's true, why didn't you say?'

'I promised her not to tell anyone.'

'Her family think she's been killed, like her dad. They're going through hell.'

'I never intended anyone to suffer. Jade wanted to keep watch over Ethan, from upstairs. I couldn't turn her away.'

'Why did she come to you?'

'She knows no one visits me here. I let her sleep in the box room, and she spent most of her time looking out of the upstairs window, quiet as a mouse. She barely touched the food I left outside the door.'

'Where the fuck is she now?'

'Jade came downstairs a few hours ago, crying. She said Ethan was in danger. The girl must have dropped that glove when she ran outside.'

'Maybe you buried her under the floorboards.'

'You're hurting me, Inspector. Let go of my wrist.'

I don't like strong-arm tactics, but my patience has worn out. The old man expects me to believe that an eleven-year-old girl chose an outcast's home as her best refuge.

'Jade's looking for Ethan, that's all I know,' he mutters.

The old man's skin is papery with exhaustion when I finally leave. Someone should stay with him, but that would take time to arrange, and instinct tells me he's speaking the truth. The man has no faith in the authorities, after they failed to protect him before, and I know the threats Jade's been facing at home. The girl must have been desperate to reassure Ethan that she's safe. She may have left him messages in the hollow oak tree, the idea leading me down the lane. When I plunge my hand into the opening, my fingers close around another glass bottle, and my frustration deepens. The killer has left yet another taunt, but this time I don't care about preserving forensic details. I hurl it at the nearest tree, then listen to it shatter. Shadow reacts badly to the sudden noise. He snarls at me, before vanishing into the night.

65

Ethan can't feel any pain except a stinging sensation in his back. His skin throbs like it's been burnt, and his piccolo is no longer tucked inside his shirt. He relied on it to keep him safe, and now there's no protection at all. The attacker will come back, and Nina has stopped talking. There's an odd gurgling sound every time she inhales.

He keeps rubbing his head across the carpet, shifting his blindfold by a centimetre. He can see a few bin bags stacked against the wall, and his dad's favourite flowers on the carpet, their cloying scent filling his airways. He doesn't want to die on the Devil's Table, buried under hundreds of yellow blooms. When he tries to move, pain sears through him like lightning, making him cry out.

'We'll be okay, Ethan.' Nina's voice whispers. 'But if they come back, stay quiet, please. Don't try and protect me.'

'Who's doing this to us?' The boy's voice creaks like a hinge in need of oil, after his long silence.

'I don't know,' she replies. 'Are you hurt?'

'My back feels weird, and I've lost my piccolo.'

'We'll find it, I promise. Help's coming soon.'

When Ethan twists his neck, Nina is curled on her side, her skin chalk pale. He knows she's badly injured, and suddenly the fear he's carried since Jade vanished is replaced by anger.

Ethan can bring the attacker's face into focus at last. He saw it, the night Jade was taken, but he's blocked it out ever since. It appears for a moment, then vanishes again, before he can repeat the name.

66

Friday 23 December

I drop onto a stile to gather my thoughts. I can't believe that Stan Hicks poses a serious threat to his grandchildren, but someone on the island is intent on doing them harm, so I need to act fast. It's 6 a.m. and the flower pickers' alarm clocks will soon be ringing, announcing a new day. If Carillian was telling the truth then Jade Minear set off to find Ethan a few hours ago, and might have enlisted help. I remember Lauren Paige saying she babysat for the Minear twins, and Jade might trust her enough to go to her house. When I look east, the island's crescent shape is exposed, Lawrence's Bay curling round to Southward Carn. It may be a wild goose chase, but I can't give up hope.

The scenery barely registers when I jog downhill, winter fields passing in a flurry of yellow and green. My mind floods with memories. This is my chance to wipe my conscience clean for another man dying in my place. If I can find Jade and Ethan, their mother's grief will be less raw.

The sky is lightening when I reach the Paiges' home in Lowertown, its whitewashed stone reflecting pink light from the east. I'm about to hammer on the door when I spot someone sitting on the garden wall. It looks like Felicity from a distance, but when I get closer, Lauren's face is clouded by blonde ringlets. She's dressed in jeans and a thick sweater, smoking a cigarette. When she turns in my direction, I can feel the dislike in her stare.

'You're up early,' I say. 'Have you been with Ivan?'

She shakes her head. 'I couldn't sleep, so I came out here.'

'Why are you lying?'

The girl's face hardens suddenly. 'You haven't got a clue, have you? You're blind, like all the rest.'

'Explain what you mean, Lauren.'

'Jade's dad got what he deserved, and Gemma's no better. They both hit Jade for talking back a few weeks ago; she was covered in bruises.'

'Why didn't you report it?'

'Jade begged me to keep quiet. They'd have punished her worse, if people knew.'

'Why would Scott hurt his favourite child?'

'To break her spirit. He wanted all the power, and Gemma's so used to violence, she passes it on.'

'Who took Jade, Lauren?'

The girl ignores my question. 'Anyone on the island

could have killed Scott Minear. He loved hurting people, that's why.'

'She's in danger. If you know who's doing all this, tell me, right now.'

'I'm sticking to my promise.'

The girl's face contains misery, as well as anger. You'd have to be full of bitterness to withhold information about a missing child, or be protecting someone you love, and suddenly my thoughts swing in a new direction.

67

Ethan's back aches when he hauls himself to a sitting position. The boy's wrists are bound together so tightly his fingers feel numb. Plastic twine has been used to tie him to a wooden table that creaks whenever he moves. Ethan looks around for ways to free himself, but his blindfold keeps slipping down, blocking his vision again. He can't see much when he drags the heavy weight across the floor. There's nothing sharp enough to cut his ties, and the killer may be waiting just outside the door.

He wishes Nina would wake up, but it sounds like she's fast asleep. He listens to the ragged sound of her breathing. Ethan's hands grope in the dark until they land on the metal fire surround. Instinct makes him start rubbing his hands across the sharp metal. It seems to make no difference, but it's his only chance.

Ethan's wrists burn as he repeats the movement, praying the plastic cord will snap. His teeth are clenched with determination, even though he can no longer feel Jade's presence. Maybe he's imagined it all along. His sister would have freed him by now if she was alive. She can't fix his problems, for the first time ever. His eyes keep returning to the door, its shape outlined by a strand of yellow light. He grits his teeth and concentrates on getting free.

68

It's 6.15 a.m. when I reach Hazel's home. The nurse's passion for Christmas is still in evidence; the fairy lights around her front door flash brightly as dawn approaches. My new theory could be wrong but it still needs testing. Ivan Teague may have been deceiving everyone, for reasons he won't share. It's Polly who opens the door. The young girl is wearing a pink dressing gown, dark hair tangled, her cheeks flushed with embarrassment.

'Is your mum at home, Polly?'

'She must be helping someone, her medical bag's gone,' the girl murmurs, rubbing her eyes. 'Ivan's asleep upstairs.'

'I need to see him.'

She looks anxious as I rush past. The boy's room is empty, and it's clear he left in a hurry; the duvet's thrown back, a crumpled T-shirt lying on the floor. Half a dozen photos of Lauren Paige are tacked to the wall above his bed. The girl's angelic smile is nothing like her frown tonight.

'I didn't hear him leave. Do you think he's okay?' Polly stands in the doorway, watching me root through his possessions, reminding me that I'm breaking the law by searching without a warrant, but there's no other choice.

Ivan's bedroom could belong to any seventeen-year-old boy, with jeans and T-shirts filling his wardrobe, a pile of trainers heaped in the corner. He's taken his phone with him, and I can't find a single item linking him to the killing.

'What are you looking for?' Polly asks.

'I'll know when I see it.'

When I glance through the window I spot an old wooden shed lying between neat flowerbeds. It reminds me that Hazel said her son was always pottering about in there. It looks ideal for a teenager's refuge.

Polly follows me when I jog back downstairs then through the garden to the shed. Ivan may have been here with Lauren recently – the air is tainted with booze and cigarettes. The space is kitted out with hammers, drills and boxes of nails. It's only when I see a workbench in the corner that my pulse rate quickens. A pair of small glass bottles are waiting to be filled, and all the paraphernalia needed to construct the ships is spread out in an arc, from needle-thin brushes to spools of thread, glue, and tweezers.

It must be Ivan that's making the ships in bottles left at the crime scenes, too crude to be Dave Carillian's work. He's stolen items from the Minears' cutting shed too. There's a harvest knife in the pocket of an old denim jacket, hanging behind the door, with the initials 'G. M.' carved into its handle. I grab my phone to warn Eddie to keep the farmhouse secure. Ivan Teague is our new suspect, and Gemma Minear his next intended victim.

69

Ethan's wrists are bleeding, the skin chafed raw by his efforts to get free. He's about to give up when Nina speaks again.

'Keep going,' she whispers. 'You're nearly there.'

When he manages to slide his blindfold back and peer through the darkness, she's still white-faced. It feels like ages since the killer left, slamming the door on their way out, but time feels endless. He doesn't even know if it's day or night. Nina makes a hushing sound when a noise reaches them from outside. Someone with a heavy tread is crossing the gravel, getting closer all the time. Ethan wrenches his hands over the metal again, and the twine finally breaks, but it may be too late. The attacker is in the hallway, waiting outside the room. Nina still sounds calm when she calls out again.

'Punishing us won't solve anything,' she says. 'We're not to blame.'

Now someone's crying. The sobbing is so loud and raw, it sounds like the noise his mother made, after his dad died.

'Talk to me, please. I know you feel too ashamed to face us. Maybe I can help you.'

The weeping stops for a moment. When it starts over it's low and guttural, the killer gulping for breath between each sob.

70

The truth dawns on me as I leave the shed. It's hard to believe such a young man would turn into a vicious murderer, especially after feigning interest in joining the police, but he must have reasons to hate the Minear family. It strikes me as bizarre that he seems determined to wipe out the entire clan. Ivan could be attacking anyone that tries to help them. My hands are shaking when I press Nina's number on my phone, and when there's no answer, a flash of panic sets my teeth on edge. I'm about to leave when Polly Teague appears. There's no sign of teenage embarrassment now, her eyes glittering with anger.

'Why did you search our shed?' she spits out the words. 'You had no right.'

'It's police business, Polly. I need to find Ivan fast.'

'He's done nothing wrong.'

'How long has he been making those ships in bottles?'

'What do you mean?'

'I saw them just now, on his workbench.'

'I found some last summer on Top Rock Hill,' she says. 'I learned how to build them on the internet. They're mine, not his.'

'You can't defend him now, Polly. Where's he hiding?'

Suddenly she's a child again, begging for mercy. 'Leave him alone, please. It's not Ivan's fault.'

'Just tell me where he is.'

The girl's eyes cloud with tears, but her mouth shuts in a hard line, keeping her secret locked inside. I blunder through the gate, then spot a flash of red in the distance, as a fresh band of fog rolls in from the sea.

71

The attacker is still crying, outside in the hallway. They're safe for now, but Ethan can tell Nina's energy is fading, her words slowing down.

'Scott hurt so many people. No one will blame you for being angry.'

Ethan manages to slip his hands free. It's only when he crawls over to Nina that he sees how badly she's hurt: her face is swollen, and blood's leaking from the corner of her eye. One of her hands is injured too, making her wince when he unties her bindings.

The boy freezes when the crying stops. The attacker is pacing up and down the corridor, and the door could fly open any minute. Another flare of pain burns through him when he rises to his feet. He grabs a table lamp with a ceramic base to use as a weapon, then stands by the door, holding it above his head. He tries to ignore the pain in his back and remember that no one else can help him now.

Nina's eyes have shut, and he can no longer hear her breathing, her body motionless on the floor.

72

The flash of red grows clearer as I run. Shadow is galloping towards me, with something trapped in his jaws. He's fifty metres away when he swerves down the path to Nina's borrowed cottage, then comes to a halt. He drops the crimson scarf in the porch, then bays at full volume. Nina has kept the place locked up, yet Shadow seems determined to get inside, scratching at the door. There's no answer when I knock. The dog is still agitated, jumping up to bark in my face.

'Calm down,' I mutter. 'You're not helping.'

The curtains are closed, even though Nina must be awake, and suddenly my heart's in my mouth. No one could sleep through so much racket. I open the letterbox and peer inside. There's not much light in the hallway but I see a figure hunched beside the living-room door, with their back turned. I'm about to force my way inside when a woman's voice interrupts me. Hazel Teague is jogging up the pathway, clutching her medical bag, panic written all over her face.

'What's happened, Ben? I got a call, saying someone's been hurt, but the line went dead. I've been looking everywhere.'

'Me too. We need to get inside,' I tell her. The nurse is such a force for good on the islands, I can't hint that Ivan's involved until I have confirmation.

I'm certain that surprise is my best advantage, so I make Hazel stand back then hurl myself at the door. My second attempt does the trick, but the figure in the hall-way has vanished when my torch beam bounces from the walls. A sudden shattering noise reaches me before I go any further. When I barge through the living-room door, a male figure is kneeling down, and shards of pottery litter the carpet. I catch sight of Ethan Minear in the corner, and it's like I'm seeing double. Another blond-haired child is gripping his hand and relief floods my system; Jade must have found a way inside, determined to help her twin.

I grab the man's shoulder and drag him away when I see that he's leaning over Nina, who's lying on the floor. Ivan Teague's face is obscured by his hooded top, and I can see he's afraid. He struggles to pull away when I yell at him.

'Stay there, you're under arrest.'

Hazel looks shocked to see her son. There's confusion on her face; the nurse seems uncertain whether to comfort the teenager or the twins first. She touches Ivan's arm, then kneels in front of Ethan and Jade, cooing words of reassurance, leaving me free to check on Nina. She's curled in a foetal position, motionless. Her face is so messed up I have to stop myself dealing out the same brutal punishment to her attacker. She's almost unconscious, thoughts of our baby choking me when I grab her hand.

'Stay awake, sweetheart. Don't go to sleep.' One of her eyes is so bloodshot, the pupil's vanished. 'Where does it hurt?'

'Everywhere.' A broken laugh spills from her lips. 'Don't punish Ivan, it's not his fault.'

'Just hang on, all right? Help's coming.'

'I said things would change, didn't I?'

When her eyes close again, I can feel her slipping away. 'No, Nina, please.'

Hazel takes over, forcing me to release her hand. Ivan is crouched on the floor, his expression stupefied.

'You fucking monster. She never laid a finger on you.'

'It's not my fault.' His voice is a flat monotone. 'Scott's to blame, for everything.'

The boy shuts his eyes to block out my questions, then someone barrels towards me from the dark corridor, knocking me sideways. Hands close around my throat, stopping me breathing, and when I look up, Stan Hicks is bearing down on me. The old man's face is flushed with rage, but tears run down his cheeks. I lash out with my vision blurring. I'm still trying to get free when Stan bellows out a scream and his grip releases. Ivan is trying to pull him away, but it's Shadow that stops the attack. My dog has sunk his teeth into

Hicks's shin, unwilling to let go, until I grab his collar. He's still barking at top volume when I use a plastic tie to secure the old man's wrists. There's resignation on Hicks's face now, but I'm baffled. I can see why he wanted Scott dead, for ruining his daughter's life and stealing his family's land, but why attack the grandkids he adores, and how did Ivan get involved?

Eddie rushes through the door before I can make sense of it. We arrange medical help for Nina first, then summon Isla to take the twins back to the farmhouse. The two killers look different now; Stan's face is devoid of expression, but Ivan's is full of rage. Maybe the boy has just realised that years of his future could be spent in a prison cell. Hazel turns her attention to her son, after placing Nina in the recovery position. No matter what he's done, she seems determined to support him, her words too quiet to hear. I catch sight of the twins from the corner of my eye, still hand in hand, but they're not my biggest concern. Eddie will have to interview Jade, to find out if Dave Carillian's story holds water.

The only person I'm worried about right now is Nina. She's got a pillow under her head and a blanket to keep her warm, but she's stopped responding. All I can do is crouch by her side, waiting for the helicopter. Clear winter sunlight streams through the window for the first time in days, the fog finally lifting as Eddie leads Stan and Ivan away.

73

Ethan and Jade haven't spoken a word, but the boy is content just to be in his sister's presence. Now that she's here his bruises no longer hurt, and the odd sensation in his chest has gone, that echoed heartbeat finally silent. Jade's hair is damp from the mist outside, and her clothes are muddy, but her face is glowing.

The twins walk home in silence beside the police officer. The boy doesn't understand who's to blame, even though he saw his grandad being led away. Jade is all that matters. She looks thinner than before, and something else has changed since they raced across the field five nights ago. Her ever-present smile is missing. It only returns when she reaches inside her jumper to produce his piccolo.

'Where did you find it?' he whispers.

'On the lane just now. I knew you'd be missing it.'

'Why did you stay away so long?'

'I missed you so much, but I thought Mum had gone crazy. It was a woman that tried to grab me in the field, I was afraid she'd hurt me again.'

Jade's words take Ethan by surprise. Until now she's been the brave one, defending him from every enemy, but tonight the tables have turned. For the first time ever he took care of himself.

'Mr Carillian helped me,' she says. 'He showed me his ships in bottles, and let me sleep in his spare room. I could see home from his top window, so I knew you were safe. Are you angry with me?'

'I knew you'd come home.'

Ethan's voice is growing stronger; the words he's kept locked inside are finally surfacing. The next time someone asks a question, he'll speak for himself, instead of relying on Jade.

The twins walk at exactly the same pace; there's no need to look at each other, or speak again. The cloud of relief that surrounds them is thicker than the fog that's finally departing from the island's shores.

74

I'm in the lane when the helicopter flies over, my arms flailing like a windmill, guiding it to the field behind the cottage. Thank God it was at St Mary's Airport, about to make the first flight back to the mainland since the bad weather. Nina's drifting in and out of consciousness, mumbling words too quiet to hear. The engine's roar drowns every noise as the helicopter takes off. I'm squeezed into a corner when the island's chief medic, Dr Tremayne, places an oxygen mask over Nina's face, ripping her T-shirt to apply a heart monitor. For once in my life I can't run or swim or punch my way out of this. Nina's breath clouds her plastic mask, but the wounds on her face are horrifying. All that matters now is her recovery. If Stan Hicks damaged those perfect features, he deserved Shadow's attack, and more.

Nina's still alive when we touch down and I remember a first-aid trainer telling me that hearing is the last sense a victim loses, so I yell at her as the gurney races across the hospital car park, not caring who hears, just so she knows I'm there. Ginny Tremayne is grim-faced when they disappear into the treatment room. The doctor has been my GP since childhood; she gave me inoculations before I could walk, and she's also Isla's mother. I trust her to give excellent care, but that doesn't stop nausea from rising in my throat when I'm made to wait outside. I sit on a bench, staring at my clenched hands while I wait for news. The phone in my pocket vibrates with messages that I choose to ignore.

I'm still waiting when the doors at the end of the corridor swing open. My uncle Ray is unmistakeable, tall and big-boned like me, steel-grey hair cropped short. He's dressed in wellingtons, ancient jeans, and an oilskin, like he's returned from a long sea voyage. Ray doesn't speak when he drops onto the bench beside me, but his presence helps. The whole island will have heard that Nina's been airlifted to hospital. He must have launched his speedboat the minute the news reached Bryher.

The doctor's face is unreadable when she finally emerges. My panic increases when she pulls up a chair and leans closer; it's the sympathy in her eyes that bothers me.

'How are you holding up, Ben?'

'Just give me the news, please.'

'Nina's a brave one, which will help in the long run.'

'How do you mean?'

'She's got a high pain threshold.' The doctor scans her clipboard. 'Three broken ribs, and a fractured eye socket. I was worried about her lungs, but her breathing's steadying. She's got no vision in her left eye currently, but that's probably due to accumulated blood behind the cornea that should clear with time. I'll get a specialist to give us a second opinion from the X-ray. The rest of her injuries are superficial.'

'She'll survive?'

Dr Tremayne's hand settles on my arm. 'She lost consciousness due to pain, not the severity of her injuries. The body has a clever way of shutting down, to prevent you from making matters worse.'

Ray leans forward to catch her eye. 'What about the baby?'

I gape at him in amazement, but the doctor only peers at her notes. 'There's a strong foetal heartbeat, which is reassuring. If one of those kicks had landed on her lower abdomen, it might have been a different story. Your baby's survived its first battle, Ben.' She pats my hand, then rises to her feet. 'Let Nina sleep for an hour before you see her. Don't worry, she knows you're both here.'

Ray's slow-dawning smile appears when the doctor takes her leave.

'When did Nina tell you she's pregnant?'

'I guessed weeks ago, when she asked if I thought you'd make a good father.'

'What did you say?'

'Probably not, on balance. If you neglect your child like your boat, it won't stand a prayer.'

Ray's sea-blue eyes glitter with amusement and I know he'll never reveal his true answer, but I'm too relieved to care. He leans against the wall, making himself comfortable, while I'm still too wired to relax. I keep my gaze on the wall clock, longing for the hour to pass.

75

Saturday 24 December

I arrive at the station at 8 a.m. on Christmas Eve, after spending the night in Nina's hospital room on a hard plastic chair. I'm full of relief, but my shoulders are stiff as a board, and the police station appears lacklustre too. The building couldn't look less Christmassy if it tried. The only sign of Yuletide is a faded string of bunting above the front door.

DCI Madron appears in the reception area when I cross the threshold. My boss offers muted congratulations on catching the killers, then stares at my five o'clock shadow and crumpled shirt with distaste. Eddie's reaction is far more human. He asks after Nina straight away, visibly relieved to hear that she's recovering. He's still quizzing me about her injuries when Madron summons me to his office.

'Go home, Kitto,' the DCI says. 'Two senior murder investigators are flying over this afternoon, and the solicitor can come back later. Let them complete the process.'

'You know I prefer to close cases myself, sir.'

'Neither of them are saying much, but Ivan Teague confessed to Scott's murder last night, to Eddie.'

'The boy pleaded innocence at the crime scene.'

'Maybe he decided to come clean.' Madron seems to have sentenced the boy already. 'It's Hazel and Elspeth I pity. Those women have served the community unstintingly for years. Stan's illness has warped his mind and Ivan's probably been looking at filth on the internet. His taste for violence comes from there, no doubt.'

'We can't prove that till we've seen his computer. Let me wrap this up, please. I know the case inside out.'

My boss takes ten minutes to cave under pressure. His constant belief that someone else will do a better job annoys me, but my irritation soon fades when I'm allowed to see the solicitor. Louise Walbert is famous for her no-nonsense approach, so I'm glad she'll be present at the interviews. She takes her legal work seriously, but her wardrobe is eccentric, bordering on clownish. She's wearing a yellow blouse and emerald-green skirt, earrings that resemble peacock feathers, her hair a wild mass of grey. I know her well enough to understand that her disguise conceals one of the sharpest minds on the islands.

Louise studies me intently when I share my intention to interview first Ivan Teague, then Stan Hicks, with Eddie assisting. She's held preliminary interviews with both suspects, which is pushing legal practice to its limit. Both suspects will need different lawyers, but right now she's the only practicing solicitor available, until we bring another over from the mainland. Ivan will need one with experience in counselling juveniles, but I can trust Louise to be compassionate until then. She lets me know that the boy has given her the silent treatment, despite his confession to Eddie last night. Stan is giving us no help either. He still appears unable to say a word or write down his thoughts.

The boy still seems dazed when he's brought from the cell in handcuffs, and it's lucky my urge to avenge Nina's injuries has passed. He gazes out of the window once he's sat down, nothing like the young man that seemed so keen to learn when he did his work experience at the station earlier this year. He looks like any other seventeen-year-old on the surface, wearing grey custody-issue joggers and a sweatshirt. It's the blankness on his face that's unsettling, because I've been there myself, and know how it feels. I've seen photos of me wearing the same dazed expression soon after my father died.

'You need to understand the terms of your arrest, Ivan. You're under suspicion of murdering Scott Minear, and assaulting Luke, Jade, and Ethan Minear. There's a final charge of grievous bodily harm for your attack on Nina Jackson last night, which caused serious bodily harm. Do you have any questions?'

'Nothing,' he mutters. 'I did all of it, by myself.'

'I'd still like to hear why. You impressed me during

your work experience. I can't believe you'd act like that without provocation.' The boy remains stony-faced as I ask the next question. 'Polly said she made those ships in bottles in your shed, but I don't buy it. How long have you been doing it?'

'No comment.' He repeats the words like a mantra when I reframe the question, but his silence only fuels my desire for the truth.

'You had a good future ahead of you, Ivan. Give us valid reasons for your actions and you could avoid a long sentence.' I can tell he's listening, despite keeping his face averted. 'Young offender institutions aren't too bad, but that's just the first three years. Then you'll go to a Category B prison, with all the rapists and other murderers. Nothing prepares you for the misery and violence.'

The boy's bleak expression speaks volumes.

'Tell us about Stan's involvement. He's faking being mute, isn't he? I know you've been visiting him. If he coerced you, the courts will be lenient.' I lean closer to study him more closely. 'Nina says you helped her last night. Maybe you just wanted Stan's violence to end. Is that right, Ivan?'

My statement brings his defences down at last. He lurches forward, fresh tears leaving circles on the knees of his joggers, but the boy's loyalties won't allow him to speak. I go on issuing questions for another fifteen minutes before calling a halt. The interview feels like bullying, if he's not prepared to answer. He may appear adult but the look in his eyes belongs to a terrified child. I still have no concrete proof that Stan Hicks hurt anyone either, or that he coerced Ivan, apart from his presence at the crime scene. It still doesn't ring true that a well-mannered teenager with a devoted girlfriend became a murderer overnight.

Eddie looks uncomfortable once Ivan is led away, clearly worried about interviewing Stan. It reminds me that everyone's connected in Scilly; his father once worked for the Hicks family, the couple doting on him like an extra grandchild.

'Madron can sit in on the next one, if you'd rather skip it,' I tell him.

'Stan's more likely to speak with me here, boss. I can see why he'd want Scott dead, but why attack his grandkids? Him and Elspeth are crazy about them.'

My deputy still looks young for his age, with a round, guileless face, but today he seems world-weary. I can understand why. It's painful when someone you respect turns out to be a liar, yet Stan Hicks looks calm when Lawrie Deane brings him into the room. The old man spent last night in a holding cell, furnished with only a mattress and a blanket, yet he appears rested. Stan looks straight through me when our interview begins. There's no sign of a reaction when I repeat the terms of his arrest.

'Start at the beginning, please, Stan. We know your silence is a pretence. Can you explain your motives for us?'

The old man's expression shows a range of emotions, but I can't guess how much he understands.

'I can see why you wanted Scott dead. He took your land, and mistreated your daughter, but the rest doesn't make sense.' I allow a long pause, hoping he'll speak. 'I assume you and Ivan went to all that trouble with the ships in bottles to make Dave Carillian look guilty. That's hard to believe from a man like you. My dad respected you, for your decency, and so did I.'

Hicks shuts his eyes.

'There's no way you and Ivan set out to kill three of your grandkids, unless you know something I don't. If you're capable of that much planning, I bet you can still write.' I push a blank piece of paper across the table, then hold out a biro. 'Someone else is involved, aren't they? Write down their name and the questions will stop.'

There's panic on the old man's face, his hands fidgeting in his lap, but he refuses my offer, so I let the pen drop onto the table. Hicks' tension makes me certain he's shielding someone, and suddenly something Elspeth said after Scott died falls into place. Ivan isn't the only one that paid regular visits to the Hicks' home after Stan's stroke.

'Wait here, please, all of you. I'm pausing the interview.'

Eddie looks startled when I leave the room, but not as surprised as Lawrie Deane when I ask him to arrest one more suspect, then deliver her to the station.

Stan's calm has vanished when I return. A babble of incoherent noises spills from his lips, like he's trying to explain at last.

'You've been played, Stan; I bet Ivan had nothing to do with it, did he? He just tried to stop the cycle of violence. I can see why you want to protect her. She's got kids to raise, but you can't shield her now. She's a menace to the whole island.'

Stan Hicks loses control without warning. Maybe it's the judgement on my face that triggers it; I'm lucky he's handcuffed when he launches his attack, trying to swipe me from my chair. The man's fury seems to give him unnatural strength, despite his age and the effects of his stroke. Eddie and I have to strong-arm him down the corridor then back into the holding cell. When I peer through the hatch, the old man is still raging. The sound of him hurling himself at the metal door echoes through the building.

76

Ethan's pain from last night's attack has eased since Maria Austell put arnica on his bruises. He's outdoors with Jade when a policeman arrives at the farmhouse. He'd like to know what the officer wants, but his sister is running ahead, like the night she disappeared. Shadow is still at his side, and the pickers are bent over the furrows, using their knives to cut each bloom so more Grand Monarch flowers can grow in their place. The boy stops to pick one. He understands why his father loved them most of all. Each flower has a yellow cup at its centre, stamens loaded with white pollen, and six flawless petals. It's their fragrance that lingers, heady and memorable. The jonquils' scent is even stronger than roses in high summer. His gaze skims over the golden fields rolling down to the sea, and grief for his father wells up suddenly. His dad loved this land more than anything. Ethan can see its beauty when he looks at the hedgerows alive with birds, and the flower crop glistening, but the past week has taught him that people matter more than fields.

The boy has left his piccolo at home; he no longer needs

it in his pocket to feel safe. Jade gets afraid sometimes too, which balances the scales. He's brave like his sister. He stood up for himself last night, without help from anyone.

Ethan is so keen to run ahead he barely notices when Shadow gives a low bark, then disappears inland to find his master. Jade is waving both arms, signalling him closer, with her red cap pulled low over her forehead. The boy sets off at running pace, just like before, following that speck of crimson down to the sea.

77

Hazel Teague is brought to the station at 10 a.m., her expression buoyant, but the tremor in her hands is a giveaway. The nurse looks stunned by the terms of her arrest, but her acting skills are waning. I've been a murder investigator long enough to understand how to use my bulk to best advantage. She bridles when I lean across the table to study her at close range. Her panic is surfacing at last, a muscle ticking below her eye.

'Start at the beginning, please, Hazel. Tell us what made you so bitter.'

'What's this about? You should release Ivan too; he's done nothing wrong.'

I rest my elbows on the table, leaving less than a metre of clear air between us. 'Let's start with your feelings for Scott Minear. You can't have loved him, or he'd still be alive.'

She gives a breathless laugh. 'This is ridiculous, Ben. Can't you see that? Gemma's my closest friend, and she's suffering right now. I should go back to the farm.'

'It's an odd way to treat your best mate; the friend-ship won't survive long when the truth comes out. One of the best forensic scientists in the UK will search your house today, and the crime scenes. She'll find out what you did in minute detail. You may as well say it in your own words.'

'All I've done is help you, and look after the victims. Nina probably wouldn't be alive if I hadn't been there last night.'

'It was you that attacked her. Now it's time to explain why.'

I let a long silence fill the room. It often does the trick when a suspect is in denial; accusations are easy to deflect, but quiet leaves you nowhere to hide. I can see her guard lowering already, her eyes blinking too fast when I speak again.

'Ivan's taking the blame. Maybe he's afraid of you, or he thinks Polly needs her mum, no matter what you've done. I admire him for that, but it's the wrong choice. Are you really going to let your son chuck his life away?'

She keeps her lips pursed shut.

'Do you want me to explain what big, ugly convicts do to pretty boys like him in jail?'

The statement hits home at last. Hazel is dry-eyed, but the regret on her face looks genuine, at last.

'How long has Ivan suspected that you killed Scott, and hurt his family?'

The nurse's gaze drops to Madron's desk, lingering

on the polished surface. 'My son's been overlooked his whole life, that's what hurts. He must have followed me to Nina's cottage last night, but I think he already knew. Maybe he followed me to the farm, the night of Luke's attack.'

'Explain it all, Hazel, from the start. You'll feel better once it's out.'

She draws in a long breath. 'Every woman on the island fancied Scott Minear when I was seventeen. He was good-looking, brash and confident, and Gemma had run off to the mainland with their kids. I fell for him, head over heels. Part of me was thrilled when I got pregnant. I thought he'd realise we should be together, but he was furious. He forced me to keep quiet about him being Ivan's dad. He needed Gemma back, to keep all that farmland.'

I acknowledge the truth with a nod. 'Tell me how Scott reacted to you being pregnant.'

'He told me to get an abortion, before I was too far gone. That bastard ended the relationship there and then.'

'That can't have been easy to hear, at seventeen.'

'My parents were furious too. They said I'd thrown my life away, but I wanted the baby, no matter what.'

Eddie looks up from his notebook. 'It was brave of you to keep it, Gemma.'

'At least you understand.' She gives him a shaky smile. 'I stayed here when my family moved away a few years later; I loved Scilly too much to leave.'

'How come you never told anyone that Scott was Ivan's dad?'

'He gave me an allowance to keep my mouth shut. He'd shove an envelope through the door each month, with just enough cash to keep us both fed. Everyone thought Ivan's dad was a seasonal worker from the hotel who'd left me high and dry.'

'And you befriended Gemma, to be near him?'

'It's a genuine friendship. Watching Scott grind her down made me hate him in the end. I killed him for both of us, not just me.'

'What makes you think she'll be grateful?'

'I've liberated her from that monster.' She stares back at me, with fury burning in her eyes. 'I asked Scott to support Ivan through university, but he just laughed. He said the minute my son turned eighteen his support would end. A father like that doesn't deserve to live, does he?'

'Your friendship with Gemma doesn't mean much though, does it? I found her harvest knife in your jacket pocket. You'd have gone after her too, for taking Scott away.'

Hazel's silence is accompanied by a slow nod.

'Tell us how you got Stan Hicks involved.'

'He trusts me completely, after our one-to-one sessions. Stan's mind's confused and so's his memory, but he's still got his physical strength, and he's been aggressive since the stroke damaged his brain. All I had to do was harness that anger. I tapped on his bedroom window at night to bring him outside while Elspeth slept. I carried a flask of whisky and gave him cigarettes, to keep him sweet, but he let me down with the twins. I wanted to catch them both, but they got away.'

'Why hurt them, or Luke? They'd done nothing to you.'

'Scott's kids will inherit his whole fortune. It's my son that deserves support, after all that neglect.'

There's a warped logic to her argument. She hated Scott so much, she was prepared to sacrifice two innocent children who trusted her completely.

'You and Stan were waiting in the field?'

'I left a message for the twins in the hollow tree. I told Stan it was just a game, and he went along with me, but it backfired. Those kids are stronger than they look.'

'I still don't get why you wanted two eleven-year-olds dead.'

'To make Scott suffer, before he died. I was planning to put their bodies in the *Galatea*.' There's remorse in her voice now, but she's already proved that she's a skilled actor. 'That boat mattered more to him than Ivan ever did. I bet he loved it more than his whole family. Stan helped me drag Scott's gig down to the sea, before we attacked him, then we lifted his body onto the Devil's Table. He hated Scott too, for ruining Gemma's life.'

'Why not take him to court instead of bludgeoning him to death?'

'I couldn't tell Gemma that Scott was Ivan's father, after keeping it secret so long.'

'You're a nurse, yet you killed a man in cold blood, weaponised Stan's anger. Elspeth said you gave him tranquillisers but I bet you slipped him uppers, to increase his aggression; we'll need to get a toxicology report on his blood. I don't believe he'd have attacked his own grandkids unless you drugged him.'

'My strategy worked, didn't it?'

'Did you get him to beat Dave Carillian up too?'

She shakes her head. 'Scott thought Carillian had taken his precious Jade, and the old man paid the price.'

'How did you lure Scott onto the moor?'

Hazel gives a twisted smile. 'His ego killed him in the end. I went down to the fields and flirted with him for a while, told him I still fancied him, after all those years. I was desperate to sleep with him again. He agreed to meet me at one a.m. on Chapel Down, like when we were young. Stan restrained him, then I beat him with hammers I threw into the sea afterwards. I'd taken his knife from the cutting shed the night before.'

'Weren't you afraid Stan would share your secret?'

'He can't talk, remember? I bet he'd forgotten it all by the next day.'

'Why bother with all the details? Chucking stones through windows, flowers, ships in bottles, the victims' own knives. You could have left Scott's body on the beach, and we'd be none the wiser.'

'It was Stan that threw the stones, not me. All I did

was write the words. It seemed wrong to leave Scott on that slab for days, even though he never considered my feelings. He cared about his flowers more than anything. Scott built his whole fucking empire out of them, so I used them as a shroud.' Hatred resonates in her voice.

'You must have loved him deeply at the start.'

'I saw his vulnerable side. He told me that he never felt close to his family, the night Ivan was conceived. We lay on the Devil's Table on a summer night, looking at the stars, and he told me his secrets. His parents were tough-minded farmers that never showed affection. But his father gave him a ship in a bottle that he'd made himself, the one thing Scott treasured as a child.'

'And you stole it?'

She smiles, like a teacher rewarding a pupil for a correct answer. 'Gemma invited me round so often, it was easy to find. I left it in the field, after trying to catch the twins, to let him know I meant business. The rest were just to keep you guessing.'

'And implicate Dave Carillian?'

She turns her face away, rejecting my question.

'Thank God Stan didn't obey all your instructions. He was crying his eyes out at the cottage last night. He realised you'd made him do something evil, even though his mind's broken.'

She makes a tutting sound under her breath. 'It was the same with Luke. Stan didn't have the nerve to watch him die.'

'Why would he kill his own grandson?'

'To please me, of course. Poor Stan loves me more than his wife.' Jealousy glitters in her eyes. 'I took him up to the farm at midnight with me. I threw pebbles at Luke's window to wake him. I knew he'd come out to see who was making noise in the cutting shed at that time.'

'I bet you'd have killed Ethan too, for disturbing you.'

'Don't you get it?' Suddenly her face contorts with rage. 'Gemma's kids will inherit millions, but Ivan won't get a penny.'

'How did your son work it out? It was more than the ships in bottles, wasn't it?'

'Ivan knew I'd been making them all year.'

'You must have spent hours in that shed in your garden, after your kids were asleep.'

'Ivan started asking questions, so I admitted Scott was his dad. He must have followed me to the Redmaynes' cottage. I thought Nina might help Ethan to remember me trying to catch him in the field, so I had to shut her up.' Her tone of voice is oddly jubilant. 'Your girlfriend's face was a mess last time I saw her.'

'She'll make a full recovery. But why target her?'

'It's like I said. I thought she'd help Ethan to accuse me.'

'That's not the reason.'

Hazel's hands screw into fists on her lap. 'Nina's got everything I wanted at seventeen: a man that loves her; a baby coming; the community's respect. I never got any of that, even though I deserved it.'

Scott's neglect seems to have warped her mind;

there's no sign of contrition on her face. I'd like to ask more questions, but my mind circles back to the start of our interview.

'Would you really have let Ivan take all the blame?'

Tears leak from her eyes at last. 'It was his idea. He begged me to go along with it, to protect Polly. She's so young, he thought she'd suffer without her mum, and he'd serve a shorter sentence than me, because he's only a teenager . . .' Her voice trails into silence, and I sense another reason for her willingness to let her son go to jail, despite her outrage about him being overlooked. She can't face the consequences of her actions – maybe she's too unbalanced even to recognise her own guilt.

When I look at her again there's no visible sign of evil. I catch a glimpse of the caring nurse, who worked hard to protect patients until jealousy and hatred broke her self-restraint.

'Look after my children, please,' she whispers. 'Don't let them suffer.'

Hazel stands up, her handcuffed arms stiff in front of her. There's no sign of rebellion when she's finally led away.

78

Ray delivers me back to St Martin's in the afternoon to find Shadow and collect my boat. I'll need it to visit Nina in hospital until she comes home, soon after Christmas. My uncle looks shocked when I pull him into an awkward man-hug on Highertown Quay. It's never fully struck me until today that he stepped into my father's shoes straight after his boat was lost at sea. I can't tell whether my physical gesture leaves Ray glad or horrified, but he wastes no time in turning around and sailing back to Bryher.

I'm hoping not to bump into anyone when I walk round Cruther's Point to one of St Martin's most picturesque bays. I'm in no mood to answer questions, still trapped in a state of disbelief. Hazel seemed like such a caring nurse, she had the whole community fooled, but her actions will have devastating consequences for her kids, and for Elspeth and Stan Hicks. The old man may have been drugged and misled by Hazel, coerced into horrifying violence, but he'll still have to face a lengthy murder trial for his part in her crimes.

I can't help thinking about all the people I wrongly accused during the investigation. My old friend Will Austell is first on my list of people that deserve an apology. He showed remarkable kindness to support the family of a man that hurt his parents by a piece of casual cruelty. I'm glad he was only subjected to one uncomfortable conversation before being allowed to go home, but I still need to say sorry.

Details from the case churn round my head like clothes in a tumble dryer, despite the peaceful scenery. The fog has finally lifted, exposing the pristine landscape that drew me back from London two years ago. I'm sitting on a boulder to admire it when a familiar sound reaches me. Shadow is barking at top volume as he races across the beach. It looks like he's been for a winter dip, his sopping wet fur drenching me when he shakes himself dry. He launches himself at me, making desperate attempts to lick my face, until I fish in my pocket for some canine treats, letting him eat them from my palm.

'I admit it, you're smarter than me. Thanks for leading me to Nina.'

He settles at my side after bolting down his reward, like he's admiring our view of Tresco's lush green slopes, and further north, Scilly's wildest islands. Tean, Men-a-Vaur, and Round Island have been uninhabited since Roman invaders built shrines there, hoping their sea God would return them home safely one day.

I'm too tired to think straight when a figure draws closer, crossing the sand at a steady pace. It's sod's law in such a tiny place that you always bump into people you'd rather avoid. I regret mistreating Dave Carillian in a crisis, but the man is too close to avoid. He looks like an elderly librarian in his grey overcoat, his tie firmly knotted, sparse strands of hair blowing in the wind, but my dog appears thrilled to see him. He trots closer until the old man leans down to stroke his head.

'I owe you an apology, Mr Carillian, for jumping to the wrong conclusion.'

The man gives a curt nod. 'You had a job to do, and you're not the first. People misinterpret me, wherever I live. Can I join you for a minute?'

'Go ahead.'

He perches on a slab of rock a few metres away. 'I hoped for a fresh start here, but that was unrealistic. I've been called odd since I was a boy. My own mother described me as a strange creature.'

'Jade Minear told my colleague you're the kindest man on the island. She says you're her new friend.'

'I always wanted my own children, but women prefer men who make them laugh and know how to pay compliments.' The man's loneliness echoes in every word.

'What are you going to do about it?'

'Nothing, of course. I'm sixty-eight years old.'

'It's never too late.'

His laughter is a dry rattle. 'I came into the world alone, they'll carry me out alone.'

'Not necessarily.' I look at him properly for the first time. He's got delicate features, his skin papery, but the light in his eyes is warm. 'Would you be prepared to try something new?'

'I very much doubt it.'

'Come to St Mary's the day after Boxing Day. The social club has a party in the church hall at three p.m. Loads of people will be there, young and old. We can go together, if it helps.'

'That's not my cup of tea, Inspector.' He's already rising to his feet.

'There are groups you could join, for walking, bird-watching, and so on. Linda Thomas at the library can give you a list.'

'I ought to be getting home.'

'Thanks for sheltering Jade when she needed it.'

The man leaves before I can say goodbye, wearing his solitude like a badge of honour, but I won't give up. My godmother will be able to befriend him. When Maggie launches a charm offensive, no one can fight it.

My thoughts shift to Hazel Teague's kids, who will grow up without their mother, but the islands are good at supporting waifs and strays. The elders will gather round, absorbing them into their families. Gemma Minear will need help too, to overcome her drinking, and come to terms with Scott's death. I'll do everything in my power to make sure Luke takes up his football trial, without Scott's shadow hanging over him. It's too soon to tell whether Amy will stay with her older man once he faces a jail sentence for tax evasion, but there's a chance she'll be reconciled with her mother, now the threat's gone.

I let my gaze catch on the sea's brightly polished surface. The horizon is studded with minute boats, even smaller than the ones Dave Carillian places inside bottles on the end of a pin. I let the waves' lullaby sooth me until the tide retreats, then rise to my feet. This Christmas will be like no other, full of DIY chores until Nina comes home, and a trip to my godmother Maggie's pub for turkey and all the trimmings. My mind moves on to tasks I must finish before the baby arrives, while the winter sun spreads its pale light across the sea.

Acknowledgements

Many thanks to my friends Rachel Greenlaw and Linda Thomas on St Mary's. Your kind welcome makes the islands even more lovely to visit. I must also thank my husband Dave Pescod, for listening to me talk endlessly about the book, and reading parts of it with great insight. Thanks to my friends Penny Hancock, Jane Horwood, and Judy Logan for chatting about plot outlines, helping me with my website, and giving me so much encouragement. Killer Women, you are all such brilliant writers! You inspire me hugely, whenever we meet.

Thanks are due to Jo Dickinson, for believing in me, and setting this series in motion. Bethan Jones and Jess Barratt at Simon and Schuster, you are a delight to work with. Many thanks to you both for your support on this book, and the series. Fraser Crichton, your copyediting skills and close knowledge of my books makes the final draft of each one a pleasure.

My Twitter pals never let me down. There are too

many of you to thank, but I'd like to call out some of your names, for raising my confidence as a writer: Polly Dymock, Jennie Blackwell, Janet Fearnley, Julie Boon, Victoria Goldman, Cassandra, Ivana, Jill Doyle, Peggy Breckin, Anna Tink, Caroline Casson, Hazel Wright, Ian Dixon, Michelle McGrath, Marni Graff, Sarah Linley, Joanna Blatchley.

I owe gratitude to everyone in Scilly for lending me so much support. I love it when people chat to me in Hugh Town Post Office or the Co-Op, and ask to be killed off in my next book. It's not just the landscape that makes the Isles of Scilly a joy to visit, but the inhabitants themselves. Fay Page is one of Scilly's talented jewellery makers. Thanks so much to you, Rob and Inga, for my tour of your workshop on St Martin's and for my fabulous earrings, which are shaped like a racing gig's paddles. I know for a fact that Val and Graham Thomas at St Martin's Vineyard and Winery make delicious wine, because I have sampled it many times. I hope you won't mind me borrowing your landscape in my story!

Particular thanks are due to Victoria, Clive, and Avril at Mumford's in Hugh Town, for hand selling my books to so many of your customers. It's always a thrill to see my books on your shelves!

Don't miss the other atmospheric locked-island thrillers featuring DI Ben Kitto from highly-acclaimed author, Kate Rhodes

'An absolute master of pace, plotting and character'
ELLY GRIFFITHS

'A vividly realised protagonist whose complex and harrowing history rivals the central crime storyline'
SOPHIE HANNAH

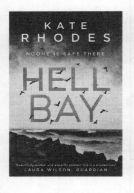 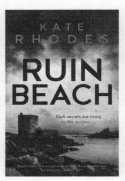 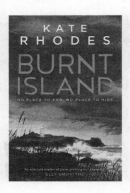 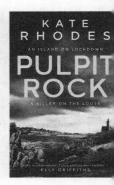

'Gripping, clever and impossible to put down' **ERIN KELLY**

'Beautifully written and expertly plotted; this is a masterclass' *GUARDIAN*

SIMON & SCHUSTER